W9-CEF-552

THE PLANET ON THE TABLE

KIM STANLEY ROBINSON

THE PLANET ON THE TABLE

A TOM DOHERTY ASSOCIATES BOOK

THE PLANET ON THE TABLE

First printing: July 1986

A TOR Book

Published by Tom Doherty Associates
49 West 24 Street
New York, N.Y. 10010

ISBN: 0-312-93595-1

Library of Congress Catalog Card Number: 85-52258

Printed in the United States

0 9 8 7 6 5 4 3 2 1

Acknowledgments

"Venice Drowned" © 1981 by Terry Carr. *Universe 11*
"Mercurial" © 1985 by Terry Carr. *Universe 15*
"Ridge Running" © 1984 by The Mercury Press. *The Magazine of Fantasy and Science Fiction*
"The Disguise" © 1977 by Damon Knight. *Orbit 19*
"The Lucky Strike" © 1984 by Terry Carr. *Universe 14*
"Coming Back to Dixieland" © 1976 by Damon Knight. *Orbit 18*
"Stone Eggs" © 1983 by Terry Carr. *Universe 13*
"Black Air" © 1983 by The Mercury Press. *The Magazine of Fantasy and Science Fiction*

Contents

Introduction

In his poem "The Planet On the Table," Wallace Stevens says,

> Ariel was glad he had written his poems.
> They were of a remembered time
> Or of something seen that he liked.

This is remarkable in my experience of Stevens: three consecutive lines that I feel I understand. More than that, I understand the feeling in them; looking at the galleys of my first short story collection, I have that feeling myself, or at least Caliban's version of it. I am glad that I have written these stories.

They were written over a period of about ten years. Some of them, as you will see, are strictly autobiographical; the rest are not. If you go on and read them, then you and I become collaborators in the strange and wonderful process that is reading fiction. My suggestion, as collaborator, is that you let some time lapse between the reading of one and the next. Perhaps one a day would be a good plan; most health experts and vitamin bottles agree on that schedule, and we want these stories as healthy as possible.

Stevens in his poem also says,

> . . . his poems, although makings of his self,
> Were no less makings of the sun.

That's a science-fictional thought, isn't it? Our star blasts a barren planet with intense radiation; and one of the results is this recombinant string of sentences. Of course there were some intermediate steps along the way: the primordial soup . . . the dinosaurs . . . the sun's radiation that I took on directly, as a child on the California beaches. . . . Or my education, the passing to me of a tradition, and some parts of a craft. This step in the movement from sun to sentence is an important one. I have been very lucky in my teachers, very lucky indeed, and I would like to thank some of them here. In San Diego, Donald Wesling, Fredric Jameson, Andrew Wright, Jack Behar, Lowry Pei, and Ursula K. Le Guin. In Boston, John Malcolm Brinnin and Charles F. Stone. In East Lansing, Samuel R. Delany, Gene Wolfe, Roger Zelazny, Joe Haldeman, Damon Knight, and Kate Wilhelm. And before these, pointing the way, Catherine Lee. I owe these people a lot.

While I'm at it, I should mention the editors who first published these stories. If you are a professional writer, then the editors buying stories in your time create a "field of play," bounded by a set of subtle but real constraints, which determine what you can write and still reasonably expect to sell. As you will see if you check the Acknowledgments page, all of the stories in this collection originally appeared in *Orbit*, in *Universe*, or in *The Magazine of Fantasy and Science Fiction*, which means I was selling them to Damon Knight, Terry Carr, or Ed Ferman. These three editors between them created a "field of play" so large that I felt free to wander off on my own, even to get lost out in the woods; and that is a wonderful freedom indeed. My thanks to these three gentlemen, fine editors all.

On the day that I got the galleys for this collection, I was living in Zürich, Switzerland. Feeling pleased to see all these strays gathered in one book, I decided to go for a run. It was January, and snowing outside, so I put on my green Goretex mountain suit, and pulled the hood up over the headphones of my Sony Walkman, and took off into the streets. Did I look a little out of place there in Zürich, Switzerland? You bet I did. I had chosen Beethoven's Third Symphony to listen to; for many of the years when I was writing the stories in this collection, Beethoven's *Eroica* had started off every single day, so it seemed appropriate. I got the volume up to a level where I could share the music a bit with the people that I passed, and the first movement began to propel me along.

Zürich lies in the valley were the Limmat River leaves the Zürichsee, and on the hills to east and west of this valley. I lived on the hillside to the east, and the top of the hill, the Zürichberg, is forested, and cut with old horsetrails; I headed up in that direction. Soon I was running on the path bordering the trees, and looking out to the west I could see the fat streak-bottomed clouds blowing in over the city, and over the pewter surface of the Zürichsee, headed right at me. The wind was pushing the tall trees back and forth, and tearing off the last of their red leaves, and making such a roar in the branches that I could hear it all round the edges of the Beethoven.

Happy at the storminess of this storm, and my little moment of being within it, I ran over the horsetrails on the Zürichberg until I came to the Friederhof Fluntern, the cemetery on the south flank of the hill. Paths wound here and there among the gravestones, not the most appropriate place to be running around, but I had the place to myself, so I kept it up. Step, step, step, up some snowy stairs, running shoes soaked, and I came upon the statue of a seated man. Well, I thought, looking at the familiar face: if it isn't James Joyce!

And so it was. I had to scrape the snow off the memorial stone, set flat in the ground, but there it was: JAMES JOYCE *Geboren 2 Februar 1882 Gestorben 13 Januar 1941*. Nora and their son George were buried in the plot as well.

The statue was an excellent one, of bronze that had darkened till it looked like iron: Joyce sitting on a block, legs crossed, elbow resting on knee, open book in one hand, cigarette in the other. Thorny walking stick leaning against him. He looked off to the side, contemplatively, through thick bronze glasses. There was an icicle hanging from one elbow, and he wore a shawl of snow.

I was well-warmed by my run up the hill, and surprised by this unexpected meeting, I sat on the low wall across from the statue. Just to hang out with him for a while, you know. I took off the headphones, turned off the Walkman. Snow drifted onto us, big flakes falling slowly sideways, and we were alone in a small white world.

James Joyce. I had always thought of him as a kind of iron man:

hard on his family, hard on his friends, hard on his creditors; hard on his readers. So I wasn't really very surprised when his neck squeaked an iron kind of squeak, and his head turned to face me. "So," he said, a bit like a ventriloquist, "you've got a story collection coming out." Even after all these years of exile his voice had a touch of the Irish in it.

"Yes!" I cried. "You've heard! Have you read it?"

He nodded.

Well. The man always had been incredibly well-read. I wanted to ask him what he thought of it, naturally, but I was afraid to. I mean, James Joyce! Think about it! So I said, "Well? What did you think?"

He shook his head: squeak, squeak. "You don't want to know." I must have looked crestfallen, because he went on: "It's not that. The truth of it is . . . it's not the past that judges you. Not the past. You should remember that."

I wasn't sure that I agreed with him, but I was willing to let it ride for the moment.

"I will say," he added, "that I didn't much like that little slur you made against Trieste. Have you ever been to Trieste?"

"Yes."

He raised his eyebrows: creak! "For how long?"

"Well, just for one day, actually."

"Hmph." He nodded, his point made, and took a drag from his cigarette. The icicle broke off his elbow as his arm moved. We watched the snow fall. He remarked on how snow in the air increases one's sense of the sight's depth of field. I asked him how his vision was doing, and he said it was improving. Then we were silent for a while. I thought about his story collection, *Dubliners*. As I recalled, he had had terrible trials getting it published; ten years of delays, the entire first edition destroyed for some reason, censorship or financial problems, I couldn't remember. . . . But it had been hard, hard. Enough to make anyone bitter. It was a fine collection, I thought, a bit uneven, but there standing at the end of it was one of the best stories ever written: "The Dead." Hmm. As I recalled, the story ended with an image of the snow falling, on all the living and all the dead; and here we were. I began to get a little cold. "Well," I said. "What should I do now?"

Squeak, squeak. "I can only tell you what I did. You're interested in science; call this the exponential program. For you must always press yourself, you see. Always. *Dubliners* was a book like many another. With the *Portrait,* however, there is a . . . strengthening. An increase in density, call it a tenfold increase for simplicity's sake. Or one magnitude, for you. *Ulysses* is again another magnitude more dense, more difficult than the *Portrait*. There aren't many books like that one; nor many people who can understand it. Then *Finnegans Wake* . . . that's yet another magnitude more difficult. . . ."

"Until even you have trouble understanding that one, hey Mr. Joyce?"

"Smartass." Always up on the latest in slang, he was, and in five languages too. He put down his book (the *Wake*? still puzzling over it? I couldn't tell) and swung his walking stick around, pointed it at me. It really was quite a thorny stick. "The point is, you must press yourself! You must go beyond what you thought yourself capable of. . . ."

"You mean I should push the outside of the envelope, I should seek new worlds, and go boldly where no man has gone before?"

"Smartass." He poked the stick at me. Shook his head. "Being an American has no doubt destroyed your mind. This book . . ." he nudged the bronze volume with his foot; was that my book he had been reading? *The Planet In the Snow*? "All these bizarre distortions from the real. . . . Well, I like that part of it, actually. And you must solve the esthetic problems of your time, it's not my problem thank God. But listen! You asked me what you should do—do you want to hear what I say?" And he jabbed me a couple of times with the end of the stick.

"Yes."

He leaned toward me, looked me right in the eye with those circular bronze specs. "Go back down there, and try again."

After that we only talked about his time, which he was much more comfortable discussing. He told me some hilarious stories about Gertrude Stein and Sylvia Beach, and tore up Dublin one more time, with a great nostalgic longing in his voice. "But I'd not be buried there, not on your life!" Of course not. The exile still, and always. We laughed over the Zürichers and their great passion for order—the tram conductors we had both seen, sticking their heads out the window, waiting to take off until the plaza clock second hand swept up to the top. . . . And he told me about writing *Finnegans Wake,* drawing on cardboard with colored crayons, so he could see the letters; the pained laughter tore out of him, creak, creak, creak! I questioned the wisdom of that particular project, and, made irritable by all those years sitting out in the snow, he got angry with me. "You haven't given it enough!" he cried. In his agitation he even stood up, squeak!, and pounded his walking stick over his sitting block, as if to soften it. "That's the best book I wrote, and you won't even work at it!" And watching him, I thought that that faith in his work, fierce, unshakeable, was his real lesson to me. Fascinated, I pressed to see more of it; he began reminiscing about the difficulties of getting the book printed properly, and I said, "Typos, in *Finnegans Wake?* How could you tell?"

And with a metallic laughing roar of a shout, he thwacked me. That stick of his had more thorns on it than I cared to face, and I had to beat a retreat; he took off after me. If anybody had been up there that day, they would have seen a strange sight: a figure in a bright green suit and running shoes, chased among tombstones by a little nearsighted bronze man wielding a stick. But the good Swiss know better than to visit a cemetery in a snowstorm, and there were no witnesses. He chased me all the way home.

Venice Drowned

By the time Carlo Tafur struggled out of sleep, the baby was squalling, the teapot whistled, the smell of stove smoke filled the air. Wavelets slapped the walls of the floor below. It was just dawn. Reluctantly he untangled himself from the bedsheets and got up. He padded through the other room of his home, ignoring his wife and child, and walked out the door onto the roof.

Venice looked best at dawn, Carlo thought as he pissed into the canal. In the dim mauve light it was possible to imagine that the city was just as it always had been, that hordes of visitors would come flooding down the Grand Canal on this fine summer morning. . . . Of course, one had to ignore the patchwork constructions built on the roofs of the neighborhood to indulge the fancy. Around the church—San Giacomo du Rialto—all the buildings had even their top floors awash, and so it had been necessary to break up the tile roofs, and erect shacks on the roofbeams made of materials fished up from below: wood, brick, lath, stone, metal, glass. Carlo's home was one of these shacks, made of a crazy combination of wood beams, stained glass from San Giacometta, and drainpipes beaten flat. He looked back at it and sighed. It was best to look off over the Rialto, where the red sun blazed over the bulbous domes of San Marco.

"You have to meet those Japanese today," Carlo's wife, Luisa, said from inside.

"I know." Visitors still came to Venice, that was certain.

"And don't go insulting them and rowing off without your pay," she went on, her voice sounding clearly out of the doorway, "like you did with those Hungarians. It really doesn't matter what they take from under the water, you know. That's the past. That old stuff isn't doing anyone any good under there, anyway."

"Shut up," he said wearily. "I know."

"I have to buy stovewood and vegetables and toilet paper and socks for the baby," she said. "The Japanese are the best customers you've got; you'd better treat them well."

Carlo reentered the shack and walked into the bedroom to dress. Between putting on one boot and the next he stopped to smoke a cigarette, the last one in the house. While smoking he stared at his pile of books on the floor, his library as Luisa sardonically called the collection: all books about Venice. They were tattered, dog-eared, mildewed, so warped by the damp that none of them would close properly, and each moldy page was as wavy as the Lagoon on a windy day. They were a miserable sight, and Carlo gave the closest stack a kick with his cold boot as he returned to the other room.

"I'm off," he said, giving his baby and then Luisa a kiss. "I'll be back late—they want to go to Torcello."

"What could they want up there?"

He shrugged. "Maybe just to see it." He ducked out the door.

Below the roof was a small square where the boats of the neighborhood were moored. Carlo slipped off the tile onto the narrow floating dock he and the neighbors had built, and crossed to his boat, a wide-beamed sailboat with a canvas deck. He stepped in, unmoored it, and rowed out of the square onto the Grand Canal.

Once on the Grand Canal he tipped the oars out of the water and let the boat drift downstream. The big canal had always been the natural course of the channel through the mud flats of the Lagoon; for a while it had been tamed, but now it was a river again, its banks made of tile rooftops and stone palaces, with hundreds of tributaries flowing into it. Men were working on roof-houses in the early morning light. Those who knew Carlo waved, hammers or rope in hand, and shouted hello. Carlo wiggled an oar perfunctorily before he was swept past. It was foolish to build so close to the Grand Canal, which now had the strength to knock the old structures down, and often did. But that was their business. In Venice they were all fools, if one thought about it.

Then he was in the Basin of San Marco, and he rowed through the Piazetta beside the Doges' Palace, which was still imposing at two stories high, to the Piazza. Traffic was heavy as usual. It was the only place in Venice that still had the crowds of old, and Carlo enjoyed it for that reason, though he shouted curses as loudly as anyone when gondolas streaked in front of him. He jockeyed his way to the basilica window and rowed in.

Under the brilliant blue and gold of the domes it was noisy. Most of the water in the rooms had been covered with a floating dock. Carlo moored his boat to it, heaved his four scuba tanks on, and clambered up after them. Carrying two tanks in each hand he crossed the dock, on which the fish market was in full swing. Displayed for sale were flats of mullet, lagoon sharks, tunny, skates, and flatfish. Clams were piled in trays, their shells gleaming in the shaft of sunlight from the stained-glass east window; men and women pulled live crabs out of holes in the dock, risking fingers in the crab-jammed traps; fishermen bawled out prices, and insulted the freshness of their neighbors' product.

In the middle of the fish market, Ludovico Salerno, one of Carlo's best friends, had his stalls of scuba gear. Carlo's two Japanese customers were there. He greeted them and handed his tanks to Salerno, who began refilling them from his machine. They conversed in quick, slangy Italian while the tanks filled. When they were done, Carlo paid him and led the Japanese back to his boat. They got in and stowed their backpacks under the canvas decking while Carlo pulled the scuba tanks on board.

''We are ready to voyage at Torcello?'' one asked, and the other smiled and repeated the question. Their names were Hamada and Taku. They had made a few jokes concerning the latter name's similarity to Carlo's own, but Taku was the one with less Italian, so the sallies hadn't gone on for long. They had hired him four days before, at Salerno's stall.

''Yes,'' Carlo said. He rowed out of the Piazza and up back canals past Campo San Maria Formosa, which was nearly as crowded as the Piazza. Beyond that the canals were empty, and only an occasional roof-house marred the look of flooded tranquility.

''That part of city Venice here not many people live,'' Hamada observed. ''Not houses on houses.''

''That's true,'' Carlo replied. As he rowed past San Zanipolo and the hospital, he explained, ''It's too close to the hospital here, where many diseases were contained. Sicknesses, you know.''

''Ah, the hospital!'' Hamada nodded, as did Taku. ''We have swam hospital in our Venice voyage previous to that one here. Salvage many fine statues from lowest rooms.''

''Stone lions,'' Taku added. ''Many stone lions with wings in room below Twenty-forty waterline.''

''Is that right,'' Carlo said. Stone lions, he thought, set up in the entryway of some Japanese businessman's expensive home around the world. . . . He tried to divert his thoughts by watching the brilliantly healthy, masklike faces of his two passengers as they laughed over their reminiscences.

Then they were over the Fondamente Nuova, the northern limit of the city, and on the Lagoon. There was a small swell from the north. Carlo rowed out a way and then stepped forward to raise the boat's single sail. The wind was from the east, so they would make good time north to Torcello. Behind them Venice looked beautiful in the morning light, as if they were miles away, and a watery horizon blocked their full view of it.

The two Japanese had stopped talking and were looking over the side. They were over the cemetery of San Michele, Carlo realized. Below them lay the island that had been the city's chief cemetery for centuries; they sailed over a field of tombs, mausoleums, gravestones, obelisks that at low tide could be a navigational hazard. . . . Just enough of the bizarre white blocks could be seen to convince one that they were indeed the result of the architectural thinking of fishes. Carlo crossed himself quickly to impress his customers, and sat back down at the tiller. He pulled the sail tight and they heeled over slightly, slapped into the waves.

In no more than twenty minutes they were east of Murano, skirting its edge. Murano, like Venice an island city crossed with canals, had been a quaint little town before the flood. But it didn't have as many tall buildings as Venice, and it was said that an underwater river had undercut its islands. In any case, it was a wreck. The two Japanese chattered with excitement.

"Can we visit to that city here, Carlo?" asked Hamada.

"It's too dangerous," Carlo answered. "Buildings have fallen into the canal."

They nodded, smiling. "Are people live here?" Taku asked.

"A few, yes. They live in the highest buildings on the

floors still above water, and work in Venice. That way they avoid having to build a roof-house in the city.''

The two faces of his companions expressed incomprehension.

''They avoid the housing shortage in Venice,'' Carlo said. ''There's a certain housing shortage in Venice, as you may have noticed.'' His listeners caught the joke this time and laughed.

''Could live on floors below if owning scuba such as that here,'' Hamada said, gesturing at Carlo's equipment.

''Yes,'' he replied. ''Or we could grow gills.'' He bugged his eyes out and wiggled his fingers at his neck to indicate gills. The Japanese loved it.

Past Murano the Lagoon was clear for a few miles, a sunbeaten blue covered with choppy waves. The boat tipped up and down, the wind tugged at the sail cord in Carlo's hand. He began to enjoy himself. ''Storm coming,'' he volunteered to the others, and pointed at the black line over the horizon to the north. It was a common sight; short, violent storms swept over Brenner Pass from the Austrian Alps, dumping on the Po Valley and the Lagoon before dissipating in the Adriatic . . . once a week, or more, even in the summer. That was one reason the fish market was held under the domes of San Marco; everyone had gotten sick of trading in the rain.

Even the Japanese recognized the clouds. ''Many rain fall soon here,'' Taku said.

Hamada grinned and said, ''Taku and Tafur, weather prophets no doubt, make big company!''

They laughed. ''Does he do this in Japan, too?'' Carlo asked.

''Yes, indeed, surely. In Japan rains every day—Taku says, 'It rains tomorrow for surely.' Weather prophet!''

After the laughter receded, Carlo said, ''Hasn't all the rain drowned some of your cities too?''

''What's that here?''

"Don't you have some Venices in Japan?"

But they didn't want to talk about that. "I don't understand . . . No, no Venice in Japan," Hamada said easily, but neither laughed as they had before. They sailed on. Venice was out of sight under the horizon, as was Murano. Soon they would reach Burano. Carlo guided the boat over the waves and listened to his companions converse in their improbable language, or mangle Italian in a way that alternately made him want to burst with hilarity or bite the gunwale with frustration.

Gradually Burano bounced over the horizon, the campanile first, followed by the few buildings still above water. Murano still had inhabitants, a tiny market, even a midsummer festival; Burano was empty. Its campanile stood at a distinct angle, like the mast of a foundered ship. It had been an island town, before 2040; now it had "canals" between every rooftop. Carlo disliked the town intensely and gave it a wide berth. His companions discussed it quietly in Japanese.

Just beyond it was Torcello, another island ghost town. The campanile could be seen from Burano, tall and white against the black clouds to the north. They approached in silence. Carlo took down the sail, set Taku in the bow to look for snags, and rowed cautiously to the edge of town. They moved between rooftops and walls that stuck up like reefs or like old foundations out of the earth. Many of the roof tiles and beams had been taken for use in construction back in Venice. This had happened to Torcello before. During the Renaissance it had been a little rival of Venice, boasting a population of twenty thousand, but during the sixteenth and seventeenth centuries it had been entirely deserted. Builders from Venice had come looking in the ruins for good marble or a staircase of the right dimensions. . . . Briefly a tiny population had returned, to make lace and host those tourists who wanted to be melancholy; but the waters rose, and Torcello died for good. Carlo pushed off a wall with his oar, and a big section of it tilted over and sank. He tried not to notice.

He rowed them to the open patch of water that had been the Piazza. Around them stood a few intact rooftops, no taller than the mast of their boat; broken walls of stone or rounded brick; the shadowy suggestion of walls just underwater. It was hard to tell what the street plan of the town would have been. On one side of the Piazza was the cathedral of Santa Maria Assunta, however, still supporting the white campanile that stood square and solid, as if over a living community.

"That here is the church we desire to dive," Hamada said.

Carlo nodded. The amusement he had felt during the sail was entirely gone. He rowed around the Piazza looking for a flat spot where they could stand and put on the scuba gear. The church outbuildings—it had been an extensive structure—were all underwater. At one point the boat's keel scraped the ridge of a roof. They rowed down the length of the barnlike nave, looked in the high windows: floored with water. No surprise. One of the small windows in the side of the campanile had been widened with sledgehammers. Directly inside it was the stone staircase and, a few steps up, a stone floor. They hooked the boat to the wall and moved their gear up to the floor. In the dim midday light the stone of the interior was pocked with shadows. It had a rough-hewn look. The citizens of Torcello had built the campanile in a hurry, thinking that the world would end at the millennium, the year 1000. Carlo smiled to think how much longer they had had than that. They climbed the steps of the staircase, up to the sudden sunlight of the bell chamber, to look around; viewed Burano, Venice in the distance . . . to the north, the shallows of the Lagoon, and the coast of Italy. Beyond that, the black line of clouds was like a wall nearly submerged under the horizon, but it was rising; the storm would come.

They descended, put on the scuba gear, and flopped into the water beside the campanile. They were above the complex of church buildings, and it was dark. Carlo slowly led the two Japanese back into the Piazza and swam down. The ground was silted, and Carlo was careful not to step on it. His charges saw the great stone chair in the center of the Piazza (it had been called the Throne of Attila, Carlo remembered from one of his moldy books, and no one had known why), and waving to each other they swam to it. One of them made ludicrous attempts to stand on the bottom and walk around in his fins; he threw up clouds of silt. The other joined him. They each sat in the stone chair, columns of bubbles rising from them, and snapped pictures of each other with their underwater cameras. The silt would ruin the shots, Carlo thought. While they cavorted, he wondered sourly what they wanted in the church.

Eventually, Hamada swam up to him and gestured at the church. Behind the mask his eyes were excited. Carlo pumped his fins up and down slowly and led them around to the big entrance at the front. The doors were gone. They swam into the church.

Inside it was dark, and all three of them unhooked their big flashlights and turned them on. Cones of murky water turned to crystal as the beams swept about. The interior of the church was undistinguished, the floor thick with mud. Carlo watched his two customers swim about and let his flashlight beam rove the walls. Some of the underwater windows were still intact, an odd sight. Occasionally the beam caught a column of bubbles, transmuting them to silver.

Quickly enough the Japanese went to the picture at the west end of the nave, a tile mosaic. Taku (Carlo guessed) rubbed the slime off the tiles, vastly improving their color. They had gone to the big one first, the one portraying the Crucifixion, the Resurrection of the Dead, and the Day of Judgement. A busy mural. Carlo swam over to have a better look. But no sooner had the Japanese wiped the wall clean than they were off to the other end of the church, where above the stalls of the apse was another mosaic. Carlo followed.

It didn't take long to rub this one clean; and when the water had cleared, the three of them floated there, their flashlight beams converged on the picture revealed.

It was the Teotaca Madonna, the God-bearer. She stood against a dull gold background, holding the Child in her arms, staring out at the world with a sad and knowing gaze. Carlo pumped his legs to get above the Japanese, holding his light steady on the Madonna's face. She looked as though she could see all time: all her child's short life, all the terror and calamity after that. . . . There were mosaic tears on her cheeks. At the sight of them, Carlo could barely check tears of his own from joining the general wetness on his face. He felt that he had suddenly been transposed to a church on the deepest floor of the ocean, the pressure of his feelings threatened to implode him, he could scarcely hold them off. The water was freezing, he was shivering, sending up a thick, nearly continuous stream of bubbles . . . and the Madonna watched. With a kick he turned and swam away. Like startled fish his two companions followed him. Carlo led them out of the church into murky light, then up to the surface, to the boat and the window casement.

Fins off, Carlo sat on the staircase and dripped. Taku and Hamada scrambled through the window and joined him. They conversed for a moment in Japanese, clearly excited. Carlo stared at them blackly.

Hamada turned to him. "That here is the picture we desire," he said. "The Madonna with Child."

"What?" Carlo cried.

Hamada raised his eyebrows. "We desire taking home that here picture to Japan."

"But it's impossible! The picture is made of little tiles stuck to the wall—there's no way to get them off!"

"Italy government permits," Taku said, but Hamada silenced him with a gesture.

"Mosaic, yes. We use instruments we take here—water torch. Archaeology method, you understand. Cut blocks out of wall, bricks, number them—construct on new place in Japan. Above water." He flashed his pearly smile.

"You can't do that," Carlo stated, deeply affronted.

"I don't understand." Hamada said. But he did. "Italian government permits us that."

"This isn't Italy," Carlo said savagely, and in his anger stood. What good would a Madonna do in Japan, anyway? They weren't even Christian. "Italy is over there," he said, in his excitement mistakenly waving to the southeast, no doubt confusing his listeners even more. "This has never been Italy! This is Venice! The Republic!"

"I don't understand." He had that phrase down pat. "Italian government has giving permit us."

"Christ," Carlo said. After a disgusted pause: "Just how long will this take?"

"Time? We work that afternoon, tomorrow; place the bricks here, go hire Venice barge to carry bricks to Venice—"

"Stay here overnight? I'm not going to stay here overnight, God damn it!"

"We bring sleeping bag for you—"

"No!" Carlo was furious. "I'm not staying, you miserable heathen hyenas—" He pulled off his scuba gear.

"I don't understand."

Carlo dried off, got dressed. "I'll let you keep your scuba tanks, and I'll be back for you tomorrow afternoon, late. *Understand?*"

"Yes," Hamada said, staring at him steadily, without expression. "Bring barge?"

"What?—yes, yes, I'll bring your barge, you miserable slime-eating catfish. Vultures . . ." He went on for a while, getting the boat out of the window.

"Storm coming!" Taku said brightly, pointing to the north.

"To hell with you!" Carlo said, pushing off and beginning to row. "Understand?"

He rowed out of Torcello and back onto the Lagoon. Indeed, a storm was coming. He would have to hurry. He put up the sail and pulled the canvas decking back until it covered everything but the seat he was sitting on. The wind was from the north now, strong but fitful. It pulled the sail taut, and the boat bucked over the choppy waves, leaving behind a wake that was bright white against the black of the sky. The clouds were drawing over the sky like a curtain, covering half of it: half black, half colorless blue, and the line of the edge was solid. It resembled that first great storm of 2040, Carlo guessed, that had pulled over Venice like a black wool blanket and dumped water for forty days. And it had never been the same again, not anywhere in the world. . . .

Now he was beside the wreck of Burano. Against the black sky he could see only the drunken campanile, and suddenly he realized why he hated the sight of this abandoned town: it was a vision of the Venice to come, a cruel model of the future. If the water level rose even three meters, Venice would become nothing but a big Burano. Even if the water didn't rise, more people were leaving Venice every year. . . . One day it would be empty. Once again the sadness he had felt looking at the Teotaca filled him, a sadness become a bottomless despair. "God damn it," he said, staring at the crippled campanile; but that wasn't enough. He didn't know words that were enough. "God *damn* it."

Just beyond Burano the squall hit. It almost blew the sail out of his hand; he had to hold on with a fierce clench, tie it to the stern, tie the tiller in place, and scramble over the pitching canvas deck to lower the sail, cursing all the while. He brought the sail down to its last reefing, which left a handkerchief-sized patch exposed to the wind. Even so, the boat yanked over the waves and the mast creaked as if it would tear loose. . . . The choppy waves had become white-caps, in the screaming wind their tops were tearing loose and flying through the air, white foam in the blackness. . . .

Best to head for Murano for refuge, Carlo thought. Then the rain started. It was colder than the Lagoon water and fell almost horizontally. The wind was still picking up. His handkerchief sail was going to pull the mast out. ''Madonna,'' he said. He got onto the decking again, slid up to the mast, took down the sail with cold and disobedient fingers. He crawled back to his hole in the deck, hanging on desperately as the boat yawed. It was almost broadside to the waves and hastily he grabbed the tiller and pulled it around, just in time to meet a large wave stern-on. He shuddered with relief. Each wave seemed bigger than the last; they picked up quickly on the Lagoon. Well, he thought, what now? Get out the oars? No, that wouldn't do; he had to keep stern-on to the waves, and besides, he couldn't row effectively in this chop. He had to go where the waves were going, he realized; and if they missed Murano and Venice, that meant the Adriatic.

As the waves lifted and dropped him, he grimly contemplated the thought. His mast alone acted like a sail in a wind of this force; and the wind seemed to be blowing from a bit to the west of north. The waves—the biggest he had ever seen on the Lagoon, perhaps the biggest *ever* on the Lagoon—pushed in about the same direction as the wind, naturally. Well, that meant he would miss Venice, which was directly south, maybe even a touch west of south. Damn, he thought. And all because he had been angered by those two Japanese and the Teotaca. What did he care what happened to a sunken mosaic from Torcello? He had helped foreigners find and cart off the one bronze horse of San Marco that had fallen . . . more than one of the stone lions of Venice, symbol of the city . . . the entire Bridge of Sighs, for Christ's sake! What had come over him? Why should he have cared about a forgotten mosaic?

Well, he had done it; and here he was. No altering it. Each wave lifted his boat stern first and slid under it until he could look down in the trough, if he cared to, and see his mast nearly horizontal, until he rose over the broken, foaming crest, each one of which seemed to want to break down his little hole in the decking and swamp him—for a second he was in midair, the tiller free and useless until he crashed into the next trough. Every time at the top he thought, this wave will catch us, and so even though he was wet and the wind and rain were cold, the repeated spurts of fear adrenaline and his thick wool coat kept him warm. A hundred waves or so served to convince him that the next one would probably slide under him as safely as the last, and he relaxed a bit. Nothing to do but wait it out, keep the boat exactly stern-on to the swell . . . and he would be all right. Sure, he thought, he would just ride these waves across the Adriatic to Trieste or Rijeka, one of those two tawdry towns that had replaced Venice as Queen of the Adriatic . . . the princesses of the Adriatic, so to speak, and two little sluts they were, too. . . . Or ride the storm out, turn around, and sail back in, better yet. . . .

On the other hand, the Lido had become a sort of reef, in most places, and waves of this size would break over it, capsizing him for sure. And, to be realistic, the top of the Adriatic was wide. Just one mistake on the top of these waves (and he couldn't go on forever) and he would be broached, capsized, and rolled down to join all the other Venetians who had ended up on the bottom of the Adriatic. And all because of that damn Madonna. Carlo sat crouched in the stern, adjusting the tiller for the particulars of each wave, ignoring all else in the howling, black, horizonless chaos of water and air around him, pleased in a grim way that he was sailing to his death with such perfect seamanship. But he kept the Lido out of mind.

And so he sailed on, losing track of time as one does when

there is no spatial referent. Wave after wave after wave. A little water collected at the bottom of his boat, and his spirits sank. That was no way to go, to have the boat sink by degrees under him. . . .

Then the high-pitched, airy howl of the wind was joined by a low booming, a bass roar. He looked over his shoulder in the direction he was being driven and saw a white line, stretching from left to right; his heart jumped, fear exploded through him. This was it. The Lido, now a barrier reef tripping the waves. They were smashing down on it, he could see white sheets bouncing skyward and blowing to nothing. He was terrifically frightened. It would have been so much easier to founder at sea.

But there—among the white breakers, off to the right—a gray finger pointing up at the black—

A campanile. Carlo was forced to look back at the wave he was under, to straighten the boat, but when he looked back it was still there. A campanile, standing there like a dead lighthouse. "Jesus!" he said aloud. It looked as if the waves were pushing him a couple hundred meters to the north of it. As each wave lifted him he had a moment when the boat was sliding down the face of the wave as fast as it was moving under him; during these moments he shifted the tiller a bit and the boat turned and surfed across the face, to the south, until the wave rose up under him to the crest, and he had to straighten it out. He repeated the delicate operation time after time, sometimes nearly broaching the boat in his impatience. But that wouldn't do—just take as much from each wave as it will give you, he thought. And pray it will add up to enough.

The Lido got closer, and it looked as if he was directly upwind of the campanile. It was the one at the Lido channel entrance, or perhaps the one at Pellestrina, farther south; he had no way of knowing, and at the moment didn't care. He was just happy that his ancestors had seen fit to construct such solid bell towers. In between waves he reached under the decking and by touch found his boat hook and the length of rope he carried. It was going to be a problem, actually, when he got to the campanile—it would not do to pass it helplessly by a few meters. On the other hand he couldn't smash into it and expect to survive either, not in these waves. In fact the more he considered it, the more exact and difficult he realized the approach would have to be, and fearfully he stopped thinking about it and concentrated on the waves.

The last one was the biggest. As the boat slid down its face, the face got steeper, until it seemed they would be swept on by this wave forever. The campanile loomed ahead, big and black. Around it waves pitched over and broke with sharp, deadly booms; from behind Carlo could see the water sucked over the breaks, as if over short but infinitely broad waterfalls. The noise was tremendous. At the top of the wave it appeared he could jump in the campanile's top windows—he got out the boat hook, shifted the tiller a touch, took a deep breath. Amid the roaring, the wave swept him just past the stone tower, smacking against it and splashing him; he pulled the tiller over hard, the boat shot into the wake of the campanile—he stood and swung the boat hook over a window casement above him. It caught, and he held on hard.

He was in the lee of the tower. Broken water rose and dropped under the boat, hissing, but without violence, and he held. One-handed, he wrapped the end of his rope around the sail-cord bolt in the stern, tied the other end to the boat hook. The hook held pretty well. He took a risk and reached down to tie the rope firmly to the bolt. Then another risk: when the boiling soupy water of another broken wave raised the boat, he leaped off his seat, grabbed the stone windowsill, which was too thick to get his fingers over—for a moment he hung by his fingertips. With desperate strength he pulled himself up, reached in with one hand and got a grasp on the inside of the sill, and pulled himself in and over. The stone floor was about four feet below the window. Quickly he pulled the boat hook in, put it on the floor, and took up the slack in the rope.

He looked out the window. His boat rose and fell, rose and fell. Well, it would sink or it wouldn't. Meanwhile, he was safe. Realizing this, he breathed deeply, let out a shout. He remembered shooting past the side of the tower, face no more than two meters from it—getting drenched by the wave slapping the front of it—why, he had done it perfectly! He couldn't do it again like that in a million tries. Triumphant laughs burst out of him, short and sharp: "Ha! Ha! Ha! Jesus Christ! Wow!"

"Whoooo's theeeerre?" called a high scratchy voice, floating down the staircase from the floor above. "Whoooooooo's there? . . ."

Carlo froze. He stepped lightly to the base of the stone staircase and peered up. Through the hole to the next floor flickered a faint light. To put it better, it was less dark up there than anywhere else. More surprised than fearful (though he was afraid), Carlo opened his eyes as wide as he could—

"Whoooooo's theeeeeerrrrrre? . . ."

Quickly he went to the boat hook, untied the rope, felt around on the wet floor until he found a block of stone that would serve as anchor for his boat. He looked out the window: boat still there; on both sides, white breakers crashing over the Lido. Taking up the boat hook, Carlo stepped slowly up the stairs, feeling that after what he had been through he could slash any ghost in the ether to ribbons.

It was a candle lantern, flickering in the disturbed air—a room filled with junk—

"Eeek! Eeek!"

"Jesus!"

"Devil! Death, away!" A small black shape rushed at him, brandishing sharp metal points.

"Jesus!" Carlo repeated, holding the boat hook out to defend himself. The figure stopped.

"Death comes for me at last," it said. It was an old woman, he saw, holding lace needles in each hand.

"Not at all," Carlo said, feeling his pulse slow back down. "Swear to God, Grandmother, I'm just a sailor, blown here by the storm."

The woman pulled back the hood of her black cape, revealing braided white hair, and squinted at him.

"You've got the scythe," she said suspiciously. A few wrinkles left her face as she unfocused her gaze.

"A boat hook only," Carlo said, holding it out for her inspection. She stepped back and raised the lace needles threateningly. "Just a boat hook, I swear to God. To God and Mary and Jesus and all the saints, Grandmother. I'm just a sailor, blown here by the storm from Venice." Part of him felt like laughing.

"Aye?" she said. "Aye, well then, you've found shelter. I don't see so well anymore, you know. Come in, sit down, then." She turned around and led him into the room. "I was just doing some lace for penance, you see . . . though there's scarcely enough light." She lifted a tomboli with the lace pinned to it. Carlo noticed big gaps in the pattern, as in the webs of an injured spider. "A little more light," she said and, picking up a candle, held it to the lit one. When it was fired, she carried it around the chamber and lit three more candles in lanterns that stood on tables, boxes, a wardrobe. She motioned for him to sit in a heavy chair by her table, and he did so.

As she sat down across from him, he looked around the chamber. A bed piled high with blankets, boxes and tables covered with objects . . . the stone walls around, and another staircase leading up to the next floor of the campanile. There was a draft. "Take off your coat," the woman said. She arranged the little pillow on the arm of her chair and began to poke a needle in and out of it, pulling the thread slowly.

Carlo sat back and watched her. "Do you live here alone?"

"Always alone," she replied. "I don't want it otherwise." With the candle before her face, she resembled Carlo's mother or someone else he knew. It seemed very peaceful in the room after the storm. The old woman bent in her chair until her face was just above her tomboli; still, Carlo couldn't help noticing that her needle hit far outside the apparent pattern of lace, striking here and there randomly. She might as well have been blind. At regular intervals Carlo shuddered with excitement and tension. It was hard to believe he was out of danger. More infrequently they broke the silence with a short burst of conversation, then sat in the candlelight absorbed in their own thoughts, as if they were old friends.

"How do you get food?" Carlo asked, after one of these silences had stretched out. "Or candles?"

"I trap lobsters down below. And fishermen come by and trade food for lace. They get a good bargain, never fear. I've never given less, despite what he said—" Anguish twisted her face as the squinting had, and she stopped. She needled furiously, and Carlo looked away. Despite the draft, he was warming up (he hadn't removed his coat, which was wool, after all), and he was beginning to feel drowsy. . . .

"He was my spirit's mate, do you comprehend me?"

Carlo jerked upright. The old woman still looked at her tomboli.

"And—and he left me here, here in this desolation when the floods began, with words that I'll remember forever and ever and ever. Until death comes . . . I wish you *had* been death!" she cried. "I wish you had."

Carlo remembered her brandishing the needles. "What is this place?" he asked gently.

"What?"

"Is this Pellestrina? San Servolo?"

"This is Venice," she said.

Carlo shivered convulsively, stood up.

"I'm the last one of them," the woman said. "The waters

rise, the heavens howl, love's pledges crack and lead to misery. I—I live to show what a person can bear and not die. I'll live till the deluge drowns the world as Venice is drowned; I'll live till all else living is dead; I'll live . . ." Her voice trailed off; she looked up at Carlo curiously. "Who are you, really? Oh, I know. I know. A sailor."

"Are there floors above?" he asked, to change the subject.

She squinted at him. Finally she spoke. "Words are vain. I thought I'd never speak again, not even to my own heart, and here I am, doing it again. Yes, there's a floor above intact; but above that, ruins. Lightning blasted the bell chamber apart, while I lay in that very bed." She stood up. "Come on, I'll show you." Under her cape she was tiny.

She picked up the candle lantern beside her, and Carlo followed her up the stairs, stepping carefully in the shifting shadows.

On the floor above, the wind swirled, and through the stairway to the floor above that, he could distinguish black clouds. The woman put the lantern on the floor, started up the stairs. "Come."

Once through the hole they were in the wind, out under the sky. The rain had stopped. Great blocks of stone lay about the floor, and the walls broke off unevenly.

"I thought the whole campanile would fall," she shouted at him over the whistle of the wind. He nodded, and walked over to the west wall, which stood chest high. Looking over it, he could see the waves approaching, rising up, smashing against the stone below, spraying back and up at him. He could feel the blows in his feet. Their force frightened him; it was hard to believe he had survived them and was now out of danger. He shook his head violently. To his right and left the white lines of crumbled waves marked the Lido, a broad swath of them against the black. The old woman was speaking, he saw; he walked back to her side and listened.

"The waters yet rise," she shouted. "See? And the lightning . . . you can see the lightning breaking the Alps to dust. It's the end, child. Every island fled away, and the mountains were not found . . . the second angel poured out his vial upon the sea, and it became as the blood of a dead man: and every living thing died in the sea.'' On and on she spoke, her voice mingling with the sound of the gale and the boom of the waves, just carrying over it all . . . until Carlo, cold and tired, filled with pity and a black anguish like the clouds rolling over them, put his arm around her thin shoulders and turned her around. They descended to the floor below, picked up the extinguished lantern, and descended to her chamber, which was still lit. It seemed warm, a refuge. He could hear her still speaking. He was shivering without pause.

''You must be cold,'' she said in a practical tone. She pulled a few blankets from her bed. ''Here, take these.'' He sat down in the big heavy chair, put the blankets around his legs, put his head back. He was tired. The old woman sat in her chair and wound thread onto a spool. After a few minutes of silence she began talking again, and as Carlo dozed and shifted position and nodded off again, she talked and talked, of storms, and drownings, and the world's end, and lost love. . . .

In the morning when he woke up, she was gone. Her room stood revealed in the dim morning light: shabby, the furniture battered, the blankets worn, the knickknacks of Venetian glass ugly, as Venetian glass always was . . . but it was clean. Carlo got up and stretched his stiff muscles. He went up to the roof; she wasn't there. It was a sunny morning. Over the east wall he saw that his boat was still there, still floating. He grinned—the first one in a few days; he could feel that in his face.

The woman was not on the floors below, either. The lowest one served as her boathouse, he could see. In it were a pair of decrepit rowboats and some lobster pots. The biggest ''boatslip'' was empty. She was probably out checking pots.

Or perhaps she hadn't wanted to talk with him in the light of day.

From the boathouse he could walk around to his craft, through water only knee-deep. He sat in the stern, reliving the previous afternoon, and grinned again at being alive.

He took off the decking and bailed out the water on the keel with his bailing can, keeping an eye out for the old woman. Then he remembered the boat hook and went back upstairs for it. When he returned there was still no sight of her. He shrugged. He'd come back and say good-bye another time. He rowed around the campanile and off the Lido, pulled up the sail, and headed northwest, where he presumed Venice was.

The Lagoon was as flat as a pond this morning, the sky cloudless, like the blue dome of a great basilica. It was amazing, but Carlo was not surprised. The weather was like that these days. Last night's storm, however, had been something else. That was the mother of all squalls, those were the biggest waves in the Lagoon ever, without a doubt. He began rehearsing his tale in his mind, for wife and friends.

Venice appeared over the horizon right off his bow, just where he thought it would be: first the great campanile, then San Marco and the other spires. The campanile . . . Thank God his ancestors had wanted to get up there so close to God—or so far off the water—the urge had saved his life. In the rain-washed air, the sea approach to the city was more beautiful than ever, and it didn't even bother him as it usually did that no matter how close you got to it, it still seemed to be over the horizon. That was just the way it was, now. The Serenissima. He was happy to see it.

He was hungry, and still very tired. When he pulled into the Grand Canal and took down the sail, he found he could barely row. The rain was pouring off the land into the Lagoon, and the Grand Canal was running like a mountain river. It was tough going. At the fire station where the canal bent back, some of his friends working on a new roof-house waved at him, looking surprised to see him going upstream so early in the day. "You're going the wrong way!" one shouted.

Carlo waved an oar weakly before plopping it back in. "Don't I know it!" he replied.

Over the Rialto, back into the little courtyard of San Giacometta. Onto the sturdy dock he and his neighbors had built, staggering a bit—careful there, Carlo.

"Carlo!" his wife shrieked from above. "Carlo, Carlo, Carlo!" She flew down the ladder from the roof.

He stood on the dock. He was home.

"Carlo, Carlo, Carlo!" his wife cried as she ran onto the dock.

"Jesus," he pleaded, "shut up." And pulled her into a rough hug.

"Where have you been, I was so worried about you because of the storm, you said you'd be back yesterday, oh, Carlo, I'm so glad to see you. . . ." She tried to help him up the ladder. The baby was crying. Carlo sat down in the kitchen chair and looked around the little makeshift room with satisfaction. In between chewing down bites of a loaf of bread he told Luisa of his adventure: the two Japanese and their vandalism, the wild ride across the Lagoon, the madwoman on the campanile. When he had finished the story and the loaf of bread, he began to fall alseep.

"But Carlo, you have to go back and pick up those Japanese."

"To hell with them," he said slurrily. "Creepy little bastards. . . . They're tearing the Madonna apart, didn't I tell you? They'll take everything in Venice, every last painting and statue and carving and mosaic and all . . . I can't stand it."

"Oh, Carlo. It's all right. They take those things all over

the world and put them up and say this is from Venice, the greatest city in the world."

"They should be here."

"Here, here, come in and lie down for a few hours. I'll go see if Giuseppe will go to Torcello with you to bring back those bricks." She arranged him on their bed. "Let them have what's under the water, Carlo. Let them have it." He slept.

He sat up struggling, his arm shaken by his wife.

"Wake up, it's late. You've got to go to Torcello to get those men. Besides, they've got your scuba gear."

Carlo groaned.

"Maria says Giuseppe will go with you. He'll meet you with his boat on the Fondamente."

"Damn."

"Come on, Carlo, we need that money."

"All right, all right." The baby was squalling. He collapsed back on the bed. "I'll do it. Don't pester me."

He got up and drank her soup. Stiffly he descended the ladder, ignoring Luisa's instructions and warnings, and got back in his boat. He untied it, pushed off, let it float out of the courtyard to the wall of San Giacometta. He stared at the wall.

Once, he remembered, he had put on his scuba gear and swum down into the church. He had kneeled behind one of the stone pews in front of the altar, adjusting his weightbelts and tank to do so, and had tried to pray through his mouthpiece and the facemask. The silver bubbles of his breath had floated up through the water toward heaven; whether his prayers had gone with them, he had no idea. After a while, feeling somewhat foolish—but not entirely—he had swum out the door. Over it he had noticed an inscription and stopped to read it, facemask centimeters from the stone. *Around This Temple Let the Merchant's Law Be Just, His*

Weight True, and His Covenants Faithful. It was an admonition to the old usurers of the Rialto, but he could make it his, he thought; the true weight could refer to the diving belts, not to overload his clients and sink them to the bottom. . . .

The memory passed and he was on the surface again, with a job to do. He took in a deep breath and let it out, put the oars in the oarlocks and started to row.

Let them have what was under the water. What lived in Venice was still afloat.

—1980

Mercurial

"She rules all of Oz," said Dorothy, "and so she rules your city and you, because you are in the Winkie Country, which is part of the Land of Oz."

"It may be," returned the High Coco-Lorum, "for we do not study geography and have never inquired whether we live in the Land of Oz or not. And any Ruler who rules us from a distance, and unknown to us, is welcome to the job."

—L. Frank Baum, *The Lost Princess of Oz*

I am not, despite the appearances, fond of crime detection. In the past, it is true, I occasionally accompanied my friend Freya Grindavik as she solved her cases, and admittedly this watsoning gave me some good material for the little tales I have written for the not-very-discriminating markets on Mars and Titan. But after The Case of the Golden Sphere of the Lion of Mercury, in which I ended up hung by the feet from the clear dome of Terminator, two hundred meters above the rooftops of the city, my native lack of enthusiasm rose to the fore. And following the unfortunate Adventure of the Vulcan Accelerator, when Freya's arch-foe Jan Johannsen tied us to a pile of hay under a large magnifying glass in a survival tent, there to await Mercury's fierce dawn, I put my foot down: no more detecting. That, so to speak, was the last straw.

So when I agreed to accompany Freya to the Solday party of Heidi Van Seegeren, it was against my better judgement. But Freya assured me there would be no business involved; and despite the obvious excesses, I enjoy a Solday party as much as the next aesthete. So when she came by my villa, I was ready.

"Make haste," she said. "We're late, and I must be before Heidi's Monet when the Great Gates are opened. I adore that painting."

"Your infatuation is no secret," I said, panting as I trailed her through the crowded streets of the city. Freya, as those of you who have read my earlier tales know, is two and a half meters tall, and broad-shouldered; she barged through the shoals of Solday celebrants rather like a whale, and I, pilot-fishlike, dodged in her wake. She led me through a group of Greys, who with carpetbeaters were busy pounding rugs saturated with yellow dust. As I coughed and brushed off my fine burgundy suit, I said, "My feeling is that you have taken me to view that antique canvas once or twice too often."

She looked at me sternly. "As you will see, on Solday it transcends even its usual beauty. You look like a bee drowning in pollen, Nathaniel."

"Whose fault is that?" I demanded, brushing my suit fastidiously.

We came to the gate in the wall surrounding Van Seegeren's town villa, and Freya banged on it loudly. The gate was opened by a scowling man. He was nearly a meter shorter than Freya, and had a balding head that bulged rather like the dome of the city. In a mincing voice he said, "Invitations?"

"What's this?" said Freya. "We have permanent invitations from Heidi."

"I'm sorry," the man said coolly. "Ms. Van Seegeren has decided her Solday parties have gotten overcrowded, and this time she sent out invitations and instructed me to let in only those who have them."

"Then there has been a mistake," Freya declared. "Get Heidi on the intercom, and she will instruct you to let me in. I am Freya Grindavik, and this is Nathaniel Sebastian."

"I'm sorry," the man said, quite unapologetically. "Every person turned away says the same thing, and Ms. Van Seegeren prefers not to be disturbed so frequently."

"She'll be more disturbed to hear we've been held up." Freya shifted toward the man. "Who are you, anyway?"

"I am Sandor Musgrave, Ms. Van Seegeren's private secretary."

"How come I've never met you?"

"Ms. Van Seegeren hired me two months ago," Musgrave said, and stepped back so he could look Freya in the eye without straining his neck. "That is immaterial, however—"

"I've been Heidi's friend for over forty years," Freya said slowly, once again shifting forward to lean over the man. "And I would wager she values her friends more than her secretaries. . . ."

Musgrave stepped back indignantly. "I'm sorry!" he snapped. "I have my orders! Good day!"

But alas for him, Freya was now standing well in the gateway, and she seemed uninclined to move; she merely cocked her head at him. Musgrave comprehended his problem, and his mouth twitched uncertainly.

The impasse was broken when Van Seegeren's maid Lucinda arrived from the street. "Oh, hello Freya, Nathaniel. What are you doing out here?"

"This new Malvolio of yours is barring our entrance," Freya said.

"Oh, Musgrave," said Lucinda. "Let these two in, or the boss will be mad."

Musgrave retreated with a deep scowl. "I've studied the ancients, Ms. Grindavik," he said sullenly. "You need not insult me."

"Malvolio was a tragic character," Freya assured him. "Read Charles Lamb's essay concerning the matter."

"I certainly will," Musgrave said stiffly, and hurried to the villa, giving us a last poisonous look.

"Of course Lamb's father," Freya said absently, staring after the man, "was a house servant. Lucinda, who is that?"

Lucinda rolled her eyes. "The boss hired him to restore some of her paintings, and get the records in order. I wish she hadn't."

The bell in the gate sounded. "I've got it, Musgrave," Lucinda shouted at the villa. She opened the gate, revealing the artist Harvey Washburn.

"So you do," said Harvey, blinking. He was high again; a bottle of the White Brother hung from his hand. "Freya! Nathaniel! Happy Solday to you—have a drink?"

We refused the offer, and then followed Harvey around the side of the villa, exchanging a glance. I felt sorry for Harvey. Most of Mercury's great collectors came to Harvey's showings, but they dissected his every brushstroke for influences, and told him what he *should* be painting, and then among themselves they called his work amateurish and unoriginal, and never bought a single canvas. I was never surprised to see him drinking.

We rounded the side of the big villa and stepped onto the white stone patio, which was made of a giant slab of England's Dover cliffs, cut out and transported to Mercury entire. Malvolio Musgrave had spoken the truth about Heidi reducing the size of her Solday party: where often the patio had been jammed, there were now less than a dozen people. I spotted George Butler, Heidi's friend and rival art collector, and Arnold Ohman, the art dealer who obtained for many of Mercury's collectors their ancient masterpieces from Earth. As I greeted them Freya led us all across the patio to the back wall of the villa, which was also fronted with white slabs of the Dover cliffs. There, all alone, hung Claude Monet's *Rouen Cathedral—Sun Effect*. "Look at it, Nathaniel!" Freya commanded me. "Isn't it beautiful?"

I looked at it. Now you must understand that, as owner of the Gallery Orientale, and by deepest personal aesthetic conviction, I am a connoisseur of Chinese art, a style in which a dozen artfully spontaneous brushstrokes can serve to delineate a mountain or two, several trees, a small village and its inhabitants, and perhaps some birds. Given my predilection, you will not be surprised to learn that merely to look at the antique rectangle of color that Freya so admired was to risk damaging my eyes. Thick scumbled layers of grainy paint scarcely revealed the cathedral of the title, which wavered under a blast of light so intense that I doubted Mercury's midday could compete with it. Small blobs of every color served to represent both the indistinct stone and a pebbly sky; both were composed of combinations principally of white, yellow, and purple, though as I say, every other color made an appearance.

"Stunning," I said, with a severe squint. "Are you sure this Monet wasn't a bit nearsighted?"

Freya glared at me, ignoring Butler's chuckles. "I suppose your comment might have been funny the first time you made it. To children, anyway."

"But I heard it was actually *true,*" I said, shielding my eyes with one hand. "Monet *was* nearsighted, and so like Goya his vision affected his painting—"

"I should hope so," Harvey said solemnly.

"—so all he could see were those blobs of color, isn't that sad?"

Freya shook her head. "You won't get a rise out of me

today, Nathaniel. You'll have to think up your dinner conversation by yourself.''

Momentarily stopped by this riposte, I retired with Arnold Ohman to Heidi's patio bar. After dialing drinks from the bartender we sat on the blocks of Dover cliffs that made up the patio's low outer wall. We toasted Solday, and contemplated the clouds of yellow talc that swirled over the orange tile rooftops below us. For those of you who have never visited it, Terminator is an oval city. The forward half of the city is flat, and projects out under the clear dome. The rear half of the oval is terraced, and rises to the tall Dawn Wall, which supports the upper rim of the dome, and shields the city from the perpetually rising sun. The Great Gates of Terminator are near the top of the Dawn Wall, and when they are opened, shafts of Sol's overwhelming light spear through the city's air, illuminating everything in a yellow brilliance. Heidi Van Seegeren's villa was about halfway up the terraced slope; we looked upon gray stone walls, orange tile roofs, and the dusty vines and lemon trees of the terrace gardens that dotted the city; outside the dome the twelve big tracks over which the city slid extended off to the horizon, circling the planet like a slender silver wedding band. It was a fine view, and I lifted my glass to the idea that Claude Monet wasn't there to paint it. For sometimes, if you ask me, reality is enough.

Ohman downed his drink in one swallow. Rumor had it that he was borrowing heavily to finance one of his big terran purchases; it was whispered he was planning to buy the closed portion of the Louvre—or the Renaissance room of the Vatican museum—or Amsterdam's Van Gogh collection. But rumors like that circulated around Arnold continuously. He was that kind of dealer. It was unlikely any of them were true; still, his silence seemed to reveal a certain tension.

''Look at the way Freya is soaking in that painting you got for Heidi,'' I said, to lift his spirits. Freya's face was within centimeters of the canvas, where she could examine it blob by blob; the people behind her could see nothing but her white-blond hair. Ohman smiled at the sight. He had brought the Monet back from his most recent terran expedition, and apparently it had been a great struggle to obtain it. Both the English family that owned it and the British government had had to be paid enormous sums to secure its release, and only the fact that Mercury was universally considered humanity's greatest art museum had cleared the matter with the courts. It had been one of Arnold's finest hours. Now he said, "Maybe we should pull her away a bit, so that others can see."

"If both of us tug on her it may work," I said. We stood and went to her side. Harvey Washburn, looking flushed and frazzled, joined us, and we convinced Freya to share the glory. Ohman and Butler conferred over something, and entered the villa through the big French doors that led into the concert room. Inside, Heidi's orchestra rolled up and down the scales of Mussorgsky's *Hut of Baba Yaga*. That meant it was close to the time when the Great Gates would open (Heidi always gets inside information about this). Sure enough, as Mussorgsky's composition burst from the *Hut of Baba Yaga* into the *Great Gates of Kiev*, two splinters of white light split the air under the dome. Shouts and fanfares rose everywhere, nearly drowning the amplified sound of our orchestra. Slowly the Great Gates opened, and as they did the shafts of light grew to thick buttery gold bars of air. By their rich, nearly blinding glare, Heidi Van Seegeren made her first entrance from her villa, timing her steps to the exaggerated Maazel ritard that her conductor Hiu employed every Solday when *Pictures at an Exhibition* was performed. This ritard shifted the music from the merely grandiose to the utterly bombastical, and it took Heidi over a minute to cross her own narrow patio; but I suppose it was not entirely silly, given the ritual nature of the moment, and the flood of light that was making the air appear a thick, quite tangible gel.

What with the light, and the uproar created by the keening Greys and the many orchestras in the neighborhood, each playing their own overture or fanfare (the *Coriolan* came from one side of us, the *1812* from the other), it was a complex and I might even say *noisy* aesthetic moment, and the last thing I needed was to take another look at the Monet monstrosity, but Freya would not have it otherwise.

"You've never seen it when the Great Gates are opened," she said. "That was the whole point in bringing you here today."

"I see." Actually I barely saw anything; as Freya had guided me by the arm to the painting I had accidentally looked directly at the incandescent yellow bars of sunlight, and brilliant blue afterimages bounced in my sight. I heard rather than saw Harvey Washburn join us. Many blinks later I was able to join the others in devoting my attention to the big canvas.

Well. The Monet positively *glowed* in the dense, lambent air; it gave off light like a lamp, vibrating with a palpable energy of its own. At the sight of it even I was impressed.

"Yes," I admitted to Freya and Harvey, "I can see how precisely he placed all those little chunks of color, and I can see how sharp and solid the cathedral is under all that goo, but it's like Solday, you know, it's a heightened effect. The result is garish, really, it's too much."

"But this is a painting of midday," Harvey said. "And as you can see, midday can get pretty garish."

"But this is Terminator! The Greys have put a lot of talc in the air to make it look this way!"

"So what?" Freya demanded impatiently. "Stop thinking so much, Nathaniel. Just *look* at it. *See* it. Isn't it beautiful? Haven't you felt things look that way sometimes, seeing stone in sunlight?"

"Well . . ." And, since I am a strictly honest person, if I had said anything at all I would have had to admit that it did have a power about it. It drew the eye; it poured light onto us as surely as the beams of sunlight extending from the gates in the Dawn Wall to the curved side of the clear dome.

"Well?" Freya demanded.

"Well yes," I said, "yes I see that cathedral front—I feel it. But there must have been quite a heat wave in old Rouen. It's as if Monet had seen Terminator on Solday, the painting fits so well with this light."

"No," Freya said, but her left eye was squinted, a sign she is thinking.

Harvey said, "We make the conditions of light in Terminator, and so it is an act of the imagination, like this painting. You shouldn't be surprised if there are similarities. We value this light because the old masters created it on their canvases."

I shook my head, and indicated the brassy bedlam around us. "No. I believe we made this one up ourselves."

Freya and Harvey laughed, with the giddiness that Solday inspires.

Suddenly a loud screech came from inside the villa. Freya hurried across the patio into the music room, and I followed her. Both of us, however, had forgotten the arrangements that Heidi made on Soldays to cast the brilliant light throughout her home, and as we ran past the silenced orchestra into a hallway we were blasted by light from a big mirror carefully placed in the villa's central atrium. Screams still echoed from somewhere inside, but we could only stumble blindly through bright pulsing afterimages, retinal Monets if you will, while unidentified persons bowled into us, and mirrors crashed to the floor. And the atrium was raised, so that occasional steps up in the hallway tripped us. "Murder!" someone cried. "Murder! There he goes!" And with that a whole group of us were off down the halls like hounds—blind hounds—baying after unknown prey. A figure leaped from behind a mirror glaring white, and Freya and I tackled it just inside the atrium.

When my vision swam back I saw it was George Butler. "What's going on?" he asked, very politely for a man who had just been jumped on by Freya Grindavik.

"Don't ask us," Freya said irritably.

"Murder!" shrieked Lucinda from the hallway that led from the atrium directly back to the patio. We jumped up and crowded into the hallway. Just beyond a mirror shattered into many pieces lay a man's body; apparently he had been crawling toward the patio when he collapsed, and one arm and finger extended ahead of him, pointing to the patio still.

Freya approached, gingerly turned the body's head. "It's that Musgrave fellow," she said, blinking to clear her sight. "He's dead all right. Struck on the head with the mirror there, no doubt."

Heidi Van Seegeren joined us. "What's going on?"

"That was my question," George Butler said.

Freya explained the situation to her.

"Call the police," Heidi said to Lucinda. "And I suppose no one should leave."

I sighed.

And so crime detection ensnared me once again. I helped Freya by circulating on the patio, calming the shocked and nervous guests. "Um, excuse me, very sorry to inform you, yes, sorry—hard to believe, yes—somebody had it in for the secretary Musgrave, it appears," all the while watching to see if anyone would jump, or turn pale, or start to run when I told them. Then, of course, I had to lead gently to the idea that everyone had gone from guest to suspect, soon to be questioned by Freya and the police. "No, no, of *course* you're not suspected of anything, furthest thing from our minds, it's just that Freya wants to know if there's anything you saw that would help," and so on. Then I had to do the difficult scheduling of Freya's interviews, at the same time I was supposed to keep an eye out for anything suspicious. Oh, the watson does the dirty work, all right. No wonder we always look dense when the detective unveils the solutions; we never have the time even to get the facts straight, much less meditate on their meaning. All I got that day were fragments: Lucinda whispered to me that Musgrave had worked for George Butler before Heidi hired him. Harvey Washburn told me that Musgrave had once been an artist, and that he had only recently moved to Mercury from Earth; this was his first Solday. That didn't give him much time to be hired by Butler, fired, and then hired by Van Seegeren. But was that of significance?

Late in the day I spoke with one of the police officers handling the case. She was relieved to have the help of Freya Grindavik; Terminator's police force is small, and often relies on the help of the city's famous detective for the more difficult cases. The officer gave me a general outline of what they had learned: Lucinda had heard a shout for help, had stepped into the atrium and seen a bloodied figure crawling down the hallway toward the patio. She had screamed and run for help, but only in the hallway was clear vision possible, and she had quickly gotten lost. After that, chaos; everyone at the party had a different tale of confusion.

After that conversation I had nothing more to do, so I got all the sequestered guests coffee and helped pick up some of the broken hall mirrors and passed some time prowling Heidi's villa, getting down on my hands and knees with the police robots to inspect a stain or two.

When Freya was finished with her interrogations, she promised Heidi and the police that she would see the case to its end—at least provisionally: "I only do this for entertainment," she told them irritably. "I'll stay with it as long as it entertains me. And I shall entertain myself with it."

"That's all right," said the police, who had heard this

before. "Just so long as you'll take the case." Freya nodded, and we left.

The Solday celebration was long since over; the Great Gates were closed, and once again through the dome shone the black sky. I said to Freya, "Did you hear about Musgrave working for Butler? And how he came from Earth just recently?" For you see, once on the scent I am committed to seeing a case solved.

"Please, Nathaniel," Freya said. "I heard all that and more. Musgrave stole the concept of Harvey Washburn's first series of paintings; he blackmailed both Butler and our host Heidi to obtain his jobs from them—or so I deduce from their protestations and certain facts concerning their recent questionable merger that I am privy to. And he tried to assault Lucinda, who is engaged to the cook Delaurence—" She let out a long sigh. "Motives are everywhere."

"It seems this Musgrave was a thoroughly despicable sort," I said.

"Yes. An habitual blackmailer."

"Nothing *suggests* itself to you?"

"No. I don't know why I agree to solve these things. Here I am committed to this headbashing, and my best clue is something that *you* suggested."

"I wasn't aware that I had suggested anything!"

"There is a fresh perspective to ignorance that can be very helpful."

"So it *is* important that Musgrave just arrived from Earth?"

She laughed. "Let's stop in the Plaza Dubrovnik and get something to eat. I'm starving."

Almost three weeks passed without a word from Freya, and I began to suspect that she was ignoring the case. Freya has no real sense of right and wrong, you see; she regards her cases as games, to be tossed aside if they prove too taxing. More than once she has cheerfully admitted defeat, and blithely forgotten any promises she may have made. She is *not* a moral person.

So I dropped by her home near Plaza Dubrovnik one evening, to rouse her from her irresponsible indifference. When she answered the door there were paint smudges on her face and hands.

"Freya," I scolded her. "How could you take up an entirely new hobby when there is a *case* to be solved?"

"Generously I allow you entrance after such a false accusation," she said. "But you will have to eat your words."

She led me downstairs to her basement laboratory, which extended the entire length and breadth of her villa. There on a big white-topped table lay Heidi Van Seegeren's Monet, looking like the three-dimensional geologic map of some minerally blessed country.

"What's this?" I exclaimed. "Why is this here?"

"I believe it is a fake," she said shortly, returning to a computer console.

"Wait a moment!" I cried. On the table around the painting were rolls of recording chart paper, lab notebooks, and what looked like black-and-white photos of the painting. "What do you mean?"

After tapping at the console she turned to me. "I mean, I believe it's a fake!"

"But I thought art forgery was extinct. It is too easy to discover a fake."

"Ha!" She waved a finger at me angrily. "You pick a bad time to say so. It is a common opinion, of course, but not necessarily true."

I regarded the canvas more closely. "What makes you think this a fake? I thought it was judged a masterpiece of its period."

"Something you said first caused me to question it," she said. "You mentioned that the painting seemed to have been created by an artist familiar with the light of Terminator. This seemed true to me, and it caused me to reflect that one of the classic signs of a fake was anachronistic sensibility—that is to say, the forger injects into his vision of the past some element of his time that is so much a part of his sensibility that he cannot perceive it. Thus the Victorians faked Renaissance faces with a sentimentality that only they could not immediately see."

"I see." I nodded sagely. "It did seem that cathedral had been struck with Solday light, didn't it."

"Yes. The trouble is, I have been able to find no sign of forgery in the physical properties of the painting." She shook her head. "And after three weeks of uninterrupted chemical analysis, that is beginning to worry me."

"But Freya," I said, as something occurred to me. "Does all this have a bearing on the Musgrave murder?"

"I think so," she replied. "And if not, it is certainly more interesting. But I believe it does."

I nodded. "So what, exactly, have you found?"

She smiled ironically. "You truly want to know? Well. The best test for anachronisms is the polonium 210, radium 226 equilibrium—"

"Please, Freya. No jargon."

"Jargon!" She raised an eyebrow to scorn me. "There is no such thing. Intelligence is like mold in a petri dish—as it eats ever deeper into the agar of reality, language has to expand with it to describe what has been digested. Each specialty provides the new vocabulary for its area of feeding and gets accused of fabricating jargon by those who know no better. I'm surprised to hear such nonsense from you. Or perhaps not."

"Very well," I said, hands up. "Still, you must communicate your meaning to me."

"I shall. First I analyzed the canvas. The material and its weave match the characteristics of the canvas made by the factory outside Paris that provided Monet throughout the painting of the Rouen cathedral series. Both the fabric and the glue appear very old, though there is no precise dating technique for them. And there was no trace of solvents that might have been used to strip paint off a genuine canvas of the period.

"I then turned to the paint. Follow so far?" she asked sharply. "Paint?"

"You may proceed without further sarcasm, unless unable to control yourself."

"The palette of an artist as famous as Monet has been studied in detail, so that we know he preferred cadmium yellow to chromium yellow or Naples yellow, that he tended to use Prussian blue rather than cobalt blue, and so on." She tapped the flecks of blue at the base of the cathedral. "Prussian blue."

"You've taken paint off the canvas?"

"How else test it? But I took very small samples, I assure you. Whatever the truth concerning the work, it remains a masterpiece, and I would not mar it. Besides, most of my tests were on the white paint, of which there is a great quantity, as you can see."

"Why the white paint?" I leaned over to stare more closely at the canvas.

"Because lead white is one of the best dating tools we have. The manufacturing methods used to make it changed frequently around Monet's time, and each change in method altered the chemical composition of the paint. After 1870, for instance, the cheaper zinc white was used to adulterate lead white, so there should be over one percent zinc in Monet's lead white."

"And is that what you found?"

"Yes. The atomic absorption spectrum showed—" She dug around in the pile of chart paper on the table— "Well, take my word for it—"

"I will."

"Nearly twelve percent. And the silver content for late nineteenth century lead white should be around four parts per million, the copper content about sixty parts per million. So it is with this paint. There is no insoluble antimony component, as there would be if the paint had been manufactured after 1940. The X-ray diffraction pattern"—she unrolled a length of chart paper and showed me where three sharp peaks in a row had been penned by the machine—"is exactly right, and there is the proper balance of polonium 210 and radium 226. That's very important, by the way, because when lead white is manufactured the radioactive balance of some of its elements is upset, and it takes a good three hundred years for them to decay back to equilibrium. And this paint is indeed back to that equilibrium."

"So the paints are Monet's," I concluded. "Doesn't that prove the work authentic?"

"Perhaps," Freya admitted. "But as I was doing all this analysis, it occurred to me that a modern forger has just as much information concerning Monet's palette as I do. With a modern laboratory it would be possible to use such information as a recipe, so to speak, and then to synthesize paints that would match the recipe exactly. Even the radioactively decayed lead white could be arranged, by avoiding the procedures that disrupt the radioactive balance in the first place!"

"Wouldn't that be terrifically complicated?"

Freya stared at me. "*Obviously,* Nathaniel, we are dealing with a very very meticulous faker here. But how else could it be done, in this day and age? Why else do it at all? The complete faker must take care to anticipate every test available, and then in a modern laboratory create the appropriate results for every one of them. It's admirable!"

"Assuming there ever was such a forger," I said dubiously. "It seems to me that what you have actually done here is prove the painting genuine."

"I don't think so."

"But even with these paints made by recipe, as you call them, the faker would still have to paint the painting!"

"Exactly. Conceive the painting, and execute it. It becomes very impressive, I confess." She walked around the table to look at the work from the correct angle. "I do believe this is one of the *best* of the Rouen cathedral series—astonishing, that a forger would be capable of it."

"That brings up another matter," I said. "Doesn't this work have a five-hundred-year-old pedigree? How could a whole history have been provided for it?"

"Good question. But I believe I have discovered the way. Let's go upstairs—you interrupted my preparations for lunch, and I'm hungry."

I followed her to her extensive kitchen, and sat in the window nook that overlooked the tile rooftops of the lower city while she finished chopping up the vegetables for a large salad.

"Do you know this painting's history?" Freya asked, looking up from a dissected head of lettuce.

I shook my head. "Up until now the thing has not been of overwhelming interest to me."

"A confession of faulty aesthetics. The work was photographed at the original exhibit in 1895; Durand-Ruel photo 5828 L8451. All of the information appended to the photo fits our painting—same name, size, signature location. Then for a century it disappeared. Odd. But it turned out to have been in the estate of an Evans family, in Aylesbury, England. When the family had some conservation work done on one corner it returned to public knowledge, and was photographed for a dozen books of the twenty-first and twenty-second centuries. After that it slipped back into obscurity, but it is as well documented as any of the series belonging to private estates."

"Exactly my point," I said. "How could such a history be forged?"

As Freya mixed the salad she smiled. "I sat and thought about that for quite some time myself. But consider it freshly, Nathaniel. How do we know what we know of the past?"

"Well," I said, somewhat at a loss. "From data banks, I suppose. And books—documents—historians—"

"From historians!" She laughed. She provided us both with bowls and sat across from me. As I filled mine she said, "So we want to know something of the past. We go to our library and sit at its terminal. We call up general reference works, or a bibliographic index, and we choose, if we want, books that we would like to have in our hands. We type in the appropriate code, our printer prints up the appropriate book, and the volume slides out of the computer into our waiting grasp." She paused to fork down several mouthfuls of salad. "So we learn about the past using computer programs. And a clever programmer, you see, can change a program. It would be possible to *insert* extra pages into these old books on Monet, and thus add the forged painting to the record of the past."

I paused, a cherry tomato hovering before my mouth. "But—"

"I searched for an original of *any* of these books containing photos of our painting," Freya said. "I called all over Mercury, and to several incunabulists in libraries on Earth—you wouldn't believe the phone bill I've run up. But the initial printings of these art volumes were very small, and although first editions probably remain *somewhere,* they are not to be found. Certainly there are no first editions of these books on Mercury, and none immediately locatable on Earth. It began to seem a very unlikely coincidence, as if these volumes contained pictures of our painting precisely because they existed only in the data banks, and thus could be altered without discovery."

She attended to her salad, and we finished eating in silence. All the while my mind was spinning furiously, and when we were done I said, "What about the original exhibit photo?"

She nodded, pleased with me. "That, apparently, is genuine. But the Durand-Ruel photos include four or five of paintings that have never been seen since. In that sense the Rouen cathedral series is a good one for a faker; from the first it has never been clear how many cathedrals Monet painted. The usual number given is thirty-two, but there are more in the Durand-Ruel list, and a faker could examine the list and use one of the lost items as a prescription for his fake. Providing a later history with the aid of these obscure art books would result in a fairly complete pedigree."

"But could such an addition to the data banks be made?"

"It would be easiest done on Earth," Freya said. "But there is no close security guarding the banks containing old art books. No one expects them to be tampered with."

"It's astonishing," I said with a wave of my fork, "it is baroque, it is *byzantine* in its ingenuity!"

"Yes," she said. "Beautiful, in a way."

"However," I pointed out to her, "you have no proof—only this perhaps over-complex theory. You have found no first edition of a book to confirm that the computer-generated volumes add Heidi's painting, and you have found no physical anachronism in the painting itself."

Gloomily she clicked her fork against her empty salad bowl, then rose to refill it. "It is a problem," she admitted. "Also, I have been working on the assumption that Sandor Musgrave discovered evidence of the forgery. But *I* can't find it."

Never let it be said that Nathaniel Sebastian has not performed a vital role in Freya Grindavik's great feats of detection. I was the first to notice the anachronism of sensibility in Heidi's painting; and now I had a truly inspired idea. "He was pointing to the patio!" I exclaimed. "Musgrave, in his last moment, struggled to point to the patio!"

"I had observed that," Freya said, unimpressed.

"But Heidi's patio—you know—it is formed out of blocks of the Dover cliffs! And thus Musgrave indicated *England!* Is it not possible? The Monet was owned by Englishmen until Heidi purchased it—perhaps Musgrave meant to convey that the original owners were the forgers!"

Freya's mouth hung open in surprise, and her left eye was squinted shut. I leaped from the window nook in triumph. "I've solved it! I've solved a mystery at last!"

Freya looked up at me and laughed.

"Come now, Freya, you must admit I have given you the vital clue."

She stood up, suddenly all business. "Yes, yes, indeed you have. Now out with you Nathaniel, I have work to do."

"So I did give you the vital clue?" I asked. "Musgrave was indicating the English owners?"

As she ushered me to her door Freya laughed. "As a detective your intuition is matched only by your confidence. Now leave me to work, and I will be in contact with you soon, I assure you." And with that she urged me into the street, and I was left to consider the case alone.

Freya was true to her word, and only two days after our crucial luncheon she knocked on the door of my town villa. "Come along," she said. "I've asked Arnold Ohman for an appointment; I want to ask him some questions about the Evans family. The city is passing the Monet museum, however, and he asked us to meet him out there."

I readied myself quickly, and we proceeded to North Station. We arrived just in time to step across the gap between the two platforms, and then we were on the motionless deck of one of the outlying stations that Terminator is always passing. There we rented a car and sped west, paralleling the dozen massive cylindrical rails along which the city slides. Soon we had left Terminator behind, and when we were seventy or eighty kilometers onto the nightside of Mercury we turned to the north, to Monet Crater.

Terminator's tracks lie very close to the thirtieth degree of latitude, in the Northern hemisphere, and Monet Crater is not far from them. We crossed Shakespeare Planitia rapidly, passing between craters named after the great artists, writers, and composers of Earth's glorious past: traversing a low pass between Brahms and Verdi, looking down at where Degas had crashed into the Brontës. "I think I understand why a modern artist on Mercury might turn to forgery," Freya said. "We are dwarfed by the past as we are by this landscape."

"But it is still a crime," I insisted. "If it were done often, we would not be able to distinguish the authentic from the fake."

Freya did not reply.

I drove our car up a short rise, and we entered the submercurial garage of the Monet museum, which is set deep in the southern rim of the immense crater named after the artist. One long wall of the museum is a window facing out over the crater floor, so that the central knot of peaks is visible, and the curving inner wall of the crater defines the horizon in the murky distance. Shutters slid down to protect these windows from the heat of Mercury's long day, but now they were open and the black wasteland of the planet formed a strange backdrop to the colorful paintings that filled the long rooms of the museum.

There were many Monet originals there, but the canvases of the Rouen cathedral series were almost all reproductions, set in one long gallery. As Freya and I searched for Arnold we also viewed them.

"You see, they're not just various moments of a single day," Freya said.

"Not unless it was a very strange day for weather." The three reproductions before us all depicted foggy days: two bluish and underwater-looking, the third a bright burning-off of yellow noontime fog. Obviously these were from a different day than the ones across the room, where a cool clear morning gave way to a midday that looked as if the sun was just a few feet above the cathedral. The museum had classified the series in color groups: "Blue Group," "White Group," "Yellow Group," and so on. To my mind that system was stupid—it told you nothing you couldn't immediately see. I myself classified them according to weather. There was a clear day that got very hot; a clear winter day, the air chill and pure; a foggy day; and a day when a rainstorm had grown and then broken. When I told Freya of my system she applauded it. "So Heidi's painting goes from the king of the White Group to the hottest moment of the hot day."

"Exactly. It's the most extreme as far as sunlight blasting the stone into motes of color."

"And thus the forger extends Monet's own thinking, you see," she said, a bit absently. "But I *don't* see Arnold, and I think we have visited every room."

"Could he be late?"

"We are already quite late ourselves. I wonder if he has gone back?"

"It seems unlikely," I said.

Purposefully we toured the museum one more time, and I ignored the color-splashed canvases standing before the dark crater, to search closely in all the various turns of the galleries. No Arnold.

"Come along," Freya said. "I suspect he stayed in Terminator, and now I want to speak with him more than ever."

So we returned to the garage, got back in our car, and drove out onto Mercury's bare, baked surface once again. Half an hour later we had Terminator's tracks in sight. They stretched before us from horizon to horizon, twelve fat silvery cylinders set five meters above the ground on narrow pylons. To the east, rolling over the flank of Wang Wei Crater so slowly that we could not perceive its movement without close attention, came the city itself, a giant clear half-egg filled with the colors of rooftops, gardens, and the gray stone of the buildings crowding the terraced Dawn Wall.

"We'll have to go west to the next station," I said. Then I saw something, up on the city track nearest us: spread-eagled over the top of the big cylinder was a human form in a light green daysuit. I stopped the car. "Look!"

Freya peered out her window. "We'd better go investigate."

We struggled quickly into the car's emergency daysuits, clamped on the helmets, and slipped through the car's lock onto the ground. A ladder led us up the nearest cylinder pylon and through a tunnel in the cylinder itself. Once on top we could stand safely on the broad hump of the rail.

The figure we had seen was only ten meters away from us, and we hurried to it.

It was Arnold, spread in cruciform fashion over the cylinder's top, secured in place by three large suction plates that had been cuffed to his wrists and ankles, and then stuck to the cylinder. Arnold turned from his contemplation of the slowly approaching city, and looked at us wide-eyed through his faceplate. Freya reached down and turned on his helmet intercom.

"—am I glad to see you!" Arnold cried, voice harsh. "These plates won't move!"

"Tied to the tracks, eh?" Freya said.

"Yes!"

"Who put you here?"

"I don't know! I went out to meet you at the Monet museum, and the last thing I remember I was in the garage there. When I came to, I was here."

"Does your head hurt?" I inquired.

"Yes. Like I was gassed, though, not hit. But—the city—it just came over the horizon a short time ago. Perhaps we could dispense with discussion until I am freed?"

"Relax," Freya said, nudging one of the plates with her boot. "Are you sure you don't know who did this, Arnold?"

"Of course! That's what I just said! Please, Freya, can't we talk after I get loose?"

"In a hurry, Arnold?" Freya asked.

"But *of course*."

"No need to be too worried," I assured him. "If we cannot free you, the cowcatchers will be out to pry you loose." I tried lifting a plate, but could not move it. "Surely they will find a way—it's their job, after all."

"True," Arnold said.

"Usually true," said Freya. "Arnold is probably not aware that the cowcatchers have become rather unreliable recently. Some weeks ago a murderer tied his victim to a track just as you have been, Arnold, and then somehow disengaged the cowcatchers' sensors. The unfortunate victim was shaved into molecules by one of the sleeves of the city. It was kept quiet to avoid any attempted repetitions, but since then the cowcatchers' sensors have continued to function erratically, and two or three suicides have been entirely too successful."

"Perhaps this isn't the best moment to tell us about this," I suggested to Freya.

Arnold choked over what I took to be his agreement.

"Well," Freya said, "I thought I should make the situation clear. Now listen, Arnold. We need to talk."

"*Please*," Arnold said. "Free me first, *then* talk."

"No, no—"

"But Terminator is only a kilometer away!"

"Your perspective from that angle is deceptive," Freya told him. "The city is at least three kilometers away."

"More like two," I said, as I could now make out individual rooftops under the Dawn Wall. In fact the city glowed like a big glass lamp and illuminated the entire landscape with a faint green radiance.

"And at three point four kilometers an hour," Freya said,

"that gives us almost an hour, doesn't it. So listen to me, Arnold. The Monet cathedral that you sold to Heidi is a fake."

"What?" Arnold cried. "It certainly is not! And I insist this isn't the time—"

"It is a fake. Now I want you to tell me the truth, or I will leave you here to test the cowcatchers." She leaned over to stare down at Arnold face to face. "I know who painted the fake, as well."

Helplessly Arnold stared up at her.

"He put you on the track here, didn't he?"

Arnold squeezed his eyes shut, nodded slowly. "I think so."

"So if you want to be let up, you must swear to me that you will abide by my plan for dealing with this forger. You *will* follow my instructions, understand?"

"I understand."

"Do you agree?"

"I agree," Arnold said, forcing the words out. "Now let me up!"

"All right." Freya straightened.

"How are we going to do it?" I asked.

Freya shrugged. "I don't know."

At this Arnold howled, he shouted recriminations, he began to wax hysterical—

"Shut up!" Freya exclaimed. "You're beginning to sound like a man who has made too many brightside crossings. These suction plates are little different from children's darts." She leaned down, grasped a plate, pulled up with all of her considerable strength. No movement. "Hmm," she said thoughtfully.

"Freya," Arnold said.

"One moment," she replied, and walked back down the hump of the cylinder to the ladder tunnel, there to disappear down it.

"She's left me," Arnold groaned. "Left me to be crushed."

"I don't think so," I said. "No doubt she has gone to the car to retrieve some useful implement." I kicked heartily at the plate holding Arnold's feet to the cylinder, and even managed to slide it a few centimeters down the curve, which had the effect of making Arnold suddenly taller. But other than that I made no progress.

When Freya returned she carried a bar, bent at one end. "Crowbar," she explained to us.

"But where did you get it?"

"From the car's tool chest, naturally. Here." She stepped over Arnold. "If we just insinuate this end of it under your cuffs, I believe we'll have enough leverage to do the trick. The cylinder being curved, the plate's grasp should be weakened—about here." She jammed the short end of the bar under the edge of the footplate's cuff, and pulled on the upper end of it. Over the intercom, breathless silence; her fair cheeks reddened; then suddenly Arnold's legs flew up and over his head, leaving his arms twisted and his neck at an awkward angle. At the same time Freya staggered off the cylinder, performed a neat somersault, and landed on her feet on the ground below us. While she made her way back up to us I tried to ease the weight on Arnold's neck, but by his squeaks of distress I judged he was still uncomfortable. Freya rejoined us, and quickly wedged her crowbar under Arnold's right wrist cuff, and freed it. That left Arnold hanging down the side of the cylinder by his left wrist; but with one hard crank Freya popped that plate free as well, and Arnold disappeared. By leaning over we could just see him, collapsed in a heap on the ground. "Are you all right?" Freya asked. He groaned for an answer.

I looked up and saw that Terminator was nearly upon us. Almost involuntarily I proceeded to the ladder tunnel; Freya followed me, and we descended to the ground. "Disturbing not to be able to trust the cowcatchers,'' I remarked as my heartbeat slowed.

''Nathaniel,'' Freya said, looking exasperated. ''I made all that up, you know that.''

''Ah. Yes, of course.''

As we joined Arnold he was just struggling to a seated position. ''My ankle,'' he said. Then the green wash of light from Terminator disappeared, as did the night sky; the city slid over us, and we were encased in a gloom interrupted by an occasional running light. All twelve of the city's big tracks had disappeared, swallowed by the sleeves in the city's broad metallic foundation. Only the open slots that allowed passage over the pylons showed where the sleeves were; for a moment in the darkness it seemed we stood between two worlds held apart by a field of pylons.

Meanwhile the city slid over us soundlessly, propelled by the expansion of the tracks themselves. You see, the alloy composing the tracks is capable of withstanding the 425 degree centigrade heat of the Mercurial day, but the cylinders do expand just a bit in this heat. Here in the terminator is the forward edge of the cylinders' expansion, and the smooth-sided sleeves above us at that moment fit so snugly over the cylinders that as the cylinders expand, the city is pushed forward toward the cooler, thinner railing to the west; and so the city is propelled by the sun, while never being fully exposed to it. The motive force is so strong, in fact, that resistance to it arranged in the sleeves generates the enormous reserves of energy that Terminator has sold so successfully to the rest of civilization.

Though I had understood this mechanism for decades, I had never before observed it from this angle, and despite the fact that I was somewhat uneasy to be standing under our fair city, I was also fascinated to see its broad, knobby silver underside, gliding majestically westward. For a long time I did nothing but stare at it.

"We'd better get to the car," Freya said. "The sun will be up very soon after the city passes, and then we'll be in trouble."

Since Arnold was still cuffed to the plates, and had at least a sprained ankle, walking with him slung between us was a slow process. While we were at it the Dawn Wall passed over us, and suddenly the twelve tracks and the stars between them were visible again. "Now we'd better hurry," said Freya. Above us the very top of the Dawn Wall flared a brilliant white; sunlight was striking that surface, only two hundred meters above us. Dawn was not far away. In the glare of reflected light we could see the heavily tire-printed ground under the cylinders perfectly, and for a while our eyes were nearly overwhelmed. "Look!" Freya cried, shielding her eyes with one hand and pointing up at the sun-washed slope of the city wall with the other. "It's the inspiration for our Monet, don't you think?"

Despite our haste, the great Rouen cathedral of Mercury pulled away from us. "This won't do," Freya said. "Only a bit more to the car, but we have to hurry. Here, Arnold, let me carry you—" and she ran, carrying Arnold piggyback, the rest of the way to the car. As we maneuvered him through the lock, a tongue of the sun's corona licked briefly over the horizon, blinding us. I felt scorched; my throat was dry. We were now at the dawn edge of the terminator zone, and east-facing slopes burned white while west-facing slopes were still a perfect black, creating a chaotic patchwork that was utterly disorienting. We rolled into the car after Arnold, and quickly drove west, passing the city, returning to the night zone, and arriving at a station where we could make the transfer into the city again. Freya laughed at my expression as we crossed the gap. "Well, Nathaniel," she said, "home again."

* * *

The very next day Freya arranged for those concerned with the case to assemble on Heidi's patio again. Four police officials were there, and one took notes. The painting of the cathedral of Rouen was back in its place on the villa wall; George Butler and Harvey Washburn stood before it, while Arnold Ohman and Heidi paced by the patio's edge. Lucinda and Delaurence, the cook, watched from behind the patio bar.

Freya called us to order. She was wearing a severe blue dress, and her white-blond hair was drawn into a tight braid that fell down her back. Sternly she said, "I will suggest to you an explanation for the death of Sandor Musgrave. All of you except for the police and Mr. Sebastian were to one extent or another suspected of killing him, so I know this will be of great interest to you."

Naturally there was an uneasy stir among those listening.

"Several of you had reason to hate Musgrave, or to fear him. The man was a blackmailer by profession, and on Earth he had obtained evidence of illegalities in the merger Heidi and George made five years ago, that gave him leverage over both of you. This and motives for the rest of you were well established during the initial investigation, and we need not recapitulate the details.

"It is also true, however, that subsequent investigations have revealed that all of you had alibis for the moment when Musgrave was struck down. Lucinda and Delaurence were together in the kitchen until Lucinda left to investigate the shout she heard; this was confirmed by caterers hired for the Solday party. Heidi left the patio shortly before Musgrave was found, but she was consulting with Hiu and the orchestra during the time in question. George Butler went into the house with Arnold Ohman, but they were together for most of the time they were inside. Eventually George left to go to the bathroom, but luckily for him the orchestra's first clarinetist was there to confirm his presence. And fortunately for

Mr. Ohman, I myself could see him from the patio, standing in the hallway until the very moment when Lucinda screamed.

"So you see"—Freya paused, eyed us one by one, ran a finger along the frame of the big painting—"the problem took on a new aspect. It became clear that, while many had a motive to kill Musgrave, no one had the opportunity. This caused me to reconsider. How, exactly, had Musgrave been killed? He was struck on the head by the frame of one of Heidi's hall mirrors. Though several mirrors were broken in the melee following Lucinda's screams, we know the one that Musgrave was struck with; it was at the bend in the hallway leading from the atrium to the patio. And it was only a couple of meters away from a step down in the hallway."

Freya took a large house plan from a table and set it before the policemen. "Sandor Musgrave, you will recall, was new to Mercury. He had never seen a Solday celebration. When the Great Gates opened and the reflected light filled this villa, my suggestion is that he was overwhelmed by fright. Lucinda heard him cry for help—perhaps he thought the house was burning down. He panicked, rushed out of the study, and blindly began to run for the patio. Unable to see the step down or the mirror, he must have pitched forward, and his left temple struck the frame a fatal blow. He crawled a few steps farther, then collapsed and died."

Heidi stepped forward. "So Musgrave died by accident?"

"This is my theory. And it explains how it was that no one had the opportunity to kill him. In fact, no one did kill him." She turned to the police. "I trust you will follow up on this suggestion?"

"Yes," said the one taking notes. "Death declared accidental by consulting investigator. Proceed from there." He exchanged glances with his colleagues. "We are satisfied this explains the facts of the case."

Heidi surveyed the silent group. "To tell you the truth, I am very relieved." She turned to Delaurence. "Let's open the bar. It would be morbid to celebrate an accidental death, but here we can say we are celebrating the absence of a murder."

The others gave a small cheer of relief, and we surrounded the bartender.

A few days later Freya asked me to accompany her to North Station. "I need your assistance."

"Very well," I said. "Are you leaving Terminator?"

"Seeing someone off."

When we entered the station's big waiting room, she inspected the crowd, then cried, "Arnold!" and crossed the room to him. Arnold saw her and grimaced. "Oh, Arnold," she said, and leaned over to kiss him on each cheek. "I'm very proud of you."

Arnold shook his head, and greeted me mournfully. "You're a hard woman, Freya," he told her. "Stop behaving so cheerfully, you make me sick. You know perfectly well this is exile of the worst sort."

"But Arnold," Freya said, "Mercury is not the whole of civilization. In fact it could be considered culturally dead, an immense museum to the past that has no real life at all."

"Which is why you choose to live here, I'm sure," he said bitterly.

"Well of course it does have some pleasures. But the really vital centers of any civilization are on the frontier, Arnold, and that's where you're going."

Arnold looked completely disgusted.

"But Arnold," I said. "Where are you going?"

"Pluto," he said curtly.

"Pluto?" I exclaimed. "But whatever for? What will you do there?"

He shrugged. "Dig ditches, I suppose."

Freya laughed. "You certainly will not." She addressed me: "Arnold has decided, very boldly I might add, to abandon his safe career as a dealer here on Mercury, to become a real artist on the frontier.''

''But *why?*''

Freya wagged a finger at Arnold. ''You must write us often.''

Arnold made a strangled growl. ''Damn you, Freya. I refuse. I refuse to go.''

''You don't have that option,'' Freya said. ''Remember the chalk, Arnold. The chalk was your signature.''

Arnold hung his head, defeated. The city interfaced with the spaceport station. ''It isn't fair,'' Arnold said. ''What am I going to do out on those barbaric outworlds?''

''You're going to live,'' Freya said sternly. ''You're going to live and you're going to paint. No more hiding. Understand?''

I, at any rate, was beginning to.

''You should be thanking me profusely,'' Freya went on, ''but I'll concede you're upset and wait for gratitude by mail.'' She put a hand on Arnold's shoulder and pushed him affectionately toward the crossing line. ''Remember to write.''

''But,'' Arnold said, a panicked expression on his face. ''But—''

''Enough!'' Freya said. ''Be gone! Or else.''

Arnold sagged, and stepped across the divide between the stations. Soon the city left the spaceport station behind.

''Well,'' Freya said. ''That's done.''

I stared at her. ''You just helped a murderer to escape!''

She lifted an eyebrow. ''Exile is a very severe punishment; in fact in my cultural tradition it was the usual punishment for murder committed in anger or self-defense.''

I waved a hand dismissively. ''This isn't the Iceland of Eric the Red. And it wasn't self-defense—Sandor Musgrave was outright murdered.''

''Well,'' she said, ''*I* never liked him.''

I told you before: she has no sense of right and wrong. It is a serious defect in a detective. I could only wave my arms in incoherent outrage; and my protests have never carried much weight with Freya, who claims not even to believe them.

We left the station. "What's that you were saying to Arnold about chalk?" I said, curiosity getting the better of me.

"That's the clue you provided, Nathaniel—somewhat transformed. As you reminded me, Musgrave was pointing at the patio, and Heidi's patio is made of a block of the Dover cliffs. Dover cliffs, as you know, are composed of *chalk*. So I returned to the painting, and cut through the back to retrieve samples of the chalk used in the underdrawing, which had been revealed to me by infrared photography." She turned a corner and led me uptown. "Chalk, you see, has its own history of change. In Monet's time, chalk was made from natural sources, not from synthetics. Sure enough, the chalk I took from the canvas was a natural chalk. But natural chalk, being composed of marine ooze, is littered with the fossil remains of unicellular algae called cocoliths. These cocoliths are different depending upon the source of the chalk. Monet used Rouen chalk, appropriately enough, which was filled with the cocoliths *Maslovella barnesae* and *Cricolithus pemmatoidens*. The cocoliths in our painting, however, are *Neococcolithes dubius*. Very dubious indeed—for this is a North American chalk, first mined in Utah in 1924."

"So Monet couldn't have used this chalk! And there you had your proof that the painting is a fake."

"Exactly."

I said doubtfully, "It seems a subtle clue for the dying Musgrave to conceive of."

"Perhaps," Freya said cheerfully. "Perhaps he was only pointing in the direction of the patio by the accident of his final movements. But it was sufficient that the coincidence gave me the idea. The solution of a crime often depends upon imaginary clues."

"But how did you know Arnold was the forger?" I asked. "And why, after taking the trouble to concoct all those paints, did he use the wrong chalk?"

"The two matters are related. It could be that Arnold only knew he needed a natural chalk, and used the first convenient supply without knowing there are differences between them. In that case it was a mistake—his only mistake. But it seems unlike Arnold to me, and I think rather that it was the forger's signature. In effect, the forger said, if you take a slide of the chalk trapped underneath the paint, and magnify it five thousand times with an electron microscope, you will find me. This chalk never used by Monet is my sign. —For on some level every forger hopes to be discovered, if only in the distant future—to receive credit for the work.

"So I knew we had a forger on Mercury, and I was already suspicious of Arnold, since he was the dealer who brought the painting to Mercury, and since he was the only guest at Heidi's party with the opportunity to kill Musgrave; he was missing during the crucial moments—"

"You *are* a liar."

"And it seems Arnold was getting desperate; I searched among his recent bills, and found one for three suction plates. So when we found him on the track I was quite sure."

"He stuck himself to the track?"

"Yes. The one on his right wrist was electronically controlled, so after setting the other two he tripped the third between his teeth. He hoped that we would discover him there after missing him at the museum, and think that there was someone else who wished him harm. And if not, the cowcatchers would pull him free. It was a silly plan, but he was desperate after I set up that appointment with him. When I confronted him with all this, after we rescued him from the tracks, he broke down and confessed. Sandor Musgrave had discovered that the Monet was a fake while blackmailing the Evans family in England, and after forcing Heidi to give him a job, he worked on the painting in secret until he found proof. Then he blackmailed Arnold into bankruptcy, and when on Solday he pressed Arnold for more money, Arnold lost his composure and took advantage of the confusion caused by the opening of the Great Gates to smack Musgrave on the head with one of Heidi's mirrors.''

I wagged a finger under her nose. ''And you set him free. You've gone too far this time, Freya Grindavik.''

She shook her head. ''If you consider Arnold's case a bit longer, you might change your mind. Arnold Ohman has been the most important art dealer on Mercury for over sixty years. He sold the Vermeer collection to George Butler, and the Goyas to Terminator West Gallery, and the Pissarros to the museum in Homer Crater, and those Chinese landscapes you love so much to the city park, and the Kandinskys to the Lion of the Greys. Most of the finest paintings on Mercury were brought here by Arnold Ohman.''

''So?''

''So how many of those, do you think, were painted by Arnold himself?''

I stopped dead in the street, stunned at the very idea. ''But—but that only makes it worse! Inestimably worse! It means there are fakes all over the planet!''

''Probably so. And no one wants to hear that. But it also means Arnold Ohman is a very great artist. And in our age that is no easy feat. Can you imagine the withering reception his work would have received if he had done original work? He would have ended up like Harvey Washburn and all the rest of them who wander around the galleries like dogs. The great art of the past crashes down on our artists like meteors, so that their minds resemble the blasted landscape we roll over. Now Arnold has escaped that fate, and his work is universally admired, even loved. That Monet, for instance—it isn't just that it passes for one of the cathedral series—it could be argued that it is the *best* of them. Now is this a level of greatness that Arnold could have achieved—would have been *allowed* to achieve—if he had done original work on this museum planet? Impossible. He was forced to forge old masters to be able to fully express his genius."

"All this is no excuse, for forgery or murder."

But Freya wasn't listening. "Now that I've exiled him, he may go on forging old paintings, but he may begin painting something new. That possibility surely justifies ameliorating his punishment for killing such a parasite as Musgrave. And there is Mercury's reputation as art museum of the system to consider. . . ."

I refused to honor her opinions with a reply, and looking around I saw that during our conversation she had led me far up the terraces. "Where are we going?"

"To Heidi's," she said. And she had the grace to look a little shamefaced—for a moment, anyway. "I need your help moving something."

"Oh, no."

"Well," Freya explained, "when I told Heidi some of the facts of the case, she insisted on giving me a token of her gratitude, and she overrode all my refusals, so . . . I was forced to accept." She rang the wall bell.

"You're joking," I said.

"Not at all. Actually, I think Heidi preferred not to own a painting she knew to be a fake, you see. So I did her a favor by taking it off her hands."

When Delaurence let us in, we found he had almost finished securing *Rouen Cathedral—Sun Effect* in a big plastic box. "We'll finish this," Freya told him.

While we completed the boxing I told Freya what I thought of her conduct. "You've taken liberties with the *law*—you lied right and left—"

"Well boxed," she said. "Let's go before Heidi changes her mind."

"And I suppose you're proud of yourself."

"Of course. A lot of lab work went into this."

We maneuvered the big box through the gate and into the street, and carried it upright between us, like a short flat coffin. We reached Freya's villa, and immediately she set to work unboxing the painting. When she had freed it she set it on top of a couch, resting against the wall.

Shaking with righteous indignation, I cried, "That *thing* isn't a product of the past! It isn't *authentic*. It is only a *fake*. Claude Monet *didn't paint it*."

Freya looked at me with a mild frown, as if confronting a slightly dense and very stubborn child. "So what?"

After I had lectured her on her immorality a good deal more, and heard all of her patient agreement, I ran out of steam. "Well," I muttered, "you may have destroyed all my faith in you, and damaged Mercury's art heritage forever, but at least I'll get a good story out of it." This was some small comfort. "I believe I'll call it 'The Case of the Thirty-third Cathedral of Rouen.' "

"What's this?" she exclaimed. "No, of course not!" And then she insisted that I keep everything she had told me that day a secret.

I couldn't believe it. Bitterly I said, "You're like those forgers. You want *somebody* to witness your cleverness, and I'm the one who is stuck with it."

She immediately agreed, but went on to list all the reasons no one else could ever learn of the affair—how so many people would be hurt—including her, I added acerbically—how so many valuable collections would be ruined, how her plan to transform Arnold into a respectable honest Plutonian artist would collapse, and so on and so forth, for nearly an hour. Finally I gave up and conceded to her wishes, so that the upshot of it was, I promised not to write down a single word concerning this particular adventure of ours, and I promised furthermore to say nothing of the entire affair, and to keep it a complete secret, forever and ever.

But I don't suppose it will do any harm to tell you.

—1983

— Ridge Running —

Three men sit on a rock. The rock is wet granite, a bouldertop surrounded by snow that has melted just enough to reveal it. Snow extends away from the rock in every direction. To the east it drops to treeline, to the west it rises to a rock wall that points up and ends at sky. The boulder the three men are on is the only break in the snow from the treeline to rock wall. Snowshoe tracks lead to the rock, coming from the north on a traverse across the slope. The men sit sunning like marmots.

One man chews snow. He is short and broad-chested, with thick arms and legs. He adjusts blue nylon gaiters that cover his boots and lower legs. His thighs are bare, he wears gray gym shorts. He leans over to strap a boot into an orange plastic snowshoe.

The man sitting beside him says, "Brian, I thought we were going to eat lunch." This second man is big, and he wears sunglasses that clip onto prescription wire-rims.

"Pe-ter," Brian drawls. "We can't eat here comfortably, there's barely room to sit. As soon as we get around that shoulder''—he points south—''the traverse will be done and we'll be at the pass.''

Peter takes in a deep breath, lets it out. ''I need to rest.''

''O.K.,'' Brian says, ''do it. I'm just going to go around to the pass, I'm tired of sitting.'' He picks up the other orange snowshoe, sticks his boot in the binding.

The third man, who is medium height and very thin, has been staring at the snow granules on his boot. Now he picks up a yellow snowshoe and kicks into it. Peter sees him do it, sighs, bends over to yank his aluminum-and-cord snowshoes out of the snow they are stuck in.

''Look at that hummingbird,'' the third man says with pleasure and points.

He is pointing at blank snow. His two companions look where he is pointing, then glance at each other uncomfortably. Peter shakes his head, looks at his boots.

''I didn't know there were hummingbirds in the Sierras,'' the third man says. ''What a beauty!'' He looks at Brian uncertainly. ''*Are* there hummingbirds in the Sierras?''

''Well,'' Brian says, ''actually, I think there are. But . . .''

''But not this time, Joe,'' Peter finishes.

''Ah,'' Joe says, and stares at the spot in the snow. ''I could have sworn . . .'' Peter looks at Brian, his face squinched up in distress. ''Maybe the light breaking on that clump of snow,'' Joe says, mystified. ''Oh, well.''

Brian stands and hoists a compact blue pack onto his shoulders, and steps off the boulder onto the snow. He leans over to adjust a binding. ''Let's get going, Joe,'' he says. ''Don't worry about it.'' And to Peter: ''This spring snow is great.''

''If you're a goddamn polar bear,'' Peter says.

Brian shakes his head, and his silvered sunglasses flash reflections of snow and Peter. ''This is the best time to be up here. If you would ever come with us in January or February you'd know that.''

"Summer!" Peter says as he picks up his long frame pack. "Summer's what I like—catch the rays, see the flowers, walk around without these damn flippers on—" He swings his pack onto his back, steps back quickly (clatter of aluminum on granite) to keep his balance. He buckles his waistbelt awkwardly, looks at the sun. It is near midday. He wipes his forehead.

"You don't even come up with us in the summer anymore," Brian points out. "What has it been, four years?"

"Time," Peter says. "I don't have any time, and that's a fact."

"Just all your life," Brian scoffs. Peter shakes off the remark with an irritated scowl, and steps onto the snow.

They turn to look at Joe, who is still inspecting the snow with a fierce squint.

"Hey, Joe!" Brian says.

Joe starts and looks up.

"Time to hike, remember?"

"Oh, yeah, just a second." Joe readies himself.

Three men snowshoeing.

Brian leads. He sinks about a foot into the snow with every step. Joe follows, placing his yellow snowshoes carefully in the prints of Brian's, so that he sinks hardly at all. Peter pays no attention to prints, and his snowshoes crash into and across the holes. His snowshoes slide left, downhill, and he slips frequently.

The slope steepens. The three men sweat. Brian slips left one time too often and stops to remove his snowshoes. They can no longer see the rock wall above them, the slope is so steep. Brian ties his snowshoes to his pack, puts the pack back on. He puts a glove on his right hand and walks canted over so he can punch into the slope with his fist.

Joe and Peter stop where Brian stops, to make the same

changes. Joe points ahead to Brian, who is now crossing a section of slope steeper than forty-five degrees.

"Strange three-legged hill animal," says Joe, and laughs. "Snoweater."

Peter looks in his pack for his glove. "Why don't we go down into the trees and avoid this damn traverse?"

"The view isn't as good."

Peter sighs. Joe waits, scuffs snow, looks at Peter curiously. Pete has put suntan oil on his face, and the sweat has poured from his forehead, so that his stubbled cheeks shine with reflected light.

He says, "Am I imagining this, or are we working really hard?"

"We're working very hard," Joe says. "Traverses are difficult."

They watch Brian, who is near the middle of the steepest section. "You guys do this snow stuff for *fun?*" Peter says.

After a moment Joe starts. "I'm sorry," he says. "What were we talking about?"

Peter shrugs, examines Joe closely. "You O.K.?" he asks, putting his gloved hand to Joe's arm.

"Yeah, yeah. I just . . . *forgot*. Again!"

"Everyone forgets sometimes."

"I know, I know." With a discouraged sigh Joe steps off into Brian's prints. Peter follows.

From above they appear little dots, the only moving objects in a sea of white and black. Snow blazes white and prisms flash from sunglasses. They wipe their foreheads, stop now and then to catch their breath. Brian pulls ahead, Pete falls behind. Joe steps out the traverse with care, talking to himself in undertones. Their gloves get wet, there are ice bracelets around their wrists. Below them solitary trees at treeline wave in a breeze, but on the slope it is windless and hot.

* * *

The slope lessens, and they are past the shoulder. Brian pulls off his pack and gets out his groundpad, sits on it. He roots in the pack. After a while Joe joins him. ''Whew!'' Joe says. ''That was a hard traverse.''

''Not really hard,'' Brian replies. ''Just boring.'' He eats some M and M's, waves a handful up at the ridge above. ''I'm tired of traversing, though, that's for sure. I'm going up to the ridge so I can walk down it to the pass.''

Joe looks at the wall of snow leading up to the ridge. ''Yeah, well, I think Pete and I will continue around the corner here and go past Lake Doris to the pass. It's almost level from here on.''

''True. I'm going to go up there anyway.''

''All right. We'll see you in the pass in a while.''

Brian looks at Joe. ''You'll be all right?''

''Sure.''

Brian gets his pack on, turns and begins walking up the slope, bending forward to take big slow strides. Watching him, Joe says to himself, ''Humped splayfoot pack beast, yes. House-backed creature. Giant snow snail. Yo ho for the mountains. Rum de dum. Rum de dum de dum.''

Peter appears around the shoulder, walking slowly and carelessly. He spreads his groundpad, sits beside Joe. After a time his breathing slows. ''Where's Brian?''

''He went up there.''

''Is that where we're going?''

''I thought we might go around to the pass the way the trail goes.''

''Thank God.''

''We'll get to go by Lake Doris.''

''The renowned Lake Doris,'' Peter scoffs.

Joe waves a finger to scold. ''It is nice, you know.''

* * *

Joe and Peter walk. Soon their breathing hits a regular rhythm. They cross a meadow tucked into the side of the range like a terrace. It is covered with suncones, small melt depressions in the snow, and the walking is uneven.

"My feet are freezing," Pete says from several yards behind Joe.

Joe looks back to reply. "It's a cooling system. Most of my blood is hot—so hot I can hold snow in my hand and my hand won't get cold. But my feet are chilled. It cools the blood. I figure there's a spot around my knees that's perfect. My knees feel great. I live there and everything's comfortable."

"My knees hurt."

"Hmm," Joe says. "Now that is a problem."

After a silence filled by the squeak of snow and the crick of boot against snowshoe, Pete says, "I don't understand why I'm getting so tired. I've been playing full-court basketball all winter."

"Mountains aren't as flat as basketball courts."

Joe's pace is a bit faster than Pete's, and slowly he pulls ahead. He looks left, to the tree-filled valley, but slips a few times and turns his gaze back to the snow in front of him. His breaths rasp in his throat. He wipes sweat from an eyebrow. He hums unmusically, then starts a breath-chant, muttering a word for each step: *animal, animal, animal, animal, animal*. He watches his snowshoes crush patterns onto the points and ridges of the pocked, glaring snow. White light blasts around the sides of his sunglasses. He stops to tighten a binding, looks up when he is done. There is a tree a few score yards ahead—he adjusts his course for it, and walks again.

After a while he reaches the tree. He looks at it; a gnarled old Sierra juniper, thick and not very tall. Around it hundreds of black pine needles are scattered, each sunk in its own tiny pocket in the snow. Joe opens his mouth several times, says "Lugwump?" He shakes his head, walks up to the tree, puts a hand on it. "I don't know who you are?" He leans in, his nose is inches from bark. The bark peels away from the tree like papery sheets of filo dough. He puts his arms out, hugs the trunk. "Tr-eeeee," he says. "Tr-eeeeeee."

He is still saying it when Peter, puffing hard, joins him. Joe steps around the tree, gestures at a drop beyond the tree, a small bowl notched high in the side of the range.

"That's Lake Doris," he says, and laughs.

Blankly Peter looks at the small circle of flat snow in the center of the bowl. "Mostly a summer phenomenon," Joe says. Peter purses his lips and nods. "But not the pass," Joe adds, and points west.

West of the lake bowl the range—a row of black peaks emerging from the snow—drops a bit, in a deep, symmetrical U, an almost perfect semicircle, a glacier road filled with blue sky. Joe smiles. "That's Rockbound Pass. There's no way you could forget a sight like that. I think I see Brian up there. I'm going to go up and join him."

He takes off west, walking around the side of the lake until he can go straight up the slope rising from the lake to the pass. The snow thins on the slope, and his plastic snowshoes grate on stretches of exposed granite. He moves quickly, takes big steps and deep breaths. The slope levels and he can see the spine of the pass. Wind blows in his face, growing stronger with every stride. When he reaches the flat of the saddle in mid-pass it is a full gale. His shirt is blown cold against him, his eyes water. He can feel sweat drying on his face. Brian is higher in the pass, descending the north spine. His high shouts are blown past Joe. Joe takes off his pack and swings his arms around, stretches them out to the west. He is in the pass.

Below him to the west is the curving bowl of a cirque, one dug by the glacier that carved the pass. The cirque's walls are nearly free of snow, and great tiers of granite gleam in the sun. A string of lakes—flat white spots—mark the valley that extends westward out of the cirque. Lower ranges lie in rows out to the haze-fuzzed horizon.

Behind him Lake Doris's bowl blocks the view of the deep valley they have left behind. Joe looks back to the west; wind slams his face again. Brian hops down the saddle to him, and Joe whoops. "It's windy again," he calls.

"It's always windy in this pass," Brian says. He strips off his pack, whoops himself. He approaches Joe, looks around. "Man, for a while there about a year ago I thought we'd never be here again." He claps Joe on the back. "I'm sure glad you're here," he says, voice full.

Joe nods. "Me, too. Me, too."

Peter joins them. "Look at this," calls Brian, waving west. "Isn't this amazing?" Peter looks at the cirque for a moment and nods. He takes off his pack and sits behind a rock, out of the wind.

"It's cold," he says. His hands quiver as he opens his pack.

"Put on a sweatshirt," Brian says sharply. "Eat some food."

Joe removes his snowshoes, wanders around the pass away from Brian and Peter. The exposed rock is shattered tan granite, covered with splotches of lichen, red and black and green. Joe squats to inspect a crack, picks up a triangular plate of rock. He tosses it west. It falls in a long arc.

Brian and Peter eat lunch, leaning against a boulder that protects them from the wind. Where they are sitting it is fairly warm. Brian eats slices of cheese cut from a big block of it. Peter puts a tortilla in his lap, squeezes peanut butter out of a plastic tube onto it. He picks up a bottle of liquid butter and squirts a stream of it over the peanut butter.

Brian looks at the concoction and squints. "That looks like shit."

"Hey," Peter says. "Food is food. I thought you were the big pragmatist."

"Yeah, but . . ."

Pete wolfs down the tortilla, Brian works on the block of cheese.

"So how did you like the morning's hike?" Brian asks.

Pete says, "I read that snowshoes were invented by Plains Indians, for level places. In the mountains, those traverses"—he takes a bite—"those traverses were terrible."

"You used to love it up here."

"That was in the summers."

"It's better now, there's no one else up here. And you can go anywhere you want over snow."

"I've noticed you think so. But I don't like the snow. Too much work."

"Work," Brian scoffs. "The old law office is warping your conception of work, Peter."

Peter chomps irritably, looking offended. They continue to eat. One of Joe's nonsense songs floats by.

"Speaking of warped brains," Peter says.

"Yeah. You keeping an eye on him?"

"I guess so. I don't know what to do when he loses it, though."

Brian arches back and turns to look over the boulder. "Hey, Joe!" he shouts. "Come eat some lunch!" They both watch Joe jerk at the sound of Brian's voice. But after a moment's glance around, Joe returns to playing with the rocks.

"He's out again," says Brian.

"That," Peter says, "is one sick boy. Those doctors really did it to him."

"That *crash* did it to him. The doctors saved his life. You didn't see him at the hospital like I did. Man, ten or twenty years ago an injury like that would have left him a vegetable for sure. When I saw him I thought he was a goner."

"Yeah, I know, I know. The man who flew through his windshield."

"But you don't know what they *did* to him."

"So what did they do to him?"

"Well, they stimulated what they call axonal sprouting in the areas where neuronal connections were busted up—which means, basically, that they grew his brain back!"

"*Grew* it?"

"Yeah! Well some parts of it—the broken connections, you know. Like the arm of a starfish. You know?"

"No. But I'll take your word for it." Peter looks over the boulder at Joe. "I hope they grew back everything, yuk yuk. He might have one of his forgetting spells and walk over the edge there."

"Nah. He just forgets how to talk, as far as I can tell. Part of the reorganization, I think. It doesn't matter much up here." Brian arches up. "Hey, JOE! FOOD!"

"It does too matter," Peter says. "Say he forgets the word *cliff*. He forgets the concept, he says to himself I'm just going to step down to that lake there, and whoops, over the edge he goes."

"Nah," Brian says. "It doesn't work that way. Concepts don't need language."

"What?" Peter cries. "Concepts don't need language? Are you kidding? Man I thought Joe was the crazy one around here."

"No seriously," Brian says, shifting rapidly from his usual reserve to interested animation. "Sensory input is already a thought, and the way we field it is conceptual. Enough to keep you from walking off cliffs anyway." Despite this assertion he looks over his shoulder again. There stands Joe nodding as if in agreement with him.

"Yes, language is a contact lens," Joe says.

Peter and Brian look at each other.

"A contact lens at the back of the eyeball. Color filters into this lens, which is made of nameglass, and its reflected to the correct corner of the brain, tree corner or rock corner."

Peter and Brian chew that one over.

"So you lose your contact lenses?" Brian ventures.

"Yeah!" Joe looks at him with an appreciative glance. "Sort of."

"So what's in your mind then?"

Joe shrugs. "I wish I knew." After a while, struggling for expression: "I feel things. I feel that something's not right. Maybe I have another language then, but I'm not sure. Nothing looks right, it's all just . . . color. The names are gone. You know?"

Brian shakes his head, involuntarily grinning.

"Hmm," Peter says. "It sounds like you might have some trouble getting your driver's license renewed." All three of them laugh.

Brian stands, stuffs plastic bags into his pack. "Ready for some ridge runnning?" he says to the other two.

"Wait a second," Peter says, "we just got here. Why don't you kick back for a while? This pass is supposed to be the high point of the trip, and we've only been here half an hour."

"Longer than that," says Brian.

"Not long enough. I'm tired!"

"We've only hiked about four miles today," Brian replies impatiently. "All of us worked equally hard. Now we can walk down a ridge all afternoon, it'll be great!"

Peter sucks air between his teeth, holds it in, decides not to speak. He begins jamming bags into his pack.

They stand ready to leave the pass, packs and snowshoes on their backs. Brian makes a final adjustment to hipbelt—

Pete looks up the spine they are about to ascend—Joe stares down at the huge bowl of rock and snow to the west. Afternoon sun glares. The shadow of a cloud hurries across the cirque toward them, jumps up the west side of the pass and they are in it, for a moment.

"Look!" Joe cries. He points at the south wall of the pass. Brian and Pete look—

A flash of brown. A pair of horns, blur of legs, the distant *clacks* of rock falling.

"Mountain goat!" says Brian. "Wow!" He hurries across the saddle of the pass to the south spine, looking up frequently. "There it is again! Come on!"

Joe and Pete hurry after him. "You guys will never catch that thing," says Peter.

The south wall is faulted and boulderish, and they zig and zag from one small shelf of snow to the next. They grab outcroppings and stick fists in cracks, and strain to push themselves up steps that are waist-high. The wind peels across the spine of the wall and keeps them cool. They breathe in gasps, stop frequently. Brian pulls ahead, Peter falls behind. Brian and Joe call to each other about the goat.

Brian and Joe top the spine, scramble up the decreasing slope. The ridge edge—a hump of shattered rock, twenty or twenty-five feet wide, like a high road—is nearly level, but still rises enough to block their view south. They hurry up to the point where the ridge levels, and suddenly they can see south for miles.

They stop to look. The range rises and falls in even swoops to a tall peak. Beyond the peak it drops abruptly and rises again, up and down and up, culminating in a huge knot of black peaks. To the east the steep snowy slope drops to the valley paralleling the range. To the west a series of spurs and cirques alternate, making a broken desert of rock and snow.

The range cuts down the middle of it all, high above everything else that can be seen. Joe taps his boot on solid rock. "Fossil backbone, primeval earth being," he says.

"I think I still see that goat," says Brian, pointing. "Where's Peter?"

Peter appears, face haggard. He stumbles on a rock, steps quickly to keep his balance. When he reaches Brian and Joe he lets his pack thump to the ground.

"This is ridiculous," he says. "I have to rest."

"We can't exactly camp here," Brian says sarcastically, and gestures at the jumble of rock they are sitting on.

"I don't care," Peter says, and sits down.

"We've only been hiking an hour since lunch," Brian objects, "and we're trying to close in on that goat!"

"Tired," Peter says. "I have to rest."

"You get tired pretty fast these days!"

An angry silence.

Joe says in a mild voice. "You guys sure are bitching at each other a lot."

A long silence. Brian and Peter look in different directions.

Joe points down at the first dip in the ridge, where there is a small flat of granite slabs and corners filled with sand. "Why don't we camp there? Brian and I can drop our packs and go on up the ridge for a walk. Pete can rest and maybe start a fire later. If you can find wood."

Brian and Pete both agree to the plan, and they descend to the saddle campsite.

Two men ridge running. They make swift progress up the smooth rise, along the jumbled road at the top of the range. The bare rock they cross is smashed into fragments, splintered by ice and lightning. Breaking out of the blackish granite are knobs of tan rock, crushed into concentric rings of shards. They marvel at boulders which look like they have sat on the range since it began to rise. They jump from rock to rock, flexing freed shoulders. Brian points ahead and calls out when he sees the goat. "Do you see it?"

"Sure do," Joe says, but without looking up. Brian notices this and snorts disgustedly.

Shadows of the range darken the valley to the east. Joe hops from foothold to foothold, babbling at Brian all the while from several yards behind him. "Name it, name it. You name it. Naammme. What an idea. I've got three blisters on my feet. I named the one on the left heel Amos." Pause to climb a shoulder-high slab of granite. "I named the one on the right heel Crouch. Then I've got one on the front of my right ankle, and I named that one Achilles. That way when I feel it it's not like pain, it's like a little joke. Twinges in my heel"—panting so he can talk—"are little hellos, hellos with every step. Amos here, hi, Joe; Crouch here, hi, Joe. It's amazing. The way I feel I probably don't need boots at all. I should take them off!"

"You'd probably better keep them on," Brian says seriously.

Joe grins.

The incline becomes steeper and the edge of the ridge narrows. They slow down, step more carefully. The shattered rock gives way to great faulted blocks of solid mountain. They find themselves straddling the ridge on all fours, left feet on the east slope and right feet on the west. Both sides drop sharply away, especially the west. Sun gilds this steeper slope. Joe runs his hand down the edge of the range.

The ridge widens out, and they can walk again. The rock is shattered, all brittle plated angular splinters, covered with lichen. "Great granite," Joe says.

"This is actually diorite," Brian says. "Diorite or gabbro. Made of feldspar and darker stuff."

"Oh, don't give me that," Joe says. "I'm doing well just to remember granite. Besides, this stuff has been granite for a lot longer than geologists have been naming things. They can't go messing with a name like that." Still, he looks more closely at the rock. "Gabbro, gabbro . . . sounds like one of my words."

They wind between boulders, spring up escarpments. They come upon a knob of quartz that rises out of the black granite. The knob is infinitely cracked, as if struck on top by a giant sledgehammer. "Rose quartz," says Brian, and moves on. Joe stares at the knob, mouth open. He kneels to pick up chunks of the quartz, peers at them. He sees that Brian is moving on. Rising, he says to himself, "I wish I knew everything."

Suddenly they are at the top. Everything is below them. Beside Brian, Joe stops short. They stand silently, inches apart. Wind whips around them. To the south the range drops and rises yet again, to the giant knob of peaks they saw when they first topped the ridge. At every point of the compass mountains drop away, white folds crumpling to every horizon. Nothing moves but the wind. Brian says, "I wonder where that goat went to."

Two men sitting on a mountaintop. Brian digs into a pile of rocks, pulls out a rusty tin box. "Aha," he says. "The goat left us a clue." He takes a piece of paper from the box. "Here's its name—Diane Hunter."

"Oh, bullshit!" cries Joe. "That's no name. Let me see that." He grabs the box out of Brian's hand and the top falls off. A shower of paper, ten or twenty pieces of it, pops out of the box and floats down to the east, spun by the wind. Joe pulls out a piece still wedged in the box. He reads, "Robert Spencer, July 20th, 2014. It's a name box. It's for people who want to leave a record of their climb."

Brian laughs. "How could anyone get into something like

that? Especially on a peak you can just walk right up to." He laughs again.

"I suppose I should try to recover as many as I can," Joe says dubiously, looking down the steep side of the peak.

"What for? It's not going to erase their experience."

"You never know," says Joe, laughing to himself. "It very well might. Just think, all over the United States the memory of this peak has popped right out of twenty people's heads." He waves to the east. "Bye-bye . . ."

They sit in silence. Wind blows. Clouds pass by. The sun closes on the horizon. Joe talks in short bursts, waves his arms. Brian listens, watches the clouds. At one point he says, "You're a new being, Joseph." Joe cocks his head at this.

Then they just sit and watch. It gets cold.

"Hawk," says Brian in a quiet voice. They watch the black dot soar on the updraft of the range.

"It's the goat," says Joe. "It's a shapechanger."

"Nah. Doesn't even move the same."

"I say it is."

The dot turns in the wind and rises, circling higher and higher above the world, coasting along the updraft with minute wing adjustments, until it hovers over the giant, angular knotpeak. Suddenly it plummets toward the peaks, stooping faster than objects fall. It disappears behind the jagged black teeth. "Hawk," Joe breathes. "Hawuck divvve."

They look at each other.

Brian says, "That's where we'll go tomorrow."

Glissading down the snow expanse, skidding five or ten feet with each stiff-legged step, the two of them make rapid progress back to camp. The walking is dreamlike as they pump left . . . right . . . left . . . right down the slope.

"So what about that goat?" says Joe. "I never did see any prints."

''Maybe we shared a hallucination,'' says Brian. ''What do they call that?''

''A folie à deux.''

''I don't like the sound of that.'' A pause while they skid down a steep bank of snow, straight-legged as if they are skiing. ''I hope Pete got a fire going. Damn cold up here.''

''A feature of the psychic landscape,'' Joe says, talking to himself again. ''Sure, why not? It looks about like what I'd expect, I'll tell you that. No wonder I'm getting things confused. What you saw was probably a fugitive thought of mine, escaping off across the waste. Bighorn sheep, sure.''

After a while they can see the saddle where they left Peter, far below them in the rocky expanse. There is a spark of yellow. They howl and shout. ''Fire! FIRE!''

In the sandy camp, situated in a dip between slabs of granite, they greet Pete and root through their packs with the speed of hungry men. Joe takes his pot, jams it with snow, puts it on the fire. He sits down beside Peter.

''You guys were gone a long time,'' Peter says. ''Did you find that goat?''

Joe shakes his head. ''It turned into a hawk.'' He moves his pot to a bigger flame. ''Sure am glad you got this fire going,'' he says. ''It must have been a bitch to start in this wind.'' He starts to pull off his boots.

''There wasn't much wood, either,'' Pete says. ''But I found a dead tree down there a ways.''

Joe prods a burning branch, frowns. ''Juniper,'' he says with satisfaction. ''Good wood.''

Brian appears, dressed in down jacket, down pants, and down booties. Pete falls silent. Glancing at Pete, Joe notices this, and frowns again. He gets up stiffly to go to his pack and get his own down booties. He returns to the fire, finishes taking off his boots. His feet are white and wrinkled, with red blisters.

"Those look sore," says Pete.

"Nah." Joe gulps down the melted snow in his pot, starts melting more. He puts his booties on.

They watch the fire in silence.

Joe says, "Remember that time you guys wrestled in the living room of our apartment?"

"Yeah, we got all those carpet burns."

"And broke the lamp that never worked anyway—"

"And then you went berserk!" Brian laughs. "You went berserk and tried to bite my ear off!" They all laugh, and Pete nods, grinning with embarrassed pride.

"Pete won that one," Joe says.

"That's right," says Brian. "Put my shoulders to the mat, or to the carpet in that case. A victory for maniacs everywhere."

Ponderously Peter nods, imitating official approval. "But I couldn't beat you tonight," he admits. "I'm exhausted. I guess I'm not up to this snow camping."

"You were strong in those days," Brian tells him. "But you hiked a radical trail with us today, I'll tell you. I don't know too many people who would have come with us, actually."

"What about Joe here? He was on his back most of last year."

"Yeah, but he's crazy now."

"I was crazy before!" Joe protests, and they laugh.

Brian pours macaroni into his pot, shifts to a rock seat beside Peter so he can tend the pot better. They begin to talk about the days when they all lived together as students. Joe grins to hear them. He nearly overturns his pot, and they call out at him. Pete says, "The black thing is the pot, Joseph, the yellow stuff is fire—try to remember that." Joe grins. Steam rises from the pots and is whipped east by the evening breeze.

* * *

Three men sitting round a fire. Joe gets up, very slowly, and steps carefully to his pack. He unrolls his groundcloth, pulls out his sleeping bag. He straightens up. The evening star hangs in the west. It's getting darker. Behind him his old friends laugh at something Pete has said.

In the east there are stars. Part of the sky is still a light velvet blue. The wind whistles softly. Joe picks up a rock, looks at it closely. "Rock," he says. He clenches the rock in his fist, shakes it at the evening star, lofts it skyward. "Rock!" A tear gleams in his eyes. He looks down the range: *black dragon back breaking out of blue-white*, like consciousness from chaos, an unbroken range of peaks—

"Hey, Joseph! You lamebrain!"

"Space case!"

"—come take care of your pot before it puts the fire out."

Joe walks to the woodpile grinning, puts more wood on the fire, until it blazes up yellow in the dusk.

—1975/1977/1983

The Disguise

I pulled open the theater door and stuck my foot against it to keep the wind that swirled in the street from slamming it shut. I swung my duffel bag through the doorway and followed it inside. The door closed with a forced hiss and the bright lights of the street were replaced by dim greys. The air was still.

My eyes adjusted, and slowly, as if candles were being lit, I perceived the narrow high room which was the foyer of the Rose Theatre. I crossed the room and peered in the ticket window. A thin young man, with eye sockets blacked, and white hair cropped close to his head, looked up at me. I dropped my bag, pulled my card from my pocket and handed it to him.

''Pallio,'' I said.

''Very good,'' he said, and looked at the card. ''Now when Velasquo arrives we'll have everyone.'' He picked up a cast list and put a check beside my name. After slotting my card into the register, he touched some keys, and the square of plastic disappeared. ''The charge is twelve percent higher now,'' he murmured. ''They're trying to tax us to death.'' The card reappeared and he handed it back to me. ''Let me take you to your room.''

I picked up my bag. The cashier appeared through a doorway beside the window and led me down the hall, looking back over his shoulder to talk: ''I don't trust this *Guise* play, I think that whole Aylesbury Collection is a Collier forgery. . . .'' I ignored him and watched the footprints he left in the thick blue-black carpet. Dull bronze-flake wallpaper shattered the light from a half-dozen gas jets. The Rose was in its full Regency splendor, for the first time in months. The halls felt as subterranean as before, however; the Rose occupied only a few bottom floors in the Barnard Tower, an eighty-story complex.

The cashier stopped at one of a series of doors and opened it for me. Light flooded over us. We went in and were on a different set; snapping Jacob's ladders and colored liquids bubbling up tubes made me look for a mad scientist. But it was only a white-coated technician, at the computer terminal. He turned around, revealing a scrubbed, precisely shaved face. ''Whom have you brought us?'' he said.

''Pallio,'' replied the cashier. I dropped my bag.

''We're ready to give you your part,'' the technician said.

The chair was dressed up like a chrome-and-glass version of the table Frankenstein's monster was born on. ''Does Bloomsman have to do this,'' I said.

''You know our director.''

''Last time I was here it was a dentist's chair.''

''Not many liked that one, as I recall.''

I got into the chair while he tapped keys at the terminal, calling up from the artificial mind a detailed description of my brain's structure. When he was done he wrapped the pharmaceutical band around my neck. ''Ready?'' he asked. He tapped a key on the chair's console and I felt the odd sensation, like flexing a stiff muscle, of the injection—a tiny witch's brew of L-dopa, bufotenine, and norepinephrine. As always my heart began hammering immediately: not because of the introduced chemicals, but because of my own adrenaline, flooding through me to combat the imagined danger of a primal violation.

We waited. The room enlarged and flattened out into a painted cylinder. "Now for the hood," said the technician, his voice like tin. The hood descended and it was dark. The goggles were cold against my face, and my scalp prickled as filaments touched it.

"Time for the implant," the technician said. "Let's have alpha waves if you please." I started the stillness behind my nose. "Fine. Here we go."

In my vision a blue field flickered at around ten cycles per second, and voices chattered in both ears, creating counterpoints of blank verse. In those connected clumps known as the limbic system, scattered across the bottom of my cerebral cortex, new neural activity began. Electrical charges skipped through the precise network of neurons until they reached the edge of the familiar; synapses fired in new directions, and were forever changed. I was growing. I felt none of it.

Memories came before me in confusing abundance, passing before I could fix on them. An afternoon by the window in an Essex library, watching green hills become invisible in the grey rain. In the colony off Jamaica just after the earthquake, when everyone was silent, feeling the pressure of the hundred fathoms of water above. The run of basses in the scherzo of Beethoven's Fifth. A strong smell of disinfectant—hospital smell—and the voice of Carlos, droning quietly: "It was in the fourth act of *Hamlet*, when I as Claudius was on my knees, attempting to pray. Hamlet was above and to one side, on the balcony, and in my peripheral vision his face distorted into a mask of fang and snout. As he finished his soliloquy he turned away from the balustrade, but his head stayed fixed, twisted entirely over one shoulder, and he continued to glare down at me. My memory flooded. The moment I understood he was the Hieronomo, he jumped the balustrade, and I leaped to my feet only to meet the falling épée blade directly in the chest. I heard the cries of shock, but nothing more. . . ."

Blackness. Then the suction pulling at my eyes as the eyepieces withdrew. The hood rose and the white room reappeared. I twisted my head back and forth.

"Got it?" asked the technician. I paused and thought. Pallio . . . yes. A series of exclamations marked his entrance in the first scene, a conference with Velasquo. I knew only my first few lines, plus cue lines, and Bloomsman's laconic blocking, appropriate to the improvisational nature of the art: "Confront Velasquo center stage." The rest of my part would come to me throughout the course of the play, irregularly, recalled by unknown cues. This was the minimum script that Bloomsman allowed one to receive; it was the preferred preparation among seasoned actors.

"Backstage is that way," the technician said. He helped me up. I swayed unsteadily. "Break a leg," he said brightly, and returned to his terminal. I picked up my costume bag and left the room.

The hall expanded near the gas jets and contracted in the dimmer sections. I stopped and leaned against the wall, concentrating to recover from the dissociation of the implant. The wallpaper was not actually flake—it had once been a smooth sheen, but had cracked and peeled away into thousands of bronze shavings. Chips broke off under me and floated to the carpet. I strode down the hall, uncertain how long I had stopped. My sense of estrangement was stronger than usual, as if I had learned more than a play.

The hall ended in a T and I could not remember which way to go. Acting on a dim intuition I turned right and found myself in a veritable maze of T-connections. I alternated turns, going first right, then left. One hall I followed dropped several steps, then turned and became a flight of stairs, which I descended. At the bottom of this stairway were three long, dim halls, all furnished (like the stairway) with the same dark carpet, bronze wallpaper, and gas jets. I chose the right-hand one and ventured on. Just as I began to think myself inextricably lost there was a door, recessed into the right wall. I opened it and was at the back of the theater, looking across the audience to the curtain.

The audience was large, about forty or fifty people. Many times I had acted in plays which no one had come to see; in those the imaginary fourth wall had become real, and we had played for ourselves, aware only of the internal universe of the play. Most actors preferred it that way. But I liked the idea of an audience watching. And it was not surprising, with this play. It wasn't often that one got to see the first performance of a play four hundred years old.

An usher appeared and propped the door open for me. Behind him a fully-armed security guard looked me over. He was there, I supposed, because of Hieronomo. The usher offered me a program and I took it. "I need to get backstage," I whispered.

He smiled. "Just go through the door by the stage," he said. "It's easier."

Backstage I stopped and looked at the program in my hand. The first page listed the dramatis personae:

THE GUISE

Pallio, Duke of Naples
Velasquo, his younger brother
Donado, a Cardinal
Sanguinetto, a Sicilian count
Orcanes } gentlemen: followers of Donado
Hamond }
Mura, a priest: attendant to Donado
Ursini } friends to Sanguinetto
Ferrando }
Elazar, a supposed doctor

Caropia, sister to Pallio and Velasquo
Leontia, wife to Donado, and sister to Orcanes
Carmen, servant to Caropia

Courtiers, Masquers, Officers and Guards, Pages, Seer.

Director: Eunice Bloomsman

The opposite page was almost filled by one of Bloomsman's learned program notes:

> *The Guise* is one of the four previously lost plays in the Aylesbury Collection, twenty-four plays and hundreds of miscellaneous papers discovered in 2052. The invaluable books and manuscripts, found at Aylesbury Manor near Oxford, had been locked in a storage trunk for over three hundred years.
>
> The copy of *The Guise* in the Collection is a quarto volume, published in 1628 "by N.O. for Thomas Archer." Stage directions have been added by an unknown 17th century hand.
>
> The text is anonymous. It was presumed that the play was by John Webster, who mentioned a work of his by the same title in the dedication to *The*

Devil's Law Case (1623). But this has been questioned. Earlier references to a *Guise* play—variously spelled *The Gwuisse,* or *The Guesse*—indicate that there was probably more than one play so named. Most of these presumably concern the de Guise family, but the plot of our play was taken from an Italian novella, *Il Travestimento di Pallio*.

Critics have made cases for the authorship of Middleton, Tourneur, and Massinger. The debates continue—even the authenticity of the entire Collection has been questioned recently. While this state of uncertainty remains, we at the Rose have thought it best not to attribute authorship.

This is the first Vancouver performance of *The Guise*.

It was less than I already knew from talking to Bloomsman. I had been one of many requesting a part; it had been worse than trying to get reservations to play Hamlet. Everyone who performed Jacobean drama had inquired, fascinated by the prospect of a new and unknown play. It had been a surprise when Bloomsman called and said, "You'll be Pallio."

I made my way through backstage corridors to the dressing room, found the cubicle with my name on it. My first costume—grey britches, white ruffled shirt-front, long blue coat—felt as familiar to me as my street clothes. The other costumes went on hooks. I sat down before the mirror, turned on its lights, and pulled my makeup kit from the bottom of the bag. My face was damp; the white powder stuck to it. I darkened my eyelids, exaggerated the curve of my upper lip. The sight of the stranger in the mirror, face white as a mask, quickened my pulse. I considered the many layers of his character, and played over his archaic language.

A small crystal perfume bottle rolled against my foot. I reached down, picked it up; still seated, I stuck my head around the partition separating me from the next cubicle. There was no one there. Dresses, white and scarlet and black, hung from the walls, making the cubicle seem smaller. Crystal bottles like the one in my hand reflected the blue light from the makeup mirror behind them.

Within the mirror there was movement. I turned my head and looked up at an auburn-haired actress, one I had never seen before. Her face was a narrow oval. Her eyes, grey as slate and flecked with black, surveyed me calmly. She looked into her cubicle and back, clearly framing her question. I lifted the bottle in explanation, and her mouth, which curved down sharply in repose, lifted as if propelled by the same motion, into a warm smile.

"Caropia?" I asked.

Her head turned aside. She walked past me into her cubicle without responding. A strand of her hair spiraled down; her slim back was splashed with tiny streaks of the powder that whitened her shoulders. I noticed that the grey eyes were still observing me from the mirror, and I quickly withdrew. Pallio's face mocked me in my own glass. Remember where you are, he said. . . . By and large, acting was as congenial an art form as any other; friends often performed plays together. But those of us who gravitated to the world of Jacobean tragedy were not a very communicative bunch. Strangers came in, played their parts, and went their separate ways into the city, remaining strangers to each other. The Hieronomo was one of us.

The stage set was large and uncluttered. The bedroom at the rear had wide black staircases bracketing it, and a narrow balcony above, so that it was deeply recessed, like a cave. I experienced the familiar wash of *déjà vu* as I viewed it; a false one, in that I had truly *already seen* the set, as part of the implanting. Real *déjà vu* would have been an uncanny feeling, I was sure; but in a world of memory implants it was as common as recollection itself. (Still, there were people addicted to the sensation. They would implant in their memory the remembrance of a world tour and then take that very tour, in a continuous state of *déjà vu*, pulse high, adrenaline running in their arteries. . . .)

In the large prop room directly behind the stage the director, Eunice Bloomsman, was holding the first and final cast meeting. Bloomsman was quite short, and very calm. Many of the players were ignoring her, expressing the common belief among them that directors were powerless lackeys, no more than the stage managers of old. But they were mistaken—directors programmed the information to be implanted in the players, and that gave them the chance to exert much subtle influence.

Bloomsman looked up at me, then continued. "All of you but one chose minimum text, so you'll have to stay alert to keep up. I've made the cues two and sometimes three lines long, so you'll have plenty of warning. In case you get lost there will be prompters in the usual places.

"This play has an extraordinary history, as you know, and there's a large audience here to see us, so let's try to do a good job. That means an absolute ban on interpolations—agreed?" There were nods from several. "Good. Now introduce yourselves so you'll know who's who."

A tall man stood, dressed in the rich red robes of stage clergy. "I'm Cardinal Donado," he said.

Two men then rose and introduced themselves as Hamond and Orcanes, followers of Donado. I had played with them before; they always performed together.

The actor next to them tugged at his black waistcoat and looked about the chamber. "Sanguinetto," he said in a harsh, low voice. I had played with him before also. He always took the part of the most deranged villain the work had to offer, which in revenge tragedy was saying a great deal. I had watched him play Iago with the most chilling bitterness; and in *Edward II* he had laughed his way through the ugly part of the murderer Lightborn. This actor took the backstage convention of silence to its limit, and never said anything but his lines. Between scenes he stood wordlessly near his next entrance. This was too much for some. Once a young actor had drawn me aside and asked me if I thought he was the Hieronomo—I had laughed. No, I told him, the Hieronomo always takes the part of the hero. Besides, he always returns with a different face, and I've seen this man before.

The others rose and identified themselves. I didn't recognize any of them. Latecomers from the dressing room arrived, and the diverse mix of costumes now included every color, creating a confusion much more plausible than any coordinated costuming could be. This was Bloomsman's idea, another of her innovations that seemed to give the players more freedom.

When the auburn-haired actress stood, she looked directly at me. Behind the mask of cosmetics (her mouth was a dangerous sickle of dark red) her grey eyes seemed colorless. "Caropia," she said. I remained expressionless, and she smiled.

Then there was a rustle and a man stepped out of a dim back corner of the room. He was dressed in black, and his short hair was a light, dull blond. He had thin lips, and a wide jaw that made his face look square.

My heart was thumping rapidly. Bloomsman turned to him. "And you are?" she inquired.

"I am Velasquo," the man said, and at that moment I felt extreme cold, as if suddenly probability had relaxed and all the air had left my side of the room. Something about the man—the turn of his nose—told me I should know him, and in my brain thoughtless energy ran through neural corridors, struggling in vain for recognition.

"That's very good," Bloomsman was saying. Everyone else was attending to their appearance, each of them preparing for his or her five thousandth, ten thousandth entrance. . . .

I felt isolated. ''The whole cast is here. Is everyone familiar with the stage?'' The question was ignored. Bloomsman pursed her lips into an expression of contempt. ''Let's begin.''

The curtain rose. Lights dimmed, and the audience was nothing but rows of white faces, which slowly became indistinct, like blobs of dough, then faded away in the deeper gloom. Small rustlings ended, and the little room was perfectly silent, perfectly dark.

A shaft of blue light, so faint that it first appeared to be only a seam in the blackness, gained strength and defined center stage. Into this conjuration of blue walked Velasquo, who stopped as if snared by it. He turned to face the audience, and from my vantage point at stage right I could see his sharp profile, and the light hair, now glazed blue, and a suddenly raised hand, in which a sheet of paper fluttered. He spoke, in a nasal tenor:

''This note commands me: I must have revenge!''

He read the note aloud. It was a garbled, nearly incoherent document, which informed him that his father the old Duke had been murdered, ''poison'd by a spider in his bed,'' and exhorted him to vengeance. It made only obscure references to the identity of the killer—''What now seems finest is most ill''—and Velasquo threw it down in disgust.

He explained to the audience that his father's death had been unexpected and mysterious; it had been attributed to overeating by Elazar, a doctor of doubtful reputation. He saw now that the foul play had been obvious. Bitterly he described the corrupt court of Naples, which, under the ''dull and amiable'' hand of his elder brother Pallio, now the Duke, had become the plaything of riotous sycophants. Pallio was too stupid to want to search for a murderer. (I listened with great interest.) The rest of the court was too evil, and probably somehow implicated in the deed. Only his sister Caropia remained untainted. As he described the rest of us, one by one, my mind reverberated with the memory of the play, which hovered just on the edge of consciousness. Suddenly I knew the end of the play; the tangled plots that led to it were still a blank, but there were tendrils of association that linked each character with his final fate, and I saw the culmination, the vivid murders, my own death, the bloody, corpse-littered stage.

Shaken, I watched Velasquo walk toward me. I had never divined the end of the play so soon before— Velasquo raised his voice, and my attention was drawn back to him. He vowed to look for the note's author, who clearly knew more than he had written, and then search for the killer:

> "I'll seek him out—to do it I'll dissemble:
> And if there be a murderer, let him tremble."

That was my cue.

I walked on stage and an aura of blue light surrounded me. Velasquo greeted me and I replied, a bit too loudly, I thought, for the size of the room. I began concentrating, working to express naturally lines I had never spoken, doing that improvisation of stance and gesture which makes ours so much different from the acting in any previous tradition.

His eyes never leaving me, Velasquo suddenly told me of the contents of the note— "Our poor father has been most foully murdered!"

My mouth fell open. "But nay," I objected, "he's dead." Velasquo ignored me and proceeded to describe the deed, in much more elaborate detail than the mysterious letter had, as if the bald mention of the crime had brought the scene up full-bloom in his imagination. At the end of the gruesome tale I said, "That's not so well done, brother!" and continued to make stupid exclamations of shock as Velasquo listed the rest of the potential assassins at court. Finally he exhorted me to vengeance, and I eagerly agreed to help him. "I'll be your constant aid. But now, what shall we tell our holy sister?"

"Nothing."

With an audible snap the stage was flooded in white and yellow light, and nearly the entire cast paraded on. Velasquo moved away from me and drifted off through the colorful throng. The Cardinal led his retinue on, and I performed my function as Duke by calling, in a clear falsetto, for order amongst the revellers. One of the Cardinal's men proposed a masque, to be held two days hence, and I gave the idea my ducal approval. At the other side of the stage Sanguinetto voiced caustic, railing asides, which were making the audience laugh; in my peripheral vision I could see their mouths opening, faint in the wash of light from the stage. The Cardinal lost several lines by speaking too soon. I had no idea what he had said, and wondered if I had been cued. It was always at this point, in the first crowd scene, that confusions were most likely to occur. . . .

Caropia entered in a white gown, holding a cross at her breast. By the obsequious gestures of the others it was clear she was revered by all. Even Sanguinetto was silent. I went to her and she held out the cross; I kissed it. Velasquo did the same, and the Cardinal bowed deeply. She went to him and they began a quick exchange that the rest of us were supposed to ignore. I remembered my blocking, voiced in Bloomsman's dry tones—"Mime dialogue with Velasquo, far stage left."

Velasquo grabbed my arm and pulled me there. I mouthed words and he stared at my forehead. His mustard-brown eyes were nearly crossed in their intensity. Again I had the overpowering sensation of *presque vu* which told me I *almost knew* him. He mouthed words and as my memory supplied his high, rasplike voice, the sensation of recognition grew to something like panic. Abruptly he turned and began his exit, yet he looked back at me, as if in response to my inner turmoil; his head swiveled almost completely over his right shoulder. At once I knew him.

I stepped back. He squinted slightly, surprised by the move. I turned and crossed the stage, unable to face him, and halted only when I was alone in the narrow corridor between the wings and the prop room.

He was the Hieronomo, I was certain of it. Was he?

Hieronomo is the hero of Thomas Kyd's *The Spanish Tragedie*, the first and most influential of English revenge dramas. In it Hieronomo's son is killed by noblemen of the Spanish court. Hieronomo feigns insanity to facilitate his revenge, but despair pushes the imitation into reality, and by the time he completes his vengeance he is mad.

Someone playing this role had apparently experienced a similar breakdown: the previous December, in a performance at the Kean Theatre, the actor playing Hieronomo's foe, the old Duke, had actually died, killed by a knife with a loose button-tip. By the time this was discovered, the Hieronomo had disappeared.

In the months following he had appeared six more times, perhaps ten, depending on how many rumors you believed; each time with a different face, and a different name, but the same deadly blade. In *Women Beware Women*, and *Antonio's Revenge,* and in three different *Hamlet*s, the end had been disrupted by the villain's death. It was said that once he had stayed to finish *Hamlet*, and had taken a round of applause before slipping away. Others reported that another Claudius had been killed at his prayers, in act four, providing a surprise ending; I knew that one to be true; I had known the actor. The rest was hearsay and rumor, spreading at differing speeds through the strange community, so that undoubtedly each of us had heard a different selection of stories, whispered to us in dressing room or lavatory.

I was sure Velasquo was he. I scoffed at the notion, aware of the power the new legend had gained among those who played in these dramas. But once the suspicion had appeared, it was impossible to expel—it was more *certainty* than suspicion, yet I resisted it. It was as likely as not that he was just another actor, doing an excellent job. In such company, how could I tell otherwise? How could I tell anything in this theater? I knew each player only as his part. It was impossible to know anything for sure—or if not, it would have to be cleverly learned.

Someone tapped my arm and I jumped. It was one of the prompters. "You're on," he said. I hurried to the stage, afraid I would have to ask him where we were, but the sight of Caropia, standing alone by the bed in the inner chamber, brought the scene to me. It was late in the act. I composed myself and walked on.

Her slim face was a shadowed mask of contemplation, and in the weak blue light she was nothing but modulations of grey. We stood frozen for long moments, until white light splashed across center stage. Then Caropia looked up. "Who's there?" she asked. "Your brother Pallio," I said, in a lower voice than I had used before, and then we rushed at each other and crashed together, to embrace and kiss with abandon. She bit at me, and I pulled my head back and laughed directly at the audience, aware of their collective gasp, which marked the pleasure of suspicions confirmed.

We desisted and I told Caropia, with suitable contempt, how Velasquo had come to me to confide that he suspected foul play in our father's death. At this her mouth set in its sharp downward curve. "You play the fool," she said, "he *is* one. Make your Sanguinetto kill him, as you had him kill our odious father. . . .'' I explained that this was impractical, since clearly someone at the court already knew what had happened. We had to dissemble and find that person out, before we could deal with Velasquo. Caropia shrugged; it was my problem, I was to solve it as I would. I reminded her that I had had the old Duke killed at her instigation—she alone had feared his discovery of our incest—but the reminder was a mistake. In harsh and dangerous tones she asked me not to mention the matter again. I agreed, but begged her to help me find the informer, and as she walked offstage she replied that she would if it pleased her. Out of the audience's sight she turned and the faintest trace of a smile lifted her mouth. She nodded at me with approval. But I still had a short soliloquy:

''Damned bitch!'' I said, ''I'd kill you too did I not lust for you.'' Then I looked to the audience.

''I love her as a man holds a wolf by the ears,'' I said, and launched myself with vigor into the soliloquy of the villain, the stage-Machiavel: glorying in my crimes, gleefully listing my subterfuges, basking in my own cleverness, wittily seducing the audience to my side. ''To lie upon my sister I have laid my father under earth—grave crimes,'' I informed them, and their laughter was an approval of sorts. I voiced the final couplet as a close confidence:

> ''. . . there's no one knows me.
> An honest simpleton still be my guise—
> Who does not seem a fool cannot be wise.''

The theater blacked out and I made my way to the staccato roll of applause. The first act was over.

I sat down on a stool just offstage and watched the second act begin. Caropia stood before the bed. She was dressed in red, a muted crimson with gold thread in it. In the sharp white-yellow light it seemed the same color as her hair, and her mouth.

Sanguinetto entered from above. He stepped down soundlessly, choosing the stairs to the right. His black doublet complemented black hair and beard; his face was powder-white. He greeted her and told her of the arrival of the seer. "Does he read dreams?" she asked, and looked pleased when Sanguinetto answered that he did.

Sanguinetto reached the stage and crossed in front of Caropia. When he came between her and the audience it was like an eclipse; the light shifted to blue, and when she reappeared it seemed she was dressed in grey. Offstage in the wings opposite me, Velasquo leaned against a wall and watched.

With contemptuous amusement, Sanguinetto was blackmailing her. His references were vague to me; apparently he referred to something I had missed in the first act. Something that Caropia had done, or was doing, had been discovered by Sanguinetto. Now he was using the information as a lever to extract sexual favors. "Thy painted visage will be naught but candied flesh," he told her, "if you lie not with me." He circled her briskly and balked her attempts to turn her back on him. She tried to forestall him by denying his accusation, but he ran his hand over her hair and mocked her; and slowly, bitterly, she acquiesced.

As they moved back to the bed, continuing the macabre dance of thrust and parry, I marveled at their skill, at the absolute verisimilitude of their every movement and intonation. This was acting of the highest order; it was impossible for me to imagine them as anyone but Caropia and Sanguinetto.

Velasquo watched the scene without expression.

With Sanguinetto's hand at her throat, Caropia sank back on the bed. The lights dimmed with her descent and the theater was black before Sanguinetto joined her.

I sat in the dark, and considered tests.

* * *

I was startled to attention by my cue lines. The next scene had already begun. I strode on stage and spoke to the audience:

"O excellent! By that he'll conquer Rome!"

The audience roared. I had no idea what I had referred to, having forgotten the cue. I retreated to the left staircase, in my confusion aware only of my blocking.

More characters arrived and the scene became complex. Everyone was involved in the central event (which I had not yet deciphered), but many were making covert conversation, or uttering malicious asides. The Cardinal spoke, and suddenly I understood the import of the scene: he was asking Caropia to take holy orders, to become a nun. He persisted with an icy calm that I couldn't interpret, and her refusals became increasingly strident. Sanguinetto, Hamond and Orcanes, Ferrando and Ursini, all publicly encouraged her while privately vilifying her. Only Velasquo actually meant his praise. I could see the dim white faces of the audience breaking into laughter, and I felt Caropia's humiliation keenly. We could make her comic for the rest of the play, if we wanted to (I recalled once playing in a *Revenger's Tragedy* in which the cast had nearly killed themselves with mirth). Finally my cue lines arrived and it was easy for me to feign Pallio's anger:

"They that mock her soon will lie in heaps
Of rotting flesh, all broken open to
The sun and flies and maggots,
And their half-empty eye sockets will stare
At naught but Pallio, astonish'd still by his
Abrupt revenge . . ."

The scene continued, but the laughter was greatly diminished. Velasquo grasped me by the arm. "Brother, I must speak to you anon,'' he said, staring at me curiously. I agreed, averting my gaze, and he slipped offstage behind me, leaving me with my heart knocking. He would have to be tested. . . .

Now Caropia approached me, ostensibly to consult in private about the question of holy orders. She drew me out on the apron just above the audience, and in a voice tight with rage demanded that I kill Sanguinetto. I asked why, and she told me a near-truth, the best sort of lie; Sanguinetto was blackmailing her, demanding sexual favors in exchange for silence concerning *my* guilt in the old Duke's death. I reacted with a lover's anger, and as I railed against Sanguinetto she stroked my arm, the softness of her hands belying the absolute implacability of her intentions.

She left with a last velvet command, and I found myself alone—the rest had exited during our dialogue. Blue light surrounded me, as tangible as if the gel covering the bulb had poured down into the cone of light. I collected myself and tried to project an assured, amused control:

''The brother that I hate, and the sister
That I hate and love (for there's
Two feelings closer to each other than
The minds of any pair of us) both press
Me now like halves of a garotte,
Yet I'll slip out and let them gnash together;
I have a plot—yet soft—Velasquo—''

He entered. My back to him, and face to the audience, I let my features slacken into those of the Pallio he knew. There was laughter, and with a sudden leer I encouraged it, for it was directed at Velasquo. I turned and greeted him. He began by complaining that he had found no clue to the murderer's identity. I informed him that I had some news that might help him, then answered his questions so foolishly that it took him some time to deduce that if Sanguinetto kept spiders, and was blackmailing Caropia, he must indeed be the villain we were searching for. I expressed amazement at his intelligence.

While the audience laughed at my duplicity, Velasquo's face darkened, his jaw muscles bunched. The laughter died away completely before he spoke: "I'd have this be vengeance all will remember," he said, in a voice so harsh that it enforced belief, made one wonder, with squeamish anticipation, what forms revenge might take. . . . He spoke no more of it, however, which made me suspect he was omitting lines; he sent me on my way, then stalked aimlessly around the stage. Suddenly he stopped and laughed, first quietly, then in a sharp howl. In the midst of this nerve-shattering mirth the blackout snapped down and terminated both light and sound.

I was conscious of a plan that had formulated itself sometime during Velasquo's ominous drunkard's walk. I had a test, one that would leave me concealed; he would know he had been tested, of course—it was an unusual test that did not reveal that—but he would not know by whom.

In the prop room Ferrando and Ursini were running over an exchange of dialogue in double-time. A prompter at the rear entrance raised a hand; they filed on, allowing two brief bursts of yellow into the dark, grainy green of the room. I went to the prop table and casually scanned the small pile of stage-notes.

The top one was the one that would betray Pallio. I picked it up, and, holding it against me, went into the lavatory. Inside a stall I took a pencil stub from my vest pocket (my ribs were sticky with sweat), and flattened the vellum against the wall with my other hand. In a clumsy, rounded imitation of Bloomsman's Italianate lettering, I listed all the plays I had ever heard connected with the Hieronomo:

The Spanish Tragedie
Hamlet
Hamlet, Act Four
Antonio's Revenge
Women Beware Women
The Atheist's Tragedy

I couldn't think of a fully appropriate tag, and so finally added *manet alta mente repostum;* it remains deep in my mind. That would do.

I had just quietly replaced the note, and was turning from the prop table, when Sanguinetto appeared from the left hallway. He watched me as he picked up the sheet of vellum and put it inside his black doublet; I couldn't tell if he had seen me return it or not. His beard, rising almost to his eyes, hid all expression, and his steady stare revealed nothing but interest. He went to the curtained opening and paused for a moment. He pushed the curtain aside, allowing blue light to wash over him, and made his final entrance.

From the rear I could see only a portion of center stage, and I feared Velasquo would be out of my sight at the crucial moment, aborting the test and leaving me with my uncertainties. Hastily I made my way through the dark to stage right, to the vantage point where I had observed most of the play.

Caropia was there; noticing my appearance, she gestured me to her and with a lift of her head directed my attention to the stage. I stood beside her and looked out, feeling her hand's pressure against my arm.

Velasquo was in disguise, wearing a black hooded cape. He was establishing his credentials—he was, he said to Sanguinetto, Pinon d'Alsquove, a fellow Sicilian, who had been forced to flee their native island because he had unfortunately murdered a gentleman of importance. Sanguinetto accepted this, exhibiting the usual Jacobean inability to see through even the simplest of disguises. They seated themselves at a dining table set out on the apron, and proceeded to drink and regale each other with tales. Strange revelers they were, both dressed in black, presented in a brilliant white-violet light that illuminated every face in the audience. They traded bloody stories, and it became clear that Pinon d'Alsquove had much in common with his fellow countryman. (There was a certain logic to this Jacobean thinking: since all Italians were depraved, it made sense that the farther south one went, the worse they became.) The crime that caused Pinon's exile had been the last in a long and gruesome series. Sanguinetto became unnaturally gay as Pinon described the various methods he had used to dispatch his enemies back in Sicily, and they quickly finished a tall, slim bottle of wine. As Sanguinetto uncorked another one Pinon spoke to the audience, in Velasquo's high voice: "In midst of all his mirth he will meet death." Then they were roaring with laughter again, at the champagne cascading from the bottle Sanguinetto held in his lap. As he drank and bit huge chunks from a turkey leg, Pinon described one of his weapons:

"... a most ingenious toy,
A tiny spring with rapier-pointed ends,
Held tight by threads of lightest leather; which
Then hidden in the victim's food, and ate,
The threads are quick digested, and the spring
Jumps to its fullest length, ripping great holes
Within thy rival's guts. Thus do Moors
Kill dogs ..."

Sanguinetto chewed on obliviously, and everyone in the theater watched him eat. "Aye," Pinon concluded,

"Methinks I know all of the finest ways
To end th' existence of a foe—"

Sanguinetto swallowed and struggled to his feet. He leaned over Pinon:

"Thou missed a way that should be known
To all Sicilians—I will show thee."

He hurried to the rear exit in long strides, knocked the curtain aside and disappeared. Pinon spoke in Velasquo's voice:

"Now I suspect I've drawn him out like snail
From shell, into the light where I may crush him."

Sanguinetto reappeared, holding at arm's length a tall glass box, like a candle lantern. Within it a thick-bodied, long-legged spider—a cane spider, I guessed—scrabbled up the walls and slid down again. Pinon leaped up, knocking his chair over. Sanguinetto pointed at the spider and leered proudly.

"This spider's of a kind known but in Sicily.
'Tis said they come out of the sides
Of fiery Aetna, as if escaped from hell.
They live in fumes, feed on the fruit that's killed
By ash, and are most poisonous."

"Tell me," Pinon said, his voice rising uncontrollably up to Velasquo's high tenor,

"... might I buy that beauty
From thee? I have a murder would be done
Most fitting thus, most artful ..."

Sanguinetto considered it, cocking his head drunkenly to one side.

"I've more of these, they breed by hundreds—aye.
Done, if you pay me well enough."

Pinon: "I'll pay you."

They made the exchange, Sanguinetto accepting a small pouch. He looked in it and grinned. Pinon was staring with an intense frown at the spider within the glass. Sanguinetto returned to the table and sat down, his back to Velasquo.

Sanguin: "We'll celebrate this sale with more revelry."
Pinon: "Indeed it is a glad occasion."
Sanguin: "I give you my assurance, who
You set that tiny demon on will die
Most painful—"

Pinon: "You'd know best, I'm certain . . ."

Now Pinon was standing right behind Sanguinetto, caped arms high so that he appeared a huge shadow, holding the glass box directly over the seated man's head. (Caropia's fingers were digging into my arm.) The spider's legs struck at the glass soundlessly. Sanguinetto reached forward and grabbed the foam-streaked bottle, raised it to his lips, tilted his head back; they froze:

Pinon pulled the floor of the box away and the spider dropped onto Sanguinetto's face. He struck at it with his free hand and it jumped to the table. As it skittered across, he smashed the bottle on it, scattering green glass everywhere. He staggered to his feet and arched back; his scream and Velasquo's high staccato laugh began simultaneously. The laughter continued longer.

On the table three or four spindly legs flailed at the air, their fine articulation destroyed. With stiff, awkward movements, Sanguinetto pulled his dagger from his belt and stabbed at the legs of the beast until they were still. He left the dagger in the table and collapsed over his chair. His voice, guttural as a rasp over metal, rose from near the floor.

"Stranger, I would thy heart were that black corse
Upon the table: surely it resembles nothing closer.
You had no cause to murder me . . ."

Velasquo pushed the hood from his head, and his face, gleaming with sweat, suffused with exhilaration, shifted as he looked about the room. He circled the table, leaning over Sanguinetto to shout at him, interspersing his lines with bursts of strained laughter:

"I did have cause; I am Velasquo, see?
My father's murder made me seek revenge!
You murdered him, 'gainst you I had revenge!
Now all that's sweet is nothing to revenge!"

"Wrong," croaked Sanguinetto.

". . . As well might I commend myself
For vengeance 'gainst you, having killed that spider,
As you to gloat o'er me, who was no more
Than insect used to slay your father—"

Vel: "What's this?"
Sanguin: "I was hired, hired by Pallio—here's my commission—"

He pulled the note from his doublet and tossed it on the floor, then twisted as spasms racked him.

"A cauldron churns and bubbles within my skull—
I see hell waiting; Death will have its fill—"

After a while he moved no more.

Velasquo kneeled at the sheet of vellum, smoothed it on his leg, read. I could feel my heart knocking at the back of my throat—

His head snapped up, his eyes, ablaze with a vicious, yellow intensity, searched from exit to exit, *looking at actors:* his expression was absolutely murderous. I wanted to flatten myself against the wall, to hide; it was difficult indeed to stand beside Caropia and feign unconcerned interest. For *his* was no acting, he had understood, he was the Hieronomo! I felt a surge of relief at the certainty of it, replaced by fear when I recalled what I was certain of. I was in mortal danger. But I *knew*.

Finally he broke the silence, in a voice that filled the room like cold air.

> ''Pallio. Pallio, the simpleton, the fool.
> That mask conceal'd a parricide most cruel.
> Though first deceiv'd by his quick cloak of lies—''

He paused then, so that the next line would contain his private reference, unaware how accurate it already was:

> ''I'll use his blood to wash away *his* guise.''

The blackout allowed me to flee to my cubicle.

Act four began, and with it the gradual acceleration and disintegration typical of revenge tragedy. Plots skipped and jumped and ran afoul of each other, twisting without evident logic to their conclusion; characters died. . . . From my cubicle I listened to the first scenes emerging tinnily from a speaker placed in the partition. Leontia, the Cardinal's wife, whom I hadn't seen since before the play began, was being strangled by the Cardinal's men. The Cardinal entreated Caropia to leave Naples, and, perfectly aware of the danger at the court, she agreed. I felt pained at that; foolishly, I had hoped we would remain lovers until the end. Caropia was then confronted by Carmen, her maid, who had been eavesdropping. Carmen demanded payment to keep her from informing me of the Cardinal's plan—I laughed at that—it was a strange world we existed in, where some plotted against others, who listened as they did it. Caropia agreed, and then promptly poisoned her. The maid's screams brought guards, and the doctor Elazar, who declared it a natural death. He too had blackmail in mind, and after the guards left, Caropia was forced to stab him and hide his body under the bed.

I stopped listening, and attempted to decide what I should do next. Nothing occurred to me. *Nothing,* I thought, remembering with disgust the century or two of experience I had to draw on: I recalled canoeing down the Amazon, fighting in the streets of New York, a thousand other like events . . .

But what I actually had done was difficult to distinguish from all the things I remembered doing. All I was sure of was that I had spent a lot of time in a chair, living in words; and on stages. It was as if I were driving a vehicle, and the rearview mirror had expanded to fill the windshield. Or as if I were the Angel of Time, flying backward into the future! Metaphors came up to me like bowling balls out of an automatic return; but no plans, nothing like a decision. Who was I to decide? Who was I?

"Pallio," said the speaker loudly. It was a prompter, calling for me. I returned to the prop room, reluctant to take to the stage again. I could no longer remember what attraction I had ever had to it.

Bloomsman herself waved at me: I was on. I stepped out upon a dark stage. There was just enough grainy, purple light leaking down to enable me to perceive the silhouettes of three men, pulling something from beneath the bed. Something about the scene—the lithe, long-limbed black figures, crouching—lacked all familiarity—*jamais vu* swept over me like nausea. I no longer understood what I saw. The dark room was a dimensionless field, and the black figures were nameless objects, ominous because they moved. Meaningless sounds rang in my ears.

I came to and found myself confronted by Ferrando and Ursini, on a brightly lit apron. Their blades were out and pointed at my throat. My first thought was that I'd left my épée in my costume bag, and was defenseless; then synapses fired, for what reason I knew not, and my lines came to me. I was safe from them.

They accused me of Sanguinetto's murder, and in a rather weak imitation of the ingenuous public Pallio I informed them that Velasquo had been the last person seen with their late master. With trembling voice I quickly shifted their suspicions to Velasquo, feeling thankful that it made sense to play Pallio as a distracted man. I left the stage, and then had to watch while Velasquo surprised them and knifed them both in the back. He did it with a verve and accuracy that left me chilled; surely their improvised blocking couldn't be so well-done: had he begun already? But in the darkness between scenes Ferrando and Ursini brushed by me, muttering and giggling together. I shook my head in hopes of clearing it, inhaled sharply, and moved back onstage.

Again the light was deep crevasse-blue. Caropia was already there: we embraced. This was to be one of our last scenes together, I knew. Surely everyone knew. I moved to the apron and saw below me, in the front row, Ferrando, Ursini, Elazar, Carmen, Leontia, and Sanguinetto. It was the custom for actors whose work was done to join the audience, but it made me uncomfortable. Given the traditions of the genre it always seemed to me that they were still in the play as ghosts, who might speak at any time. I resisted the impulse to move to the other side of the apron.

My attention shifted back to Caropia. In her slim face the

pebble-grey eyes were large, and filled with pain. I had so many disparate images of her to link . . . and yet, within the play and without, I knew nothing real about her. Our backstage silence augmented the Jacobean notion that the other sex was unknowable, a different species, an alien intelligence. Still, watching her bowed head, her slender arms moving nervously, I felt Pallio's emotions as my own, and I wanted to break into the play and experience that incestuous closeness. I spoke, infusing my lines with all these illusory feelings, to the invisible actress inside her, the one who made them both a mystery. I spoke tenderly of our love, and lamented our situation: "We are so far in blood . . ." " 'Tis payment," Caropia cried, and railed against the sequence of unchangeable events she found herself trapped in. Bitterly she blamed our incest: "Our sin of lust has webbed these plots around us, so I've dreamt—" I interrupted:

> "Why shouldst thou not love best the one known best?
> It is no crime, and were it, it has gain'd
> Us more than lost . . ."

She spoke of the church and we argued religion. Finally I interrupted again:

> "In this world all are quite alone,
> All efforts grasp for union. Who's succeeded
> More than thou and I? We shar'd the womb,
> The universe of childhood; lov'd
> As lovers in the lust of youth—"

And Caropia, thinking no doubt of her pact with the Cardinal, replied:

> "Thou know'st me well as one can know another."

I smiled, a tremendous effort, and continued:

"Thus be calm—thy dreams are naught but visions
Of thine other self, beheld while in
The timeless void of sleep. We've fears enough
In this world."

I turned from her and the tone of reassurance left me. I voiced my real concern:

". . . I fear Velasquo's
Found me out; his eyes shout 'murderer'
With all the brutal energy of horror.
He greets me mornings, dines with me at noon,
And stalks the palace grounds at night,
As if he were a hungry wolf, and I
A man alone on the trackless waste—"

Velasquo entered, several lines too early. Unable to finish in his presence, I moved to the other side of the apron and returned his baleful glare. Below me Sanguinetto was smiling.

There was silence. It was the first time the three of us had been onstage by ourselves, and the triangle we formed was the focus of all the tension we had managed to create. Beneath our polite exchange (Velasquo was inquiring if Caropia would accompany him to the masque) were layers: the reality of the play, the reality of the players . . . Velasquo's crafted jests probed at me with an intensity I alone could understand, although all that he did made perfect sense in the context of the play; indeed it must have appeared that he was doing a superb job. Only small stresses in his intonation revealed the danger, like swirls in a river, indicating swift undercurrents. I replied with a brittle hostility that had little acting in it, and we snapped at each other like the two poles of a Jacob's ladder:

Pallio: "She goes with me, keep you away from her—"

Vel: "Would you be kicked?"

Pallio: "Would you have your neck broke?"

The audience's silence was a measure of their absorption. Despite my earlier revulsion, and the blank nausea of the *jamais vu*, I felt growing within me, insidiously, the pleasure of acting, the chill tingling one feels when a scene is going very well.

This pleasure in the scene's success was soon overwhelmed by the fear which was making it succeed; Velasquo's thinly veiled attack was strengthening. His pale eyes glared at me intently, looking for some involuntary movement or expression that would show me to be the one who had recognized him. I struggled to keep only Pallio's wariness on my face, but it was a delicate distinction, one becoming more and more difficult to make. . . . I exited to the sound of his high laughter

Once off, I hurried around toward the dressing room. Caropia's was the only voice emerging from the wall-speakers in the narrow corridor, and footsteps were padding behind me. I almost ran, remembering the early death in *Hamlet*. But it was only the Cardinal, completing errands of his own.

The dressing room was momentarily empty. I took my épée from my costume bag and once again locked myself in a lavatory stall. The steel of the blade gleamed as I pulled away the leather scabbard.

It was an old épée, once used in competitive electric fencing. I had polished the half-sphere bell and removed the plug socket from inside it to convert it to a theater sword. The wire running down a slot in the blade was still there, as was the tip, a small spring-loaded cylinder. The blade was stiff, and curved down slightly. At the bell it was triangular in cross-section, a short, wide-based triangle, with the base uppermost. It narrowed to a short cylindrical section at the end, which screwed into the tip.

I tried to unscrew the tip, certain that what I was doing was not real, that I was acting for myself. Surely the thing to do was to stop the play (I winced) and proclaim Velasquo's identity to all. Or to slip away, out the back, and escape him entirely.

Yet naming him before all would not do—where was my proof? Even my own conviction was shaken by the question of evidence. There wasn't any. The first real *proof* I would get would be a sudden hard lunge for my throat, with a sharp blade. . . .

The tip wouldn't unscrew. I twisted until my fingers and hands were imprinted with red bars and semicircles, but it felt as if tip and blade were a solid piece. I clamped the tip between two molars and turned, but succeeded only in hurting my teeth. I needed pliers. I stared at the tip.

And if I were to escape, the Hieronomo would also. Surgery would change his face and voice, and he would return. I knew that in that case I would never be able to perform again without wondering if it were him again, playing opposite me. . . .

I put the tip on the floor under my boot sole. Holding it flat against the floor, I pulled up on the blade. When I lifted my foot, the tip stuck out at right angles from the blade. I put it back on the floor, and carefully stepped on the new bend until it was straight again. I repeated the operation delicately; I knew, from years of fencing, how easily the blades would snap. Presently there appeared behind the tip a ripple, a weak spot that would break when struck hard enough. I slipped the scabbard back on, satisfied that the épée could be swiftly transformed into a weapon that would kill.

At some level unknown to me I had decided. I left the stall and stared at the white face in the mirror, feeling a stranger to myself.

Back in the dressing room, Caropia and Velasquo were in earnest conference. When they saw me, Caropia returned to her cubicle and Velasquo, looking angry, crossed to the other side of the room.

I sat down beside Caropia and listened to the speaker above us. The Cardinal was arranging, with whom I could not tell, to have Hamond and Orcanes poisoned at the masque. Apparently the masque was to take place very soon. As I changed my coat I could feel my pulse throbbing in my arms.

"Disguise," said a voice in my ear. I jumped and turned to see Velasquo, his square face set close to mine.

"It's an odd word," he continued. "Shouldn't it be enguise, or beguise? Doesn't *dis*guise imply the opposite of what you want it to mean?"

I stared at him, in an agony of apprehension that he might go on, that he might reveal (disguise?) himself openly, and dare me to act—"*Dis* can also be used to intensify a verb," I finally stammered.

"You are disguised," he said, and scrutinized me closely. Then he walked away.

In my brain a chemical typhoon whirled. The exchange had been so—dramatic . . . suddenly I was stunned by the horrible suspicion that all our words were lines, all the events backstage part of a larger play . . . Bloomsman, Bloomsman . . . By coincidence (or perhaps not) Caropia appeared to sense this thought. She stuck her head around the partition and said, with a sardonic smile, "You learnt it of no fencer to shake thus," a line from a play that I myself had once spoken. I picked up my épée and strode away in agitation, all my certainties shattered.

Caropia caught up with me just outside the prop room, and touched my hand. I watched her and tried to conceal the fact that I was still trembling. She smiled and slipped her arm under mine. The archaic gesture seemed fraught with emotion. For the first time I understood that it was not just another dominant/submissive signal from the past, that it had been able to express one human's support for another. My confusion lessened. One way or other I would know, soon enough.

The prop room was filled with actors getting ready for the masque. Bloomsman had done her usual meticulous prop work; the masks were bright animal heads that covered one to the shoulders. A menagerie composed chiefly of pigs, tigers, and horses, we stared at each other and whispered with excitement. Bloomsman handed us our masks and smiled—a smile that now seemed to be filled with ominous possibility. "It's going fine," she said. "Let's do this last scene right." She put on a mask herself, a remorselessly grinning gargoyle.

I looked at my mask: a red fox. I could guess what Velasquo's would be. Caropia's was an exact model of her own head, with holes cut out for her eyes and mouth. The result, once on, was grotesque. She looked in a wall-mirror and laughed. "I'm animal enough already," she said. The gargoyle shrugged and said, in Bloomsman's calm voice, "I thought it the right thing."

Velasquo was already on stage, announcing his plans to the audience. Somehow he had learned of the relationship between Caropia and me. Long after everyone else in the theater, he had seen through her guise. His desire for vengeance now focused as much on her as me. She was to die of poison placed in her drinking cup. Beside me, she watched the cup, still on the prop table, and shivered. I felt fear for her then, and great affection, and heedlessly I whispered to her, "Don't drink from it."

She stared at me, and began to laugh. But I did not and she stopped. Her grey eyes surveyed me and slowly widened, as if in fear of me. "I won't," she whispered in a soothing voice. She disengaged her arm and moved away, glancing back once with an expression I could not read, but which could have been one of . . . terror.

The stage was divided by two long tables, both laden with silver and gold, fruits and meat, candles and flasks of liqueurs. As the stage filled with masquers, servants—in masks that were faceless white blanks—continued to load the tables. The fantastic menagerie milled about slowly and randomly seating themselves. Lines were shouted simultaneously, creating a cacophony that could only have been Bloomsman's doing.

I stood behind Caropia, at one end of the front table, peering through the eyeholes of my fox-face in search of Velasquo. My black, shiny nose protruded far before me. I saw that the Cardinal was not masked—he was still in his red robes, but a papal coronet was tilted back on his head. He viewed the uproar with an indulgent smile. Around him goats in formal dress drank wine.

My eye was caught by a movement above. A tall figure dressed in black leaned over the balcony and observed the activity; his mask was a skull. I glanced into the audience, and the backwash from the multicolored glare was enough illumination to confirm my suspicion. Sanguinetto was gone. It was he on the balcony, playing the medieval death-figure. He began to descend the stairs, pausing for several seconds after each step.

The masque gained energy. A plate piled high with meat was tipped over; people rose from their seats, shouting witticisms. A long body of glittering red liquid flashed through the air and drenched one of the Cardinal's goats. There was still no sign of Velasquo. An orange fight started between tables, and the noise reached a frantic pitch, timed by the metronome of Sanguinetto's steps. Two women, both with tiger masks, began to claw at each other.

At the height of the cacophony a long scream cut through the sound, making its ragged descant. When it ended there was silence and the company was still, forming a bizarre tableau. A man with a pig's head and red doublet staggered to the apron. He tore at his snout and pulled the mask off, to reveal Orcanes. His face was bloated and purple. He clutched his throat, sank to his knees. As he collapsed another scream ripped the air. Another player, also in pig mask, fell to the floor and drummed out his death. Sanguinetto, now on the stage, paced between tables.

The Cardinal stood, his face grim. "Who can account for these untimely deaths?" he demanded.

"Pallio," a voice behind me called. I spun around and saw the wolf's face, fangs protruding, yellow eyes agleam. I tore off my mask and stepped back to increase the distance between us.

"Who is this man?" I asked, my voice preternaturally calm. "He must be mad."

"Your brother I," he said, and pulled off his mask. "Velasquo."

"Velasquo!" I cried, and spoke to the Cardinal:

"Why, he kill'd Sanguinetto, Ferrando
And Ursini; yea, perhaps the old Duke too.
These new deaths without doubt are also his devise—"

Vel: "He's false; he is the murd'rer of our father.
Here's proof—"

Velasquo threw Sanguinetto's note down. I picked it up and looked at it. Penciled beneath my Latin tag, in a fine imitation of Bloomsman's hand, was another title: *The Guise*. Proof indeed.

I crumpled the sheet and tossed it to the floor. "A forgery," I said, voice still calm. "He tries usurping me."

I pulled my épée from my scabbard. Velasquo did the same. The company drew back, pulling the front table with them to make room. The Cardinal made his way forward. Sanguinetto stood beside him. The two of them linked arms, and the Cardinal spoke:

"The truth is in Fate's hands. Let them fence."

And in my mind I heard the blocking instruction, in Bloomsman's dry voice: "Fence."

Finally, finally the light became red, a bright crimson glare that bathed us both in blood. We circled each other warily. I watched his wrist, his stance, and in my concentration the world contracted to the two of us. Adrenaline flooded through me and my pulse was trip-hammer fast.

His blade had a tip on it, but that meant nothing; I knew it would slide back on contact, releasing the sharp point. The Hieronomo had used it before.

We began tentatively. He lunged, I parried, and we established a simple parry-riposte pattern, often used in practice, at very high speed. The flashing blades and the rapid clicking of clean parries were highly dramatic, but meant little.

After a short pause to regain balance, Velasquo lunged again, more fully this time, and we bouted with increased speed, using the full variety of tactics. The scrape and ring of steel against steel, the wooden thumping of our footwork, our hoarse breathing were the only sounds in the theater.

The exchange ended and we stared at each other, breathing heavily. A wrinkle of concentration appeared between his eyes. I was sure he now realized that my knowledge of fencing was not implanted, that it was learned from actual experience. Implanted fencing was adequate for theatrics, but it consisted entirely of conscious moves and strategies, it was a verbal memory. Fencing learned by experience was remembered to a large extent in the cerebellum, where movement and balance are controlled, and thus reactions were nearly reflex-fast. Velasquo was certainly aware of this, and now he knew that he had been discovered by someone capable of besting him.

Suddenly he lunged with great violence. The thrust avoided my parry and I had to leap back to dodge his blade. The real fight had begun. He lunged in straightforward attacks that were easy enough to parry, but when I did so he remised, continued to attack. He was ignoring my tipped weapon, which was clearly harmless. When I understood this, I jumped back and slapped my épée against the floor. The tip stayed on. I had to retreat and parry for my life, watching nothing but his blade, and striking it aside desperately each time it thrust at me.

My heel hit the bottom of the left stairway and I nearly stumbled. I stepped up backward, and Velasquo followed, negating my height advantage with the energy of his attack. I turned and ran up to the balcony, swinging my épée against the bannister all the way. The tip stayed on. I turned and lunged fiercely at my pursuer. He halted, lead foot three steps above his hind foot, and we engaged in a grim slashing battle, as if we were fighting with sabers. I didn't want him to reach the balcony. It was hopeless; still unafraid of my épée, he drove me back by degrees and managed, step by step, to make his way up to my level. When he reached the balcony I turned and sprinted down the other staircase four steps at a time, spinning and slashing once to impede his pursuit, and slamming my blade viciously against the side wall all the way down.

When I got to the stage, I saw that my tip had snapped off and disappeared. Exultantly I turned, parried Velasquo's running attack, and riposted straight at his chest. He leaped to one side to avoid the thrust. Several feet separated us; we stood panting.

He saw the change in my blade, invisible from more than a few feet away, and his expression became one of alarm—the idea struck him, perhaps, that tonight we had reversed roles; tonight I had become the Hieronomo. He looked up to my face, and I smiled.

Instinctively he lunged and in a fury of desperate motion drove me back across the stage. But now we were armed evenly, he had to respect my blade, and I wasn't forced to retreat for long. We battled with a sweaty, intense, total concentration.

He stopped and our blades circled each other: mine jagged and blunt, but slender; his still tipped by the treacherous false button. He started a complicated, deceptive attack. I stole the offensive from him with a stop thrust, lunged for his chest and hit just below the sternum. Amazingly, the blade did not bend and push my hand back, as it always had before: *it slid right in.*

Velasquo dropped his épée, stumbled back and fell, tugging free of my blade. I lifted it; the steel was streaked with blood, unnaturally red in the light. It dripped like water. Velasquo rolled onto his belly.

I looked up and surveyed the stage. Most of the cast had moved into the wings, which were blocked.

Caropia stepped forward, her tall cup still in her hands. Her eyes and mouth were black holes in a face as white as the mask she had long since removed. She appeared confused, but spoke her lines nevertheless, in a dry, airy voice:

> "There lies he, chok'd in his own blood,
> A ravenous wolf whom all the world thought good."

Velasquo rolled over. Caropia's cup toppled to the floor. Sanguinetto, his mask still on, stepped toward me. I swung my épée in his direction and he stopped. I walked toward the rear exit, keeping the blade pointed at him.

Above me on the balcony, the gargoyle waved an arm, and the curtain jerked downward. The audience leaped to their feet, and I thought *They're after me, I'm caught;* but they were clapping, cheering, it was an ovation—the gargoyle bowed—I fled.

An unfamiliar door in the dressing room gave me access to a dark storage room. I crossed it, entered another hallway. It turned and almost immediately I was lost, running without plan down hallways and through dark rooms. Muffled shouts of pursuit reverberated through the walls from time to time, spurring me on. I tried to work my way in a single direction. A short set of stairs led me up to a little closet theater, stage no bigger than a sitting room. Hearing voices backstage, I crouched down between two rows of seats. I looked through the slot between two seat backs and watched a red-coated guard, one of the extras from our play, run on stage and halt. I held my breath. He surveyed the room quickly, then left as quickly as he had entered. The voices receded like echoes and I got up and ran again, out the back of the theater.

I was in a long white hallway with a very high ceiling. Green light poured from long strips in the wall. To my left, at the end of the hall, was a door. I ran for it. As I approached I saw words printed on the door, above the horizontal bar that opened it: EMERGENCY EXIT—ALARM WILL SOUND.

The moment I comprehended the words, the dry, ineffable presence of *déjà vu* filled me: *this had happened before*. In a flash I knew everything, I understood all that had occurred in the theater, it stood before me in my mind like a crystalline sphere. But just as quickly the entire matrix of thought collapsed, leaving no trace except the memory of its existence: *presque vu,* almost seen.

I slammed into the bar crossing the door, and it flew open. To the sharp blast of a siren I leaped out into the chill air, and back into the world.

—1976

The Lucky Strike

War breeds strange pastimes. In July of 1945 on Tinian Island in the North Pacific, Captain Frank January had taken to piling pebble cairns on the crown of Mount Lasso—one pebble for each B-29 takeoff, one cairn for each mission. The largest cairn had four hundred stones in it. It was a mindless pastime, but so was poker. The men of the 509th had played a million hands of poker, sitting in the shade of a palm around an upturned crate sweating in their skivvies, swearing and betting all their pay and cigarettes, playing hand after hand after hand, until the cards got so soft and dog-eared you could have used them for toilet paper. Captain January had gotten sick of it, and after he lit out for the hilltop a few times some of his crewmates started trailing him. When their pilot Jim Fitch joined them it became an official pastime, like throwing flares into the compound or going hunting for stray Japs. What Captain January thought of the development he didn't say. The others grouped near Captain Fitch, who passed around his battered flask. "Hey, January," Fitch called. "Come have a shot."

January wandered over and took the flask. Fitch laughed at

his pebble. "Practicing your bombing up here, eh, Professor?"

"Yah," January said sullenly. Anyone who read more than the funnies was Professor to Fitch. Thirstily January knocked back some rum. He could drink it any way he pleased up here, out from under the eye of the group psychiatrist. He passed the flask on to Lieutenant Matthews, their navigator.

"That's why he's the best," Matthews joked. "Always practicing."

Fitch laughed. "He's best because I make him be best, right, Professor?"

January frowned. Fitch was a bulky youth, thick-featured, pig-eyed—a thug, in January's opinion. The rest of the crew were all in their mid-twenties like Fitch, and they liked the captain's bossy roughhouse style. January, who was thirty-seven, didn't go for it. He wandered away, back to the cairn he had been building. From Mount Lasso they had an overview of the whole island, from the harbor at Wall Street to the north field in Harlem. January had observed hundreds of B-29s roar off the four parallel runways of the north field and head for Japan. The last quartet of this particular mission buzzed across the width of the island, and January dropped four more pebbles, aiming for crevices in the pile. One of them stuck nicely.

"There they are!" said Matthews. "They're on the taxiing strip."

January located the 509th's first plane. Today, the first of August, there was something more interesting to watch than the usual Superfortress parade. Word was out that General Le May wanted to take the 509th's mission away from it. Their commander Colonel Tibbets had gone and bitched to Le May in person, and the general had agreed the mission was theirs, but on one condition: one of the general's men was to make a test flight with the 509th, to make sure they were fit for combat over Japan. The general's man had arrived, and now he was down there in the strike plane, with Tibbets and the whole first team. January sidled back to his mates to view the takeoff with them.

"Why don't the strike plane have a name, though?" Haddock was saying.

Fitch said, "Lewis won't give it a name because it's not his plane, and he knows it." The others laughed. Lewis and his crew were naturally unpopular, being Tibbets' favorites.

"What do you think he'll do to the general's man?" Matthews asked.

The others laughed at the very idea. "He'll kill an engine at takeoff, I bet you anything," Fitch said. He pointed at the wrecked B-29s that marked the end of every runway, planes whose engines had given out on takeoff. "He'll want to show that he wouldn't go down if it happened to him."

" 'Course he wouldn't!" Matthews said.

"You hope," January said under his breath.

"They let those Wright engines out too soon," Haddock said seriously. "They keep busting under the takeoff load."

"Won't matter to the old bull," Matthews said. Then they all started in about Tibbets' flying ability, even Fitch. They all thought Tibbets was the greatest. January, on the other hand, liked Tibbets even less than he liked Fitch. That had started right after he was assigned to the 509th. He had been told he was part of the most important group in the war, and then given a leave. In Vicksburg a couple of fliers just back from England had bought him a lot of whiskies, and since January had spent several months stationed near London they had talked for a good long time and gotten pretty drunk. The two were really curious about what January was up to now, but he had stayed vague on it and kept returning the talk to the blitz. He had been seeing an English nurse, for instance, whose flat had been bombed, family and neighbors killed. . . . But they had really wanted to know. So he had told them he was onto something special, and they had flipped out their badges and told him they were Army Intelligence, and that if he ever broke security like that again he'd be transferred to Alaska. It was a dirty trick. January had gone back to Wendover and told Tibbets so to his face, and Tibbets had turned red and threatened him some more. January despised him for that. The upshot was that January was effectively out of the war, because Tibbets really played his favorites. January wasn't sure he really minded, but during their year's training he had bombed better than ever, as a way of showing the old bull he was wrong to write January off. Every time their eyes had met it was clear what was going on. But Tibbets never backed off no matter how precise January's bombing got. Just thinking about it was enough to cause January to line up a pebble over an ant and drop it.

"Will you cut that out?" Fitch complained. "I swear you must hang from the ceiling when you take a shit so you can practice aiming for the toilet." The men laughed.

"Don't I bunk over you?" January asked. Then he pointed. "They're going."

Tibbets' plane had taxied to runway Baker. Fitch passed the flask around again. The tropical sun beat on them, and the ocean surrounding the island blazed white. January put up a sweaty hand to aid the bill of his baseball cap.

The four props cut in hard, and the sleek Superfortress quickly trundled up to speed and roared down Baker. Three-quarters of the way down the strip the outside right prop feathered.

"Yow!" Fitch crowed. "I told you he'd do it!"

The plane nosed off the ground and slewed right, then pulled back on course to cheers from the four young men around January. January pointed again. "He's cut number three, too."

The inside right prop feathered, and now the plane was pulled up by the left wing only, while the two right props windmilled uselessly. "Holy smoke!" Haddock cried. "Ain't the old bull something?"

They whooped to see the plane's power, and Tibbets' nervy arrogance.

"By God, Le May's man will remember this flight," Fitch hooted. "Why, look at that! He's banking!"

Apparently taking off on two engines wasn't enough for Tibbets; he banked the plane right until it was standing on its dead wing, and it curved back toward Tinian.

Then the inside left engine feathered.

War tears at the imagination. For three years Frank January had kept his imagination trapped, refusing to give it any play whatsoever. The dangers threatening him, the effects of the bombs, the fate of the other participants in the war, he had refused to think about any of it. But the war tore at his control. That English nurse's flat. The missions over the Ruhr. The bomber just below him blown apart by flak. And then there had been a year in Utah, and the viselike grip that he had once kept on his imagination had slipped away.

So when he saw the number two prop feather, his heart gave a little jump against his sternum and helplessly he was up there with Ferebee, the first team bombardier. He would be looking over the pilots' shoulders. . . .

"Only one engine?" Fitch said.

"That one's for real," January said harshly. Despite himself he *saw* the panic in the cockpit, the frantic rush to power the two right engines. The plane was dropping fast and Tibbets leveled it off, leaving them on a course back toward the island. The two right props spun, blurred to a shimmer. January held his breath. They needed more lift; Tibbets was trying to pull it over the island. Maybe he was trying for the short runway on the south half of the island.

But Tinian was too tall, the plane too heavy. It roared right into the jungle above the beach, where 42nd Street met their East River. It exploded in a bloom of fire. By the time the sound of the explosion struck them they knew no one in the plane had survived.

Black smoke towered into white sky. In the shocked silence on Mount Lasso insects buzzed and creaked. The air left January's lungs with a gulp. He had been with Ferebee there at the end, he had heard the desperate shouts, seen the last green rush, been stunned by the dentist-drill-all-over pain of the impact.

"Oh my God," Fitch was saying. "Oh my God." Matthews was sitting. January picked up the flask, tossed it at Fitch.

"C-come on," he stuttered. He hadn't stuttered since he was sixteen. He led the others in a rush down the hill. When they got to Broadway a jeep careened toward them and skidded to a halt. It was Colonel Scholes, the old bull's exec. "What happened?"

Fitch told him.

"Those damned Wrights," Scholes said as the men piled in. This time one had failed at just the wrong moment; some welder stateside had kept flame to metal a second less than usual—or something equally minor, equally trivial—and that had made all the difference.

They left the jeep at 42nd and Broadway and hiked east over a narrow track to the shore. A fairly large circle of trees was burning. The fire trucks were already there.

Scholes stood beside January, his expression bleak. "That was the whole first team," he said.

"I know," said January. He was still in shock, in imagination crushed, incinerated, destroyed. Once as a kid he had tied sheets to his arms and waist, jumped off the roof and landed right on his chest; this felt like that had. He had no way of knowing what would come of this crash, but he had a suspicion that he had indeed smacked into something hard.

Scholes shook his head. A half hour had passed, the fire was nearly out. January's four mates were over chattering with the Seabees. "He was going to name the plane after his mother," Scholes said to the ground. "He told me that just this morning. He was going to call it *Enola Gay*."

At night the jungle breathed, and its hot wet breath washed over the 509th's compound. January stood in the doorway of his Quonset barracks hoping for a real breeze. No poker tonight. Voices were hushed, faces solemn. Some of the men had helped box up the dead crew's gear. Now most lay on their bunks. January gave up on the breeze, climbed onto his top bunk to stare at the ceiling.

He observed the corrugated arch over him. Cricketsong sawed through his thoughts. Below him a rapid conversation was being carried on in guilty undertones, Fitch at its center.

"January is the best bombardier left," he said. "And I'm as good as Lewis was."

"But so is Sweeney," Matthews said. "And he's in with Scholes."

They were figuring out who would take over the strike. January scowled. Tibbets and the rest were less than twelve hours dead, and they were squabbling over who would replace them.

January grabbed a shirt, rolled off his bunk, put the shirt on.

"Hey, Professor," Fitch said. "Where you going?"

"Out."

Though midnight was near it was still sweltering. Crickets shut up as he walked by, started again behind him. He lit a cigarette. In the dark the MPs patrolling their fenced-in compound were like pairs of walking armbands. The 509th, prisoners in their own army. Fliers from other groups had taken to throwing rocks over the fence. Forcefully January expelled smoke, as if he could expel his disgust with it. They were only kids, he told himself. Their minds had been shaped in the war, by the war, and for the war. They knew you couldn't mourn the dead for long; carry around a load like that and your own engines might fail. That was all right with January. It was an attitude that Tibbets had helped to form, so it was what he deserved. Tibbets would *want* to be forgotten in favor of the mission, all he had lived for was to drop the gimmick on the Japs, he was oblivious to anything else, men, wife, family, anything.

So it wasn't the lack of feeling in his mates that bothered January. And it was natural of them to want to fly the strike they had been training a year for. Natural, that is, if you were a kid with a mind shaped by fanatics like Tibbets, shaped to take orders and never imagine consequences. But January was not a kid, and he wasn't going to let men like Tibbets do a thing to his mind. And the gimmick . . . the gimmick was not natural. A chemical bomb of some sort, he guessed. Against the Geneva Convention. He stubbed his cigarette against the sole of his sneaker, tossed the butt over the fence. The tropical night breathed over him. He had a headache.

For months now he had been sure he would never fly a strike. The dislike Tibbets and he had exchanged in their looks (January was acutely aware of looks) had been real and strong. Tibbets had understood that January's record of pinpoint accuracy in the runs over the Salton Sea had been a way of showing contempt, a way of saying *you can't get rid of me even though you hate me and I hate you*. The record had forced Tibbets to keep January on one of the four second-string teams, but with the fuss they were making over the gimmick January had figured that would be far enough down the ladder to keep him out of things.

Now he wasn't so sure. Tibbets was dead. He lit another cigarette, found his hand shaking. The Camel tasted bitter. He threw it over the fence at a receding armband, and regretted it instantly. A waste. He went back inside.

Before climbing onto his bunk he got a paperback out of

his footlocker. "Hey, Professor, what you reading now?" Fitch said, grinning.

January showed him the blue cover. *Winter's Tales*, by an Isak Dinesen. Fitch examined the little wartime edition. "Pretty racy, eh?"

"You bet," January said heavily. "This guy puts sex on every page." He climbed onto his bunk, opened the book. The stories were strange, hard to follow. The voices below bothered him. He concentrated harder.

As a boy on the farm in Arkansas, January had read everything he could lay his hands on. On Saturday afternoons he would race his father down the muddy lane to the mailbox (his father was a reader too), grab *The Saturday Evening Post* and run off to devour every word of it. That meant he had another week with nothing new to read, but he couldn't help it. His favorites were the Hornblower stories, but anything would do. It was a way off the farm, a way into the world. He had become a man who could slip between the covers of a book whenever he chose.

But not on this night.

The next day the chaplain gave a memorial service, and on the morning after that Colonel Scholes looked in the door of their hut right after mess. "Briefing at eleven," he announced. His face was haggard. "Be there early." He looked at Fitch with bloodshot eyes, crooked a finger. "Fitch, January, Matthews—come with me."

January put on his shoes. The rest of the men sat on their bunks and watched them wordlessly. January followed Fitch and Matthews out of the hut.

"I've spent most of the night on the radio with General Le May," Scholes said. He looked them each in the eye. "We've decided you're to be the first crew to make a strike."

Fitch was nodding, as if he had expected it.

"Think you can do it?" Scholes said.

"Of course," Fitch replied. Watching him January understood why they had chosen him to replace Tibbets: Fitch was like the old bull, he had that same ruthlessness. The young bull.

"Yes, sir," Matthews said.

Scholes was looking at him. "Sure," January said, not wanting to think about it. "Sure." His heart was pounding directly on his sternum. But Fitch and Matthews looked serious as owls, so he wasn't going to stick out by looking odd. It was big news, after all; anyone would be taken aback by it. Nevertheless, January made an effort to nod.

"Okay," Scholes said. "McDonald will be flying with you as copilot." Fitch frowned. "I've got to go tell those British officers that Le May doesn't want them on the strike with you. See you at the briefing."

"Yes, sir."

As soon as Scholes was around the corner Fitch swung a fist at the sky. "Yow!" Matthews cried. He and Fitch shook hands. "We did it!" Matthews took January's hand and wrung it, his face plastered with a goofy grin. "We did it!"

"Somebody did it, anyway," January said.

"Ah, Frank," Matthews said. "Show some spunk. You're always so cool."

"Old Professor Stoneface," Fitch said, glancing at January with a trace of amused contempt. "Come on, let's get to the briefing."

The briefing hut, one of the longer Quonsets, was completely surrounded by MPs holding carbines. "Gosh," Matthews said, subdued by the sight. Inside it was already smoky. The walls were covered by the usual maps of Japan. Two blackboards at the front were draped with sheets. Captain Shepard, the naval officer who worked with the scientists on the gimmick, was in back with his assistant Lieutenant Stone, winding a reel of film onto a projector. Dr. Nelson, the group psychiatrist, was already seated on a front bench near the wall. Tibbets had recently sicced the psychiatrist on the group—another one of his great ideas, like the spies in the bar. The man's questions had struck January as stupid. He hadn't even been able to figure out that Easterly was a flake, something that was clear to anybody who flew with him, or even played him in a single round of poker. January slid onto a bench beside his mates.

The two Brits entered, looking furious in their stiff-upper-lip way. They sat on the bench behind January. Sweeney's and Easterly's crews filed in, followed by the other men, and soon the room was full. Fitch and the rest pulled out Lucky Strikes and lit up; since they had named the plane only January had stuck with Camels.

Scholes came in with several men January didn't recognize, and went to the front. The chatter died, and all the smoke plumes ribboned steadily into the air.

Scholes nodded, and two intelligence officers took the sheets off the blackboards, revealing aerial reconnaissance photos.

"Men," Scholes said, "these are the target cities."

Someone cleared his throat.

"In order of priority they are Hiroshima, Kokura, and Nagasaki. There will be three weather scouts: *Straight Flush* to Hiroshima, *Strange Cargo* to Kokura, and *Full House* to Nagasaki. *The Great Artiste* and *Number 91* will be accompanying the mission to take photos. And *Lucky Strike* will fly the bomb."

There were rustles, coughs. Men turned to look at January and his mates, and they all sat up straight. Sweeney stretched back to shake Fitch's hand, and there were some quick laughs. Fitch grinned.

"Now listen up," Scholes went on. "The weapon we are going to deliver was successfully tested stateside a couple of weeks ago. And now we've got orders to drop it on the enemy.'' He paused to let that sink in. ''I'll let Captain Shepard tell you more.''

Shepard walked to the blackboard slowly, savoring his entrance. His forehead was shiny with sweat, and January realized he was excited or nervous. He wondered what the psychiatrist would make of that.

''I'm going to come right to the point,'' Shepard said. ''The bomb you are going to drop is something new in history. We think it will knock out everything within four miles.''

Now the room was completely still. January noticed that he could see a great deal of his nose, eyebrows, and cheeks; it was as if he were receding back into his body, like a fox into its hole. He kept his gaze rigidly on Shepard, steadfastly ignoring the feeling. Shepard pulled a sheet back over a blackboard while someone else turned down the lights.

''This is a film of the only test we have made,'' Shepard said. The film started, caught, started again. A wavery cone of bright cigarette smoke speared the length of the room, and on the sheet sprang a dead gray landscape: a lot of sky, a smooth desert floor, hills in the distance. The projector went *click-click-click-click, click-click-click-click*. ''The bomb is on top of the tower,'' Shepard said, and January focused on the pinlike object sticking out of the desert floor, off against the hills. It was between eight and ten miles from the camera, he judged; he had gotten good at calculating distances. He was still distracted by his face.

Click-click-click-click, click—then the screen went white for a second, filling even their room with light. When the picture returned the desert floor was filled with a white bloom of fire. The fireball coalesced and then quite suddenly it leaped off the earth all the way into the *stratosphere*, by God, like a tracer bullet leaving a machine gun, trailing a whitish pillar of smoke behind it. The pillar gushed up and a growing ball of smoke billowed outward, capping the pillar.

January calculated the size of the cloud, but was sure he got it wrong. There it stood. The picture flickered, and then the screen went white again, as if the camera had melted or that part of the world had come apart. But the flapping from the projector told them it was the end of the film.

January felt the air suck in and out of his open mouth. The lights came on in the smoky room and for a second he panicked, he struggled to shove his features into an accepted pattern, the psychiatrist would be looking around at them all—and then he glanced around and realized he needn't have worried, that he wasn't alone. Faces were bloodless, eyes were blinky or bug-eyed with shock, mouths hung open or were clamped whitely shut. For a few moments they all had to acknowledge what they were doing. January, scaring himself, felt an urge to say, "Play it again, will you?" Fitch was pulling his curled black hair off his thug's forehead uneasily. Beyond him January saw that one of the Limeys had already reconsidered how mad he was about missing the flight. Now he looked sick. Someone let out a long *whew,* another whistled. January looked to the front again, where the psychiatrist watched them, undisturbed.

Shepard said, "It's big, all right. And no one knows what will happen when it's dropped from the air. But the mushroom cloud you saw will go to at least thirty thousand feet, probably sixty. And the flash you saw at the beginning was hotter than the sun."

Hotter than the sun. More licked lips, hard swallows, readjusted baseball caps. One of the intelligence officers passed out tinted goggles like welder's glasses. January took his and twiddled the opacity dial.

Scholes said, "You're the hottest thing in the armed forces, now. So no talking, even among yourselves." He took a deep breath. "Let's do it the way Colonel Tibbets would have wanted us to. He picked every one of you because you were the best, and now's the time to show he was right. So—so let's make the old man proud."

The briefing was over. Men filed out into the sudden sunlight. Into the heat and glare. Captain Shepard approached Fitch. "Stone and I will be flying with you to take care of the bomb," he said.

Fitch nodded. "Do you know how many strikes we'll fly?"

"As many as it takes to make them quit." Shepard stared hard at all of them. "But it will only take one."

War breeds strange dreams. That night January writhed over his sheets in the hot wet vegetable darkness, in that frightening half sleep when you sometimes know you are dreaming but can do nothing about it, and he dreamed he was walking . . .

. . . walking through the streets when suddenly the sun swoops down, the sun touches down and everything is instantly darkness and smoke and silence, a deaf roaring. Walls of fire. His head hurts and in the middle of his vision is a bluewhite blur as if God's camera went off in his face. Ah—the sun fell, he thinks. His arm is burned. Blinking is painful. People stumbling by, mouths open, horribly burned—

He is a priest, he can feel the clerical collar, and the wounded ask him for help. He points to his ears, tries to touch them but can't. Pall of black smoke over everything, the city has fallen into the streets. Ah, it's the end of the world. In a park he finds shade and cleared ground. People crouch under bushes like frightened animals. Where the park meets the river red and black figures crowd into steaming water. A figure gestures from a copse of bamboo. He enters it, finds five or six faceless soldiers huddling. Their eyes have melted, their mouths are holes. Deafness spares him their words. The sighted soldier mimes drinking. The soldiers are thirsty. He nods and goes to the river in search of a container. Bodies float downstream.

Hours pass as he hunts fruitlessly for a bucket. He pulls people from the rubble. He hears a bird screeching and he realizes that his deafness is the roar of the city burning, a roar like the blood in his ears but he is not deaf, he only thought he was deaf because there are no human cries. The people are suffering in silence. Through the dusky night he stumbles back to the river, pain crashing through his head. In a field men are pulling potatoes out of the ground that have been baked well enough to eat. He shares one with them. At the river everyone is dead—

—and he struggled out of the nightmare drenched in rank sweat, the taste of dirt in his mouth, his stomach knotted with horror. He sat up and the wet rough sheet clung to his skin. His heart felt crushed between lungs desperate for air. The flowery rotting jungle smell filled him and images from the dream flashed before him so vividly that in the dim hut he saw nothing else. He grabbed his cigarettes and jumped off the bunk, hurried out into the compound. Trembling he lit up, started pacing around. For a moment he worried that the idiot psychiatrist might see him, but then he dismissed the idea. Nelson would be asleep. They were all asleep. He shook his head, looked down at his right arm and almost dropped his cigarette—but it was just his stove scar, an old scar, he'd had it most of his life, since the day he'd pulled the frypan off the stove and onto his arm, burning it with oil. He could still remember the round O of fear that his mother's mouth had made as she rushed in to see what was wrong. Just an old burn scar, he thought, let's not go overboard here. He pulled his sleeve down.

For the rest of the night he tried to walk it off, cigarette after cigarette. The dome of the sky lightened until all the compound and the jungle beyond it was visible. He was forced by the light of day to walk back into his hut and lie down as if nothing had happened.

Two days later Scholes ordered them to take one of Le May's men over Rota for a test run. This new lieutenant colonel ordered Fitch not to play with the engines on takeoff. They flew a perfect run. January put the dummy gimmick right on the aiming point just as he had so often in the Salton Sea, and Fitch powered the plane down into the violent bank that started their 150-degree turn and flight for safety. Back on Tinian the lieutenant colonel congratulated them and shook each of their hands. January smiled with the rest, palms cool, heart steady. It was as if his body were a shell, something he could manipulate from without, like a bombsight. He ate well, he chatted as much as he ever had, and when the psychiatrist ran him to earth for some questions he was friendly and seemed open.

"Hello, doc."

"How do you feel about all this, Frank?"

"Just like I always have, sir. Fine."

"Eating well?"

"Better than ever."

"Sleeping well?"

"As well as I can in this humidity. I got used to Utah, I'm afraid." Dr. Nelson laughed. Actually January had hardly slept since his dream. He was afraid of sleep. Couldn't the man see that?

"And how do you feel about being part of the crew chosen to make the first strike?"

"Well, it was the right choice, I reckon. We're the b—the best crew left."

"Do you feel sorry about Tibbets' crew's accident?"

"Yes, sir, I do." You better believe it.

After the jokes and firm handshakes that ended the interview January walked out into the blaze of the tropical noon and lit a cigarette. He allowed himself to feel how much he despised the psychiatrist and his blind profession at the same time he was waving good-bye to the man. Ounce brain. Why couldn't he have seen? Whatever happened it would be his fault. . . . With a rush of smoke out of him January realized how painfully easy it was to fool someone if you wanted to. All action was no more than a mask that could be perfectly manipulated from somewhere else. And all the while in that somewhere else January lived in a *click-click-click* of film, in the silent roaring of a dream, struggling against images he couldn't dispel. The heat of the tropical sun—ninety-three million miles away, wasn't it?—pulsed painfully on the back of his neck.

As he watched the psychiatrist collar their tail-gunner Kochenski, he thought of walking up to the man and saying *I quit*. I don't want to do this. In imagination he saw the look that would form in the man's eye, in Fitch's eye, in Tibbets' eye, and his mind recoiled from the idea. He felt too much contempt for them. He wouldn't for anything give them a means to despise him, a reason to call him coward. Stubbornly he banished the whole complex of thought. Easier to go along with it.

And so a couple of disjointed days later, just after midnight of August 9th, he found himself preparing for the strike. Around him Fitch and Matthews and Haddock were doing the same. How odd were the everyday motions of getting dressed when you were off to demolish a city, to end a hundred thousand lives! January found himself examining his hands, his boots, the cracks in the linoleum. He put on his survival vest, checked the pockets abstractedly for fishhooks, water kit, first aid package, emergency rations. Then the parachute harness, and his coveralls over it all. Tying his bootlaces took minutes; he couldn't do it when watching his fingers so closely.

"Come on, Professor!" Fitch's voice was tight. "The big day is here."

He followed the others into the night. A cool wind was blowing. The chaplain said a prayer for them. They took jeeps down Broadway to runway Able. *Lucky Strike* stood in a circle of spotlights and men, half of them with cameras, the rest with reporter's pads. They surrounded the crew; it reminded January of a Hollywood premiere. Eventually he escaped up the hatch and into the plane. Others followed. Half an hour passed before Fitch joined them, grinning like a movie star. They started the engines, and January was thankful for their vibrating, thought-smothering roar. They taxied away from the Hollywood scene and January felt relief for a moment until he remembered where they were going. On runway Able the engines pitched up to their twenty-three hundred rpm whine, and looking out the clear windscreen he saw the runway paint-marks move by ever faster. Fitch kept them on the runway till Tinian had run out from under them, then quickly pulled up. They were on their way.

When they got to altitude January climbed past Fitch and McDonald to the bombardier's seat and placed his parachute on it. He leaned back. The roar of the four engines packed around him like cotton batting. He was on the flight, nothing to be done about it now. The heavy vibration was a comfort, he liked the feel of it there in the nose of the plane. A drowsy, sad acceptance hummed through him.

Against his closed eyelids flashed a black eyeless face and he jerked awake, heart racing. He was on the flight, no way out. Now he realized how easy it would have been to get out of it. He could have just said he didn't want to. The simplicity of it appalled him. Who gave a damn what the psychiatrist or Tibbets or anyone else thought, compared to this? Now there was no way out. It was a comfort, in a way. Now he could stop worrying, stop thinking he had any choice.

Sitting there with his knees bracketing the bombsight January dozed, and as he dozed he daydreamed his way out. He could climb the step to Fitch and McDonald and declare he had been secretly promoted to major and ordered to redirect the mission. They were to go to Tokyo and drop the bomb in the bay. The Jap War Cabinet had been told to watch this demonstration of the new weapon, and when they saw that fireball boil the bay and bounce into heaven they'd run and sign surrender papers as fast as they could write, kamikazes or not. They weren't crazy, after all. No need to murder a whole city. It was such a good plan that the generals back home were no doubt changing the mission at this very minute, desperately radioing their instructions to Tinian, only to find out it was too late . . . so that when they returned to Tinian January would become a hero for guessing what the generals really wanted, and for risking all to do it. It would be like one of the Hornblower stories in *The Saturday Evening Post*.

Once again January jerked awake. The drowsy pleasure of the fantasy was replaced with desperate scorn. There wasn't a chance in hell that he could convince Fitch and the rest that he had secret orders superseding theirs. And he couldn't go up there and wave his pistol around and *order* them to drop the bomb in Tokyo Bay, because he was the one who had to actually drop it, and he couldn't be down in front dropping the bomb and up ordering the others around at the same time. Pipe dreams.

Time swept on, slow as a second hand. January's thoughts, however, matched the spin of the props; desperately they cast about, now this way now that, like an animal caught by the leg in a trap. The crew was silent. The clouds below were a white scree on the black ocean. January's knee vibrated against the squat stand of the bombsight. He was the one who had to drop the bomb. No matter where his thoughts lunged they were brought up short by that. He was the one, not Fitch or the crew, not Le May, not the generals and scientists back home, not Truman and his advisors. Truman—suddenly January hated him. Roosevelt would have done it differently. If only Roosevelt had lived! The grief that had filled January when he learned of Roosevelt's death reverberated through him again, more strongly than ever. It was unfair to have worked so hard and then not see the war's end. And FDR would have ended it differently. Back at the start of it all he had declared that civilian centers were never to be bombed, and if he had lived, if, if, if. But he hadn't. And now it was smiling bastard Harry Truman, ordering *him*, Frank January, to drop the sun on two hundred thousand women and children. Once his father had taken him to see the Browns play before twenty thousand, a giant crowd— "I never voted for you," January whispered viciously, and jerked to realize he had spoken aloud. Luckily his microphone was off. But Roosevelt would have done it differently, he *would have*.

The bombsight rose before him, spearing the black sky and blocking some of the hundreds of little cruciform stars. *Lucky Strike* ground on toward Iwo Jima, minute by minute flying four miles closer to their target. January leaned forward and put his face in the cool headrest of the bombsight, hoping that its grasp might hold his thoughts as well as his forehead. It worked surprisingly well.

His earphones crackled and he sat up. "Captain January." It was Shepard. "We're going to arm the bomb now, want to watch?"

"Sure thing." He shook his head, surprised at his own duplicity. Stepping up between the pilots, he moved stiffly to the roomy cabin behind the cockpit. Matthews was at his desk taking a navigational fix on the radio signals from Iwo Jima and Okinawa, and Haddock stood beside him. At the back of the compartment was a small circular hatch, below the larger tunnel leading to the rear of the plane. January opened it, sat down and swung himself feet first through the hole.

The bomb bay was unheated, and the cold air felt good. He stood facing the bomb. Stone was sitting on the floor of the bay; Shepard was laid out under the bomb, reaching into it. On a rubber pad next to Stone were tools, plates, several cylindrical blocks. Shepard pulled back, sat up, sucked a scraped knuckle. He shook his head ruefully: "I don't dare wear gloves with this one."

"I'd be just as happy myself if you didn't let something slip," January joked nervously. The two men laughed.

"Nothing can blow till I change those green wires to the red ones," Stone said.

"Give me the wrench," Shepard said. Stone handed it to him, and he stretched under the bomb again. After some awkward wrenching inside it he lifted out a cylindrical plug. "Breech plug," he said, and set it on the mat.

January found his skin goose-pimpling in the cold air. Stone handed Shepard one of the blocks. Shepard extended under the bomb again. "Red ends toward the breech." "I know." Watching them January was reminded of auto mechanics on the oily floor of a garage, working under a car. He had spent a few years doing that himself, after his family moved to Vicksburg. Hiroshima was a river town. One time a flatbed truck carrying bags of cement powder down Fourth Street hill had lost its brakes and careened into the intersection with River Road, where despite the driver's efforts to turn it smashed into a passing car. Frank had been out in the yard playing, had heard the crash and saw the cement dust rising. He had been one of the first there. The woman and child in the passenger seat of the Model T had been killed. The woman driving was okay. They were from Chicago. A group of folks subdued the driver of the truck, who kept trying to help at the Model T, though he had a bad cut on his head and was covered with white dust.

"Okay, let's tighten the breech plug." Stone gave Shepard the wrench. "Sixteen turns exactly," Shepard said. He was sweating even in the bay's chill, and he paused to wipe his forehead. "Let's hope we don't get hit by lightning." He put the wrench down and shifted onto his knees, picked up a circular plate. Hubcap, January thought. Stone connected wires, then helped Shepard install two more plates. Good old American know-how, January thought, goose pimples rippling across his skin like cat's paws over water. There was Shepard, a scientist, putting together a bomb like he was an auto mechanic changing oil and plugs. January felt a tight rush of rage at the scientists who had designed the bomb. They had worked on it for over a year down there in New Mexico, had none of them in all that time ever stopped to think what they were doing?

But none of them had to drop it. January turned to hide his face from Shepard, stepped down the bay. The bomb looked like a big long trash can, with fins at one end and little antennae at the other. Just a bomb, he thought, damn it, it's just another bomb.

Shepard stood and patted the bomb gently. "We've got a live one now." Never a thought about what it would do. January hurried by the man, afraid that hatred would crack his shell and give him away. The pistol strapped to his belt caught on the hatchway and he imagined shooting Shepard—shooting Fitch and McDonald and plunging the controls forward so that *Lucky Strike* tilted and spun down into the sea like a spent tracer bullet, like a plane broken by flak, following the arc of all human ambition. Nobody would ever know what had happened to them, and their trash can would be dumped at the bottom of the Pacific where it belonged. He could even shoot everyone and parachute out, and perhaps be rescued by one of the Superdumbos following them. . . .

The thought passed and remembering it January squinted with disgust. But another part of him agreed that it was a possibility. It could be done. It would solve his problem. His fingers explored his holster snap.

"Want some coffee?" Matthews asked.

"Sure," January said, and took his hand from the gun to reach for the cup. He sipped: hot. He watched Matthews and Benton tune the loran equipment. As the beeps came in Matthews took a straightedge and drew lines from Okinawa and Iwo Jima on his map table. He tapped a finger on the intersection. "They've taken the art out of navigation," he said to January. "They might as well stop making the navigator's dome," thumbing up at the little Plexiglas bubble over them.

"Good old American know-how," January said.

Matthews nodded. With two fingers he measured the distance between their position and Iwo Jima. Benton measured with a ruler.

"Rendezvous at five thirty-five, eh?" Matthews said. They were to rendezvous with the two trailing planes over Iwo.

Benton disagreed: "I'd say five-fifty."

"What? Check again, guy, we're not in no tugboat here."

"The wind—"

"Yah, the wind. Frank, you want to add a bet to the pool?"

"Five thirty-six," January said promptly.

They laughed. "See, he's got more confidence in me," Matthews said with a dopey grin.

January recalled his plan to shoot the crew and tip the plane into the sea, and he pursed his lips, repelled. Not for anything would he be able to shoot these men, who, if not friends, were at least companions. They passed for friends. They meant no harm.

Shepard and Stone climbed into the cabin. Matthews offered them coffee. "The gimmick's ready to kick their ass, eh?" Shepard nodded and drank.

January moved forward, past Haddock's console. Another

plan that wouldn't work. What to do? All the flight engineer's dials and gauges showed conditions were normal. Maybe he could sabotage something? Cut a line somewhere?

Fitch looked back at him and said, "When are we due over Iwo?"

"Five-forty, Matthews says."

"He better be right."

A thug. In peacetime Fitch would be hanging around a pool table giving the cops trouble. He was perfect for war. Tibbets had chosen his men well—most of them, anyway. Moving back past Haddock, January stopped to stare at the group of men in the navigation cabin. They joked, drank coffee. They were all a bit like Fitch: young toughs, capable and thoughtless. They were having a good time, an adventure. That was January's dominant impression of his companions in the 509th; despite all the bitching and the occasional moments of overmastering fear, they were having a good time. His mind spun forward and he saw what these young men would grow up to be like as clearly as if they stood before him in businessmen's suits, prosperous and balding. They would be tough and capable and thoughtless, and as the years passed and the great war receded in time they would look back on it with ever-increasing nostalgia, for they would be the survivors and not the dead. Every year of this war would feel like ten in their memories, so that the war would always remain the central experience of their lives—a time when history lay palpable in their hands, when each of their daily acts affected it, when moral issues were simple, and others told them what to do—so that as more years passed and the survivors aged, bodies falling apart, lives in one rut or another, they would unconsciously push harder and harder to thrust the world into war again, thinking somewhere inside themselves that if they could only return to world war then they would magically be again as they were in the last one—young, and free, and happy. And by that time they would hold the positions of power, they would be capable of doing it.

So there would be more wars, January saw. He heard it in Matthews' laughter, saw it in their excited eyes. "There's Iwo, and it's five thirty-one. Pay up! I win!" And in future wars they'd have more bombs like the gimmick, hundreds of them no doubt. He saw more planes, more young crews like this one, flying to Moscow no doubt or to wherever, fireballs in every capital, why not? And to what end? To what end? So that the old men could hope to become magically young again. Nothing more sane than that.

They were over Iwo Jima. Three more hours to Japan. Voices from *The Great Artiste* and *Number 91* crackled on the radio. Rendezvous accomplished, the three planes flew northwest, toward Shikoku, the first Japanese island in their path. January went aft to use the toilet. "You okay, Frank?" Matthews asked. "Sure. Terrible coffee, though." "Ain't it always." January tugged at his baseball cap and hurried away. Kochenski and the other gunners were playing poker. When he was done he returned forward. Matthews sat on the stool before his maps, readying his equipment for the constant monitoring of drift that would now be required. Haddock and Benton were also busy at their stations. January maneuvered between the pilots down into the nose. "Good shooting," Matthews called after him.

Forward it seemed quieter. January got settled, put his headphones on and leaned forward to look out the ribbed Plexiglas.

Dawn had turned the whole vault of the sky pink. Slowly the radiant shade shifted through lavender to blue, pulse by pulse a different color. The ocean below was a glittering blue plane, marbled by a pattern of puffy pink cloud. The sky above was a vast dome, darker above than on the horizon. January had always thought that dawn was the time when you could see most clearly how big the earth was, and how high above it they flew. It seemed they flew at the very upper edge of the atmosphere, and January saw how thin it was, how it was just a skin of air really, so that even if you flew up to its top the earth still extended away infinitely in every direction. The coffee had warmed January, he was sweating. Sunlight blinked off the Plexiglas. His watch said six. Plane and hemisphere of blue were split down the middle by the bombsight. His earphones crackled and he listened in to the reports from the lead planes flying over the target cities. Kokura, Nagasaki, Hiroshima, all of them had six-tenths cloud cover. Maybe they would have to cancel the whole mission because of weather. "We'll look at Hiroshima first," Fitch said. January peered down at the fields of miniature clouds with renewed interest. His parachute slipped under him. Readjusting it he imagined putting it on, sneaking back to the central escape hatch under the navigator's cabin, opening the hatch . . . he could be out of the plane and gone before anyone noticed. Leave it up to them. They could bomb or not but it wouldn't be January's doing. He could float down onto the world like a puff of dandelion, feel cool air rush around him, watch the silk canopy dome hang over him like a miniature sky, a private world.

An eyeless black face. January shuddered; it was as though the nightmare could return any time. If he jumped nothing would change, the bomb would still fall—would he feel any better, floating on his Inland Sea? Sure, one part of him shouted; maybe, another conceded; the rest of him saw that face. . . .

Earphones crackled. Shepard said, "Lieutenant Stone has now armed the bomb, and I can tell you all what we are carrying. Aboard with us is the world's first atomic bomb."

Not exactly, January thought. Whistles squeaked in his earphones. The first one went off in New Mexico. Splitting atoms: January had heard the term before. Tremendous energy in every atom, Einstein had said. Break one, and—he had seen the result on film. Shepard was talking about radiation, which brought back more to January. Energy released in the form of X rays. Killed by X rays! It would be against the Geneva Convention if they had thought of it.

Fitch cut in. "When the bomb is dropped Lieutenant Benton will record our reaction to what we see. This recording is being made for history, so watch your language." Watch your language! January choked back a laugh. Don't curse or blaspheme God at the sight of the first atomic bomb incinerating a city and all its inhabitants with X rays!

Six-twenty. January found his hands clenched together on the headrest of the bombsight. He felt as if he had a fever. In the harsh wash of morning light the skin on the backs of his hands appeared slightly translucent. The whorls in the skin looked like the delicate patterning of waves on the sea's surface. His hands were made of atoms. Atoms were the smallest building block of matter, it took billions of them to make those tense, trembling hands. Split one atom and you had the fireball. That meant that the energy contained in even one hand . . . he turned up a palm to look at the lines and the mottled flesh under the transparent skin. A person was a bomb that could blow up the world. January felt that latent power stir in him, pulsing with every hard heart-knock. What beings they were, and in what a blue expanse of a world! —And here they spun on to drop a bomb and kill a hundred thousand of these astonishing beings.

When a fox or raccoon is caught by the leg in a trap, it lunges until the leg is frayed, twisted, perhaps broken, and only then does the animal's pain and exhaustion force it to quit. Now in the same way January wanted to quit. His mind hurt. His plans to escape were so much crap—stupid, useless. Better to quit. He tried to stop thinking, but it was hopeless. How could he stop? As long as he was conscious he would be thinking. The mind struggles longer in its traps than any fox.

Lucky Strike tilted up and began the long climb to bombing altitude. On the horizon the clouds lay over a green island. Japan. Surely it had gotten hotter, the heater must be broken, he thought. Don't think. Every few minutes Matthews gave Fitch small course adjustments. "Two seventy-five, now. That's it." To escape the moment January recalled his childhood. Following a mule and plow. Moving to Vicksburg (rivers). For a while there in Vicksburg, since his stutter made it hard to gain friends, he had played a game with himself. He had passed the time by imagining that everything he did was vitally important and determined the fate of the world. If he crossed a road in front of a certain car, for instance, then the car wouldn't make it through the next intersection before a truck hit it, and so the man driving would be killed and wouldn't be able to invent the flying boat that would save President Wilson from kidnappers—so he had to wait for that car because everything afterward depended on it. Oh damn it, he thought, damn it, think of something *different*. The last Hornblower story he had read—how would *he* get out of this? The round O of his mother's face as she ran in and saw his arm— The Mississippi, mud-brown behind its levees— Abruptly he shook his head, face twisted in frustration and despair, aware at last that no possible avenue of memory would serve as an escape for him now, for now there was no part of his life that did not apply to the situation he was in, and no matter where he cast his mind it was going to shore up against the hour facing him.

Less than an hour. They were at thirty thousand feet, bombing altitude. Fitch gave him altimeter readings to dial into the bombsight. Matthews gave him windspeeds. Sweat got in his eye and he blinked furiously. The sun rose behind them like an atomic bomb, glinting off every corner and edge of the Plexiglas, illuminating his bubble compartment with a fierce glare. Broken plans jumbled together in his mind, his breath was short, his throat dry. Uselessly and repeatedly he damned the scientists, damned Truman. Damned the Japanese for causing the whole mess in the first place, damned yellow killers, they had brought this on themselves. Remember Pearl. American men had died under bombs when no war had been declared; they had started it and now it was coming back to them with a vengeance. And they deserved it. And an invasion of Japan would take years, cost millions of lives—end it now, end it, they deserved it, they deserved it steaming river full of charcoal people silently dying damned stubborn race of maniacs!

"There's Honshu," Fitch said, and January returned to the world of the plane. They were over the Inland Sea. Soon they would pass the secondary target, Kokura, a bit to the south. Seven-thirty. The island was draped more heavily than the sea by clouds, and again January's heart leaped with the idea that weather would cancel the mission. But they did deserve it. It was a mission like any other mission. He had dropped bombs on Africa, Sicily, Italy, all Germany. . . . He leaned forward to take a look through the sight. Under the X of the crosshairs was the sea, but at the lead edge of the sight was land. Honshu. At two hundred and thirty miles an hour that gave them about a half hour to Hiroshima. Maybe less. He wondered if his heart could beat so hard for that long.

Fitch said, "Matthews, I'm giving over guidance to you. Just tell us what to do."

"Bear south two degrees," was all Matthews said. At last their voices had taken on a touch of awareness, even fear.

"January, are you ready?" Fitch asked.

"I'm just waiting," January said. He sat up, so Fitch could see the back of his head. The bombsight stood between his legs. A switch on its side would start the bombing sequence; the bomb would not leave the plane immediately upon the flick of the switch, but would drop after a fifteen-second radio tone warned the following planes. The sight was adjusted accordingly.

"Adjust to a heading of two sixty-five," Matthews said. "We're coming in directly upwind." This was to make any side-drift adjustments for the bomb unnecessary. "January, dial it down to two hundred and thirty-one miles per hour."

"Two thirty-one."

Fitch said, "Everyone but January and Matthews, get your goggles on."

January took the darkened goggles from the floor. One needed to protect one's eyes or they might melt. He put them on, put his forehead on the headrest. They were in the way. He took them off. When he looked through the sight again there was land under the crosshairs. He checked his watch. Eight o'clock. Up and reading the papers, drinking tea.

"Ten minutes to AP," Matthews said. The aiming point was Aioi Bridge, a T-shaped bridge in the middle of the delta-straddling city. Easy to recognize.

"There's a lot of cloud down there," Fitch nodded. "Are you going to be able to see?"

"I won't be sure until we try it," January said.

"We can make another pass and use radar if we need to," Matthews said.

Fitch said. "Don't drop it unless you're sure, January."

"Yes, sir."

Through the sight a grouping of rooftops and gray roads was just visible between broken clouds. Around it green forest. "All right," Matthews exclaimed, "here we go! Keep it right on this heading, Captain! January, we'll stay at two thirty-one."

"And same heading," Fitch said. "January, she's all yours. Everyone make sure your goggles are on. And be ready for the turn."

January's world contracted to the view through the bomb-sight. A stippled field of cloud and forest. Over a small range of hills and into Hiroshima's watershed. The broad river was mud brown, the land pale hazy green, the growing network of roads flat gray. Now the tiny rectangular shapes of buildings covered almost all the land, and swimming into the sight came the city proper, narrow islands thrusting into a dark blue bay. Under the crosshairs the city moved island by island, cloud by cloud. January had stopped breathing, his fingers were rigid as stone on the switch. And there was Aioi Bridge. It slid right under the crosshairs, a tiny T right in a gap in the clouds. January's fingers crushed the switch. Deliberately he took a breath, held it. Clouds swam under the crosshairs, then the next island. "Almost there," he said calmly into his microphone. "Steady." Now that he was committed his heart was humming like the Wrights. He counted to ten. Now flowing under the crosshairs were clouds alternating with green forest, leaden roads. "I've turned the switch, but I'm not getting a tone!" he croaked into the mike. His right hand held the switch firmly in place. Fitch was shouting something—Matthews' voice cracked across it— "Flipping it b-back and forth," January shouted, shielding the bombsight with his body from the eyes of the pilots. "But *still*—wait a second—"

He pushed the switch down. A low hum filled his ears. "That's it! It started!"

"But where will it land?" Matthews cried.

"Hold steady!" January shouted.

Lucky Strike shuddered and lofted up ten or twenty feet. January twisted to look down and there was the bomb, flying just below the plane. Then with a wobble it fell away.

The plane banked right and dove so hard that the centrifugal force threw January against the Plexiglas. Several thousand feet lower Fitch leveled it out and they hurtled north.

"Do you see anything?" Fitch cried.

From the tailgun Kochenski gasped "Nothing." January struggled upright. He reached for the welder's goggles, but they were no longer on his head. He couldn't find them. "How long has it been?" he said.

"Thirty seconds," Matthews replied.

January clamped his eyes shut.

The blood in his eyelids lit up red, then white.

On the earphones a clutter of voices: "Oh my God. Oh my God." The plane bounced and tumbled, metallically shrieking. January pressed himself off the Plexiglas. "Nother shockwave!" Kochenski yelled. The plane rocked again, bounced out of control, this is it, January thought, end of the world, I guess that solves my problem.

He opened his eyes and found he could still see. The engines still roared, the props spun. "Those were the shockwaves from the bomb," Fitch called. "We're okay now. Look at that! Will you look at that sonofabitch go!"

January looked. The cloud layer below had burst apart, and a black column of smoke billowed up from a core of red fire. Already the top of the column was at their height. Exclamations of shock clattered painfully in January's ears. He stared at the fiery base of the cloud, at the scores of fires feeding into it. Suddenly he could see past the cloud, and his fingernails cut into his palms. Through a gap in the clouds he saw it clearly, the delta, the six rivers, there off to the left of the tower of smoke: the city of Hiroshima, untouched.

"We missed!" Kochenski yelled. "We missed it!"

January turned to hide his face from the pilots; on it was a grin like a rictus. He sat back in his seat and let the relief fill him.

Then it was back to it. "God damn it!" Fitch shouted down at him. McDonald was trying to restrain him. "January, get up here!"

"Yes, sir." Now there was a new set of problems.

January stood and turned, legs weak. His right fingertips throbbed painfully. The men were crowded forward to look out the Plexiglas. January looked with them.

The mushroom cloud was forming. It roiled out as if it might continue to extend forever, fed by the inferno and the black stalk below it. It looked about two miles wide, and a half mile tall, and it extended well above the height they flew at, dwarfing their plane entirely. "Do you think we'll all be sterile?" Matthews said.

"I can taste the radiation," McDonald declared. "Can you? It tastes like lead."

Bursts of flame shot up into the cloud from below, giving a purplish tint to the stalk. There it stood: lifelike, malignant, sixty thousand feet tall. One bomb. January shoved past the pilots into the navigation cabin, overwhelmed.

"Should I start recording everyone's reactions, Captain?" asked Benton.

"To hell with that," Fitch said, following January back. But Shepard got there first, descending quickly from the navigation dome. He rushed across the cabin, caught January on the shoulder, "You bastard!" he screamed as January stumbled back. "You lost your nerve, coward!"

January went for Shepard, happy to have a target at last, but Fitch cut in and grabbed him by the collar, pulled him around until they were face to face—

"Is that right?" Fitch cried, as angry as Shepard. "Did you screw up on purpose?"

"No," January grunted, and knocked Fitch's hands away from his neck. He swung and smacked Fitch on the mouth, caught him solid. Fitch staggered back, recovered, and no doubt would have beaten January up, but Matthews and Benton and Stone leaped in and held him back, shouting for order. "Shut up! Shut up!" McDonald screamed from the cockpit, and for a moment it was bedlam, but Fitch let himself be restrained, and soon only McDonald's shouts for quiet were heard. January retreated to between the pilot seats, right hand on his pistol holster.

"The city was in the crosshairs when I flipped the switch," he said. "But the first couple of times I flipped it nothing happened—"

"That's a lie!" Shepard shouted. "There was nothing wrong with the switch, I checked it myself. Besides, the bomb exploded *miles* beyond Hiroshima, look for yourself! That's *minutes.*" He wiped spit from his chin and pointed at January. "You did it."

"You don't know that," January said. But he could see the men had been convinced by Shepard, and he took a step back. "You just get me to a board of inquiry, quick. And leave me alone till then. If you touch me again," glaring venomously at Fitch and then Shepard, "I'll shoot you." He turned and hopped down to his seat, feeling exposed and vulnerable, like a treed raccoon.

"They'll shoot *you* for this," Shepard screamed after him. "Disobeying orders—treason—" Matthews and Stone were shutting him up.

"Let's get out of here," he heard McDonald say. "I can taste the lead, can't you?"

January looked out the Plexiglas. The giant cloud still burned and roiled. One atom . . . Well, they had really done it to that forest. He almost laughed but stopped himself, afraid of hysteria. Through a break in the clouds he got a clear view of Hiroshima for the first time. It lay spread over its islands like a map, unharmed. Well, that was that. The inferno at the base of the mushroom cloud was eight or ten miles around the shore of the bay and a mile or two inland. A certain patch of forest would be gone, destroyed—utterly blasted from the face of the earth. The Japs would be able to go out and investigate the damage. And if they were told it was a demonstration, a warning—and if they acted fast—well, they had their chance. Maybe it would work.

The release of tension made January feel sick. Then he recalled Shepard's words and he knew that whether his plan worked or not he was still in trouble. In trouble! It was worse than that. Bitterly he cursed the Japanese, he even wished for a moment that he *had* dropped it on them. Wearily he let his despair empty him.

A long while later he sat up straight. Once again he was a trapped animal. He began lunging for escape, casting about for plans. One alternative after another. All during the long grim flight home he considered it, mind spinning at the speed of the props and beyond. And when they came down on Tinian he had a plan. It was a long shot, he reckoned, but it was the best he could do.

The briefing hut was surrounded by MPs again. January stumbled from the truck with the rest and walked inside. He was more than ever aware of the looks given him, and they were hard, accusatory. He was too tired to care. He hadn't slept in more than thirty-six hours, and had slept very little since the last time he had been in the hut, a week before. Now the room quivered with the lack of engine vibration to stabilize it, and the silence roared. It was all he could do to hold on to the bare essentials of his plan. The glares of Fitch and Shepard, the hurt incomprehension of Matthews, they had to be thrust out of his focus. Thankfully he lit a cigarette.

In a clamor of question and argument the others described the strike. Then the haggard Scholes and an intelligence officer led them through the bombing run. January's plan made it necessary to hold to his story: ". . . and when the AP was under the crosshairs I pushed down the switch, but got no signal. I flipped it up and down repeatedly until the tone kicked in. At that point there was still fifteen seconds to the release."

"Was there anything that may have caused the tone to start when it did?"

"Not that I noticed immediately, but—"

"It's impossible," Shepard interrupted, face red. "I checked the switch before we flew and there was nothing wrong with it. Besides, the drop occurred over a minute—"

"Captain Shepard," Scholes said. "We'll hear from you presently."

"But he's obviously lying—"

"Captain Shepard! It's not at all obvious. Don't speak unless questioned."

"Anyway," January said, hoping to shift the questions away from the issue of the long delay, "I noticed something about the bomb when it was falling that could explain why it stuck. I need to discuss it with one of the scientists familiar with the bomb's design."

"What was that?" Scholes asked suspiciously.

January hesitated. "There's going to be an inquiry, right?"

Scholes frowned. "This is the inquiry, Captain January. Tell us what you saw."

"But there will be some proceeding beyond this one?"

"It looks like there's going to be a court-martial, yes, Captain."

"That's what I thought. I don't want to talk to anyone but my counsel, and some scientist familiar with the bomb."

"*I'm* a scientist familiar with the bomb," Shepard burst out. "You could tell me if you really had anything, you—"

"I said I need a scientist!" January exclaimed, rising to face the scarlet Shepard across the table. "Not a G-God damned mechanic." Shepard started to shout, others joined in and the room rang with argument. While Scholes restored order January sat down, and he refused to be drawn out again.

"I'll see you're assigned counsel, and initiate the court-martial," Scholes said, clearly at a loss. "Meanwhile you are under arrest, on suspicion of disobeying orders in combat." January nodded, and Scholes gave him over to the MPs.

"One last thing," January said, fighting exhaustion. "Tell General Le May that if the Japs are told this drop was a warning, it might have the same effect as—"

"I told you!" Shepard shouted. "I told you he did it on purpose!"

Men around Shepard restrained him. But he had convinced most of them, and even Matthews stared at him with surprised anger.

January shook his head wearily. He had the dull feeling that his plan, while it had succeeded so far, was ultimately not a good one. "Just trying to make the best of it." It took all of his remaining will to force his legs to carry him in a dignified manner out of the hut.

His cell was an empty NCO's office. MPs brought his meals. For the first couple of days he did little but sleep. On the third day he glanced out the office's barred window, and saw a tractor pulling a tarpaulin-draped trolley out of the compound, followed by jeeps filled with MPs. It looked like a military funeral. January rushed to the door and banged on it until one of the young MPs came.

"What's that they're doing out there?" January demanded.

Eyes cold and mouth twisted, the MP said, "They're making another strike. They're going to do it right this time."

"No!" January cried. "No!" He rushed the MP, who knocked him back and locked the door. *"No!"* He beat the door until his hands hurt, cursing wildly. "You don't *need* to do it, it isn't *necessary*." Shell shattered at last, he collapsed on the bed and wept. Now everything he had done would be rendered meaningless. He had sacrificed himself for nothing.

A day or two after that the MPs led in a colonel, an iron-haired man who stood stiffly and crushed January's hand when he shook it. His eyes were a pale, icy blue.

"I am Colonel Dray," he said. "I have been ordered to defend you in court-martial." January could feel the dislike pouring from the man. "To do that I'm going to need every fact you have, so let's get started."

"I'm not talking to anybody until I've seen an atomic scientist."

"I am your *defense* counsel—"

"I don't care who you are," January said. "Your defense of me depends on you getting one of the scientists *here*. The higher up he is, the better. And I want to speak to him alone."

"I will have to be present."

So he would do it. But now January's lawyer, too, was an enemy.

"Naturally," January said. "You're my lawyer. But no one else. Our atomic secrecy may depend on it."

"You saw evidence of sabotage?"

"Not one word more until that scientist is here."

Angrily the colonel nodded and left.

Late the next day the colonel returned with another man. "This is Dr. Forest."

"I helped develop the bomb," Forest said. He had a crew cut and dressed in fatigues, and to January he looked more Army than the colonel. Suspiciously he stared back and forth at the two men.

"You'll vouch for this man's identity on your word as an officer?" he asked Dray.

"Of course," the colonel said stiffly, offended.

"So," Dr. Forest said. "You had some trouble getting it off when you wanted to. Tell me what you saw."

"I saw nothing," January said harshly. He took a deep breath; it was time to commit himself. "I want you to take a message back to the scientists. You folks have been working on this thing for years, and you must have had time to consider how the bomb should have been used. You know we could have convinced the Japs to surrender by showing them a demonstration—''

''Wait a minute,'' Forest said. ''You're saying you didn't see anything? There wasn't a malfunction?''

''That's right,'' January said, and cleared his throat. ''It wasn't *necessary*, do you understand?''

Forest was looking at Colonel Dray. Dray gave him a disgusted shrug. ''He told me he saw evidence of sabotage.''

''I want you to go back and ask the scientists to intercede for me,'' January said, raising his voice to get the man's attention. ''I haven't got a chance in that court-martial. But if the scientists defend me then maybe they'll let me live, see? I don't want to get shot for doing something every one of you scientists would have done.''

Dr. Forest had backed away. Color rising, he said, ''What makes you think that's what we would have done? Don't you think we considered it? Don't you think men better qualified than you made the decision?'' He waved a hand— ''God damn it—what made you think you were competent to decide something as important as that!''

January was appalled at the man's reaction; in his plan it had gone differently. Angrily he jabbed a finger at Forest. ''Because *I* was the man doing it, *Doctor* Forest. You take even one step back from that and suddenly you can pretend it's not your doing. Fine for you, but *I was there*.''

At every word the man's color was rising. It looked like he might pop a vein in his neck. January tried once more. ''Have you ever tried to imagine what one of your bombs would do to a city full of people?''

''I've had enough!'' the man exploded. He turned to Dray. ''I'm under no obligation to keep what I've heard here confidential. You can be sure it will be used as evidence in Captain January's court-martial.'' He turned and gave January a look of such blazing hatred that January understood it. For these men to admit he was right would mean admitting that they were wrong—that every one of them was responsible for his part in the construction of the weapon January had refused to use. Understanding that, January knew he was doomed.

The bang of Dr. Forest's departure still shook the little office. January sat on his cot, got out a smoke. Under Colonel Dray's cold gaze he lit one shakily, took a drag. He looked up at the colonel, shrugged. "It was my best chance," he explained. That did something—for the first and only time the cold disdain in the colonel's eyes shifted to a little, hard, lawyerly gleam of respect.

The court-martial lasted two days. The verdict was guilty of disobeying orders in combat and of giving aid and comfort to the enemy. The sentence was death by firing squad.

For most of his remaining days January rarely spoke, drawing ever further behind the mask that had hidden him for so long. A clergyman came to see him, but it was the 509th's chaplain, the one who had said the prayer blessing the *Lucky Strike*'s mission before they took off. Angrily January sent him packing.

Later, however, a young Catholic priest dropped by. His name was Patrick Getty. He was a little pudgy man, bespectacled and, it seemed, somewhat afraid of January. January let the man talk to him. When he returned the next day January talked back a bit, and on the day after that he talked some more. It became a habit.

Usually January talked about his childhood. He talked of plowing mucky black bottom land behind a mule. Of running down the lane to the mailbox. Of reading books by the light of the moon after he had been ordered to sleep, and of being beaten by his mother for it with a high-heeled shoe. He told the priest the story of the time his arm had been burnt, and about the car crash at the bottom of Fourth Street. ''It's the truck driver's face I remember, do you see, Father?''

''Yes,'' the young priest said. ''Yes.''

And he told him about the game he had played in which every action he took tipped the balance of world affairs. ''When I remembered that game I thought it was dumb. Step on a sidewalk crack and cause an earthquake—you know, it's stupid. Kids are like that.'' The priest nodded. ''But now I've been thinking that if everybody were to live their whole lives like that, thinking that every move they made really was important, then . . . it might make a difference.'' He waved a hand vaguely, expelled cigarette smoke. ''You're accountable for what you do.''

''Yes,'' the priest said. ''Yes, you are.''

''And if you're given orders to do something wrong, you're still accountable, right? The orders don't change it.''

''That's right.''

''Hmph.'' January smoked a while. ''So they say, anyway. But look what happens.'' He waved at the office. ''I'm like the guy in a story I read—he thought everything in books was true, and after reading a bunch of westerns he tried to rob a train. They tossed him in jail.'' He laughed shortly. ''Books are full of crap.''

''Not all of them,'' the priest said. ''Besides, you weren't trying to rob a train.''

They laughed at the notion. ''Did you read that story?''

''No.''

''It was the strangest book—there were two stories in it, and they alternated chapter by chapter, but they didn't have a thing to do with each other! I didn't get it.''

'' . . . Maybe the writer was trying to say that everything connects to everything else.''

''Maybe. But it's a funny way to say it.''

''I like it.''

And so they passed the time, talking.

* * *

So it was the priest who was the one to come by and tell January that his request for a Presidential pardon had been refused. Getty said awkwardly, ''It seems the President approves the sentence.''

''That bastard,'' January said weakly. He sat on his cot.

Time passed. It was another hot, humid day.

''Well,'' the priest said. ''Let me give you some better news. Given your situation I don't think telling you matters, though I've been told not to. The second mission—you know there was a second strike?''

''Yes.''

''Well, they missed too.''

''What?'' January cried, and bounced to his feet. ''You're kidding!''

''No. They flew to Kokura, but found it covered by clouds. It was the same over Nagasaki and Hiroshima, so they flew back to Kokura and tried to drop the bomb using radar to guide it, but apparently there was a—a genuine equipment failure this time, and the bomb fell on an island.''

January was hopping up and down, mouth hanging open, ''So we n-never—''

''We never dropped an atom bomb on a Japanese city. That's right.'' Getty grinned. ''And get this—I heard this from my superior—they sent a message to the Japanese government tellng them that the two explosions were warnings, and that if they didn't surrender by September first we would drop bombs on Kyoto and Tokyo, and then wherever else we had to. Word is that the Emperor went to Hiroshima to survey the damage, and when he saw it he ordered the Cabinet to surrender. So . . .''

''So it worked,'' January said. He hopped around, ''It worked, it worked!''

''Yes.''

''Just like I said it would!'' he cried, and hopping before the priest he laughed.

Getty was jumping around a little too, and the sight of the priest bouncing was too much for January. He sat on his cot and laughed till the tears ran down his cheeks.

''So—'' he sobered quickly. ''So Truman's going to shoot me anyway, eh?''

''Yes,'' the priest said unhappily. ''I guess that's right.''

This time January's laugh was bitter. ''He's a bastard, all right. And proud of being a bastard, which makes it worse.'' He shook his head. ''If Roosevelt had lived . . .''

''It would have been different,'' Getty finished. ''Yes. Maybe so. But he didn't.'' He sat beside January. ''Cigarette?'' He held out a pack, and January noticed the white wartime wrapper. He frowned.

''You haven't got a Camel?''

''Oh. Sorry.''

''Oh well. That's all right.'' January took one of the Lucky Strikes, lit up. ''That's awfully good news.'' He breathed out. ''I never believed Truman would pardon me anyway, so mostly you've brought good news. Ha. They *missed*. You have no idea how much better that makes me feel.''

''I think I do.''

January smoked the cigarette.

''. . . So I'm a good American after all. I *am* a good American,'' he insisted, ''no matter what Truman says.''

''Yes,'' Getty replied, and coughed. ''You're better than Truman any day.''

''Better watch what you say, Father.'' He looked into the eyes behind the glasses, and the expression he saw there gave him pause. Since the drop every look directed at him had been filled with contempt. He'd seen it so often during the court-martial that he'd learned to stop looking; and now he had to teach himself to see again. The priest looked at him as if he were . . . as if he were some kind of hero. That wasn't exactly right. But seeing it . . .

January would not live to see the years that followed, so he would never know what came of his action. He had given up casting his mind forward and imagining possibilities, because there was no point to it. His planning was ended. In any case he would not have been able to imagine the course of the post-war years. That the world would quickly become an armed camp pitched on the edge of atomic war, he might have predicted. But he never would have guessed that so many people would join a January Society. He would never know of the effect the Society had on Dewey during the Korean crisis, never know of the Society's successful campaign for the test ban treaty, and never learn that thanks in part to the Society and its allies, a treaty would be signed by the great powers that would reduce the number of atomic bombs year by year, until there were none left.

Frank January would never know any of that. But in that moment on his cot looking into the eyes of young Patrick Getty, he guessed an inkling of it—he felt, just for an instant, the impact on history.

And with that he relaxed. In his last week everyone who met him carried away the same impression, that of a calm, quiet man, angry at Truman and others, but in a withdrawn, matter-of-fact way. Patrick Getty, a strong force in the January Society ever after, said January was talkative for some time after he learned of the missed attack on Kokura. Then he became quieter and quieter, as the day approached. On the morning that they woke him at dawn to march him out to a hastily constructed execution shed, his MPs shook his hand. The priest was with him as he smoked a final cigarette, and they prepared to put the hood over his head. January looked at him calmly. "They load one of the guns with a blank cartridge, right?"

"Yes," Getty said.

"So each man in the squad can imagine he may not have shot me?"

"Yes. That's right."

A tight, unhumorous smile was January's last expression. He threw down the cigarette, ground it out, poked the priest in the arm. "But I *know*." Then the mask slipped back into place for good, making the hood redundant, and with a firm step January went to the wall. One might have said he was at peace.

—1983

Coming Back to Dixieland

It figures, just as sure as shift-start, that on our big day there'd be trouble. It's a law of physics, the one miners know best: things tend to fuck up.

I woke first out of the last of several nervous catnaps, and wandered down to the hotel bar to get something a little less heavyweight than the White Brother for my nerves. On one level I was calm as could be, but on another I was feeling a bit shaky (Shaky Barnes, that's me). Now, we drank the Brother during performances back on the rocks, of course, between sets sitting at the tables, or during the last songs when someone offered it; and Hook would make his announcement, "We never know if this'll make us play better or worse, but it sure is fun finding out," and then pass it around. Which was the point; we *had* to play good this day, so I wanted something soothing, with a little less pop to it than the White Brother we'd brought with us, which amplifies your every feeling, including fear.

So when I threaded my way through the hotel (which was as big as the whole operation on Hebe or Iris) back to our rooms, I expected the band to still be there sleeping. But when I'd finished stepping over all the scattered chairs, tables, mattresses and such (the remains of the previous shift's practice session) I could find only three of them, all tangled up in the fancy sheets: Fingers, Crazy, and Washboard. I wasn't surprised that my brother Hook was gone—he often was—but Sidney shouldn't have been missing; he hadn't gone off by himself since we left Ceres Central.

"Hey!" I said, still not too worried. "Where'd they go, you slag-eaters!" They mumbled and grunted and tried to ignore me. I gave Washboard a shove with my foot. "Where's Hook? Where's Sidney?" I said a little louder.

"Quit shouting," Washboard said fuzzily. "Hook's probably gone back to the Tower of Bible to visit the Jezebels again." He buried his head in the pillow, like a snoutbit diving into bubblerock; suddenly it popped back out. "*Sidney's* gone?"

"You see him?"

Fingers propped himself up on his elbow. "You better find Hook," he said in his slow way. "Hook, he'll know where Sidney gone to."

"Well, did Hook *say* he was going to the Tower of Bible?" No one spoke. Crazy crawled over to a bed and sat up. He reached behind the bed and pulled out a tall thin bottle, still half filled with cloudy white liquid. He put it to his mouth and tilted it up; the level dropped abruptly a couple of times.

"Crazy, I never seen you hit the White Brother so early in the dayshift before," I said.

"Shaky," he replied, "you never seen me get the chance."

"You going to get us in trouble," I said, remembering certain misadventures of the past.

"No, I'm not," Crazy said. "Now why don't you run down Hook, I'm pretty sure he's in Sodom and Gomorrah, he liked that place''—he took another swallow—''and we'll hold down the fort and wait for Sidney to come back.''

''He better come back,'' I said. ''Shit. Here it is the biggest day in our lives and you guys don't even have the sense to stay in one spot.''

''Don't worry,'' Crazy said. ''Things'll go fine, I'll see to it.''

I took one of the slow cars through the track-webbed space between our hotel and the Tower of Bible. The Tower is one of Titania's biggest experiments in Neo-Archeo-Ritualism, sometimes called Participatory Art. Within the huge structure, set right against the wall of the Titania Gap, the setting for every chapter in the Bible is contained, which means you can participate in a wide variety of activities. The lobby of the Tower was unusually crowded for the early hours of the dayshift, but it was Performance Day, I remembered, and people were starting early. I worked from ramp to ramp, trying to make my way through the oddly assorted crowd to the elevator that would take me to Sodom and Gomorrah. Finally I slid through the closing doors and took my place in the mass of future Sodomites.

''What I want to know,'' one of them said happily, ''is do they periodically sulfurize everyone in the room?''

''Every two hours,'' a woman with round eyes replied, ''and does it feel real! But then they unfreeze you and you get to begin again!'' She laughed.

''Oh,'' said the man, blinking.

The elevator opened and the group surged past me toward Costumes. I stood and looked down some of the smoky streets of Gomorrah, hoping to see my brother in the crowd. Just as I decided to get one of the costumes and start searching, I saw him coming out of the door marked JEZEBELS, one arm wrapped around a veiled woman.

''Why, he must have just got here,'' I said aloud, and took off after him. ''Hook!'' I called. ''Hook!''

He heard me and quickly steered the woman into a side street. I started running. Sure enough, when I rounded the corner they had disappeared; I made a lucky guess and opened the door to a house made of sediments, and caught up with them moving up the narrow stairs. "Hook, God damn it," I said.

"Later," he mumbled back at me, face buried in the Jezebel's neck.

"Hook, it's important."

He waved his right arm back at me in a brush-away motion, and the metal rods of his hand flashed in my face. "Not important!" he bellowed. I grabbed his arm and pulled on it.

"How can you say that?" I cried. "Today's the day! The six bands those judges pick today get to go to Earth and everywhere—"

He finally stopped dragging us all up the stairs. "I know all that, Shaky, but that don't happen for a few hours yet, so why don't you go down to Psalms or Proverbs and calm down some? No reason for you to be so anxious."

"Yes, there is," I said, "a real good reason. Sidney's gone."

Hook tucked his chin into his neck. "Sidney's gone?" he repeated.

"Nobody's seen him all shift."

His three metal fingers waved up and down, scissoring the air; it was the same nervous sign of thought he'd made when he had his hand, and played the trumpet. "Did you search the hotel good?" he said after a bit. "I don't think he'd leave the hotel."

I shook my head. "I came here, I thought you'd know where he is."

"Well, he's probably in the hotel somewhere, take a look why don't you?"

"What if he's not there? Come on, Hook, if we don't find him we're sunk."

"All right," he said. "Shit. You're as bad as Sidney. I've been playing with that man near twenty years, and I never seen him so scared."

"You think he's scared?" That had never occurred to me. Sidney was quiet, not too forward, but I'd never seen him scared of playing music.

"Sure he's scared." He looked at the Jezebel, who hadn't made a sound so far. "I got to find Sidney," he explained. "I'll be back to celebrate tomorrow."

Her veiled head nodded, and I could see the flash of teeth. "We better hurry," Hook said. "We're due to be turned into a pillar of salt any minute now." We ran back and dived into the elevator, just behind the man who had been asking questions on the way up. Down in the lobby we dodged through a group of wide-eyed Venusian monks and then through a stumbling crowd of wet people from one of the aquatic scenes. Then we made it to the exit, jumped in a car, and popped out into the Gap.

"That Participatory Art," Hook said, "is really something."

"Sidney's probably hiding in the hotel somewhere, the bar or maybe the baggage rooms," Hook said as we neared our hotel.

I could see that he was as worried as I was. Despite his easygoing speculations, his nervous trumpet fingering gave him away. Sidney's absence was a serious matter, partly because it was so unexpected; Sidney was never gone, never sick, never hurt; there was nothing that could keep Sidney from playing. And how he could play that clarinet! It was more than notes, it had to do with what was inside the man, the strength and the feeling; there's no way I can describe it to you but by telling a story here; a little blues:

After the long shift's ending, when I was just a kid and still working the sheds, I'd go down to the Heel Bar to sip beer and listen to Sidney play his clarinet. At this time he was playing with just Washboard and a piano man, Christy Morton, who later got killed in the big tunnel collapse on Troilus; and they were working out all the old tunes he'd discovered in the Benson Curtis tapes.

Sidney was as quiet and unassuming then as always. It didn't matter how much stomping and shouting he stirred up, or how much Washboard and Christy sang into the tune; old Sidney would stand there, head bowed, horn cradled in his arm when he wasn't playing, as silent and bashful as a child. Then he'd raise that horn to his mouth, and when he played it was clear he had found his way of talking to the world. All the clamoring in the room channeled into him, he was transformed, and, sweat-bright with the effort, he'd wrench those songs into a sound as clean and live as a welding arc. Listening to him my cheeks would flush with blood, my heart would pound like Washboard's cowbell.

One time, late in the graveyard shift, I was joined at my front table by a Metis mute, one of the miners whose vocal cords had been ruined by the zinc blowout on Metis. Between sets Sidney sat with us, asked me how Hook was doing (this was right after his accident), and talked about Earth. He told us about New Orleans in the old times, when the jazz bands played in the streets. Telling it, he got so excited I didn't need to prod him with questions; he spoke on his own, even told us his one childhood memory of Earth: "That ocean, it was like a flat blue plate, big as Jupiter from Io, speckled with shadows from clouds; and the horizon was straight as a rail, edge to edge cutting off a sky that was a blue I can't describe." When he went back to play I was under the spell of Dixieland; and by the gleam in the mute's eye I could tell he felt it too. When Sidney played a good break the mute would put back his head and laugh, mouth split wide open, silent as space.

So when Sidney was done we decided to take the mute along to Sidney's place, to give the mute some floor to sleep on; he didn't have any money or anywhere to go. Now at this time (this was on Achilles) Sidney lived in a cubbyhole behind one of the Supervisor's big homes. When we got there Sidney wanted us to hold back while he went to check if his sister-in-law was awake—she didn't like him bringing folks home. Sidney explained this, but the mute didn't appear to understand; he must have thought he was being left, because every time Sidney walked a few steps and turned around, he found the mute right behind him, grinning and dragging me along. So there was a lot of waving and explaining going on when the JM police suddenly appeared; we didn't even have time to run.

"Where you going?" one of them asked.

"Home," Sidney said.

"I suppose you live here?" the cop said, pointing at the Supervisor's place.

"Yeah," Sidney said, and before he had time to explain, they were taking us off to jail.

We were hardly inside the jail door when they went to work on the Metis mute. Kicked him and beat him till he couldn't stand. His face was so bloody. Sidney and I stood shaking against the wall, expecting we'd be next, but they let us alone. Turned out one of the cops' wives had been killed on Metis, and he'd been after the mutes ever since. So when they were done with him they slammed us all into the bullpen.

There's not much JM can do to make its jails any worse than its mines, but what they can do they have done. The cell we were in was cold and dark, like a tunnel in a power breakdown, except for the gravity, which felt like it was over 1.00. I crawled over the rock floor, unable to see, and quietly called Sidney's name.

"Steve?" his voice said. "Where you gone to?" His hand caught my arm, and he set me down beside him.

"Quit that snuffling," he said to me. "This is your first time in jail? Is that right? Well, it won't be your last, no, not a miner kid like you. They'll put you here many times before you're done." He paused. "Look at all these folks."

A dim light gleamed through the door grating, and when my eyes adjusted I saw shapes huddled on the floor. They were gathered in knots, feet on each other's stomachs, using the survival techniques JM had taught them.

"They going to let us die?" I asked fearfully; the only times I had seen men curled together like that was when they carried the bodies, two by two, out of breakdowns.

"No, no," he said. "They just like us, just put in here for nothing, to be cold and hungry and heavy for a shift or two, to remind them who's boss on these rocks." He sounded old and tired; and yet when I looked up at him, I saw that he was pulling the parts of his clarinet out of his big old coat and putting them together. He was sitting against the rock wall of the cell, with the mute propped up beside him. When his horn was together he put it to his mouth, gave the reed a lick, commenced to play.

He started soft, barely sounding the notes, and played "Burgundy Street Blues" all the way through without raising his voice. As he played "What Did I Do" some of the huddled figures slowly sat up and listened, backs and heads to the wall, looking up at the ceiling or the yellow squares of the grate.

Then he played the new songs, written by miners' bands and only heard in the bars scattered through their asteroids. He played "Ceres," and "Hidalgo," and "Vesta Joys"; he played his "Shaft Bucket Blues" and "I Got Me a Feeling."

Then he played "Don't God Live Out This Far," one of the first of the miner blues, which made it about twenty years old; and people began to join him. These were miners, men who seldom sang in the bars, seldom did more than stomp their boots or shout something between phrases; and at first their singing was an awkward sort of growl, barely in tune or time with Sidney. But he picked them up and more joined in, hesitantly, till you could make out the words of the refrain:

"Up at the shift-start,
Down in the mine shaft,
Spend my life throwing dirt on a car—
Ain't got nothing to do
But sing me the blues—
Hey don't God live out this far."

There were about thirty verses to the song. It was about a miner who keeps getting in trouble, till JM decides to finish him: "Super comes at shift-start for me to be hung, on account of something that I hadn't done." The Supervisor believes he's innocent, but there's no proof. It was the same old, old thing.

When the singing got loud enough Sidney took off from the melody and floated up above it. And they sang! There was something in it that seemed to take my lungs away, so I could only breathe quick and shallow; it was what they had of the music inside themselves. Just hearing someone's voice in the dark, and knowing his life has a long way to go . . .

The light from the door just caught the plumes of breath frosting out from the men singing. I looked over at the mute. His eyes were open, staring out somewhere in space. As I watched he lifted up his hands and started a little syncopated clap, very soft, giving as much to the music as he could. When Sidney heard it he looked down at him, then looked back up; he played louder, filling the room with his sound, till the clarinet was all we heard or needed to hear, and the last verse came to its end.

"Oh yeah," said a quiet voice.

Sidney looked at the mute, smiled, shook his head. "A little blues for us, eh, brother?" he said. "A little slave music."

The mute nodded and grinned, which made his lip crack open again and spill blood down his chin.

Sidney laughed at him and wiped some of the blood from the mute's face. "Oh yeah," he said softly, "a little miner music."

We found Sidney just where Hook guessed he might be, huddled in the room where our baggage and instruments were stored. He was perched up on the box that Crazy's tuba traveled in, with his shoulders hunched and his legs crossed. When we burst into the room he jumped and then settled back, head down, staring sullenly across at us. His clarinet lay fitted in his arms. We all stood still, barred and hidden in the shadows thrown by the single bulb behind us, waiting for somebody to say something. The wisps of hair Sidney combed across his head looked thicker because of the shadows they cast on his bald pate. He looked like one of the tunnel-gnomes men claim to see on Pallas; creatures who were once men maybe, who escaped JM by living in the old shafts. I had never noticed how small he was.

"You scared?" Hook asked.

Sidney raised his head to stare at Hook better. "Yeah, I am," he said suddenly, loud in the dim room, "shouldn't I be?"

"Hey, Sidney." I said, "you don't got no reason to be scared—"

"Don't got no reason!" He pointed at me, clarinet still in hand. "Don't you say that shit to me, Shaky. I got the best reason possible to be scared." He jumped down from the box. "The best reason possible. This is a contest, boy, we ain't playing to please these folks, we playing to show them that we better musicianers than all them others! And if we don't show them that, if we don't win one of them grants, we gone. We back to the mines, boy, and we'll work in those shafts until JM has broke us so we can't work no more, and we'll never get to see the Earth. So don't tell me I got no reason to be scared."

"Come on, Sidney, you can't think like that," I said, searching for something I could say to him. "It ain't so bad as—"

"Sidney," Hook said, like I hadn't been talking at all (suddenly I see a picture in my head, of Sidney crouched down and shifting through a four-foot-high tunnel, Hook straddled senseless across his back, one of his hands clamped white around Hook's wrist, which ended in a tangle of bloody filaments; shouting instructions in furious fearful high voice to the men trying to get the airlock opened); I stepped back and let Hook talk to him.

"Sidney," he said, "you ain't thought this out. They been putting one over on you. You're talking like this contest is a big vital thing, like we got some chance of going out there and *winning* one of them grants. Sidney, we got *no* chance, don't you realize that?"

"Hook—" I objected.

"No, you listen to me, we *got no chance*. You seen all those other musicianers here—those folks been doing nothing but play music all their *lives*, they playing all those fancy machines and doing things with music we don't even know about! And we just a bunch of miners playing some old Earth-type of music that just showed up a few years back, and only 'cause JM salvaged a ship full of band instruments and give them to us so we'd stay out of fights! And you still think we got a *chance?*"

Sidney and I stared at him.

"No way," he continued grimly, "no more'n there's a chance that JM will retire us at forty and send us to Mars. They got us here just so they can say they got folks from everywhere, even the rocks, and they going to give the grants to those fancy-ass musicianers, not us. So just exactly what you said is going to happen, Sidney, when this thing is over they going to send us back to the rocks to work and work, every third shift, till some equipment catches you or some tunnel collapses"—waving his hooks so they flashed silver in front of us—"and then, if you're still alive, they'll dump you on Vesta rock and wait for you to die.

"And the only way you got to show how you feel about that, Sidney, is through that horn, through that skinny black horn of yours. When you get out there they going to be looking down on you, just like they always have, and all you can do about it is to *play* that thing! play it so hard they *got* to see you! play it and show them what kind of music a man plays when he works all his life digging in those fucking rocks!"

He stopped, gulped in some air. Sidney and I didn't make a sound. Suddenly he turned and walked over to the baggage, rummaged around a bit, then found the trunk he wanted and pulled it around so he could unstrap it and fling it open. He reached in and pulled out a long white bottle, held it high in the dim light while he unscrewed it. He turned it upside down to his mouth and took a long pull.

"Eeeow!" he whooped. He held it out toward Sidney. "So what say we have a drink of the White Brother, brother, and then go play us some music."

I looked at Sidney. I don't think I'd ever seen him indulge in the White Brother; he hardly even drank beer.

"I believe I will," Sidney said, and swallowed near half the bottle.

* * *

Back up in our rooms Crazy was leading Fingers and Washboard in the ''Emperor Norton Stomp,'' running up the walls as high as he could and then diving off onto the unmade and trampled beds. He saw us standing in the doorway and from his position high on the wall he dived straight for us and bounced on the floor.

''Crazy,'' Hook said cheerfully, ''you are crazy.'' He stepped over him and made his way through the stuff heaped on the floor. He pulled his trombone out of the pile beside his bed.

''Let's roll,'' he said.

''Wait!'' Crazy cried. He poured some White Brother into cups and passed them around. When Sidney took one he didn't say a word, just grinned and pointed. Sidney paid him no attention.

We raised our cups in the air. ''To the Hot Six,'' I said. ''Play that thing!'' We downed the Brother; I could feel him slide into my stomach and explode there, making my blood pound and my vision jump.

We got our instruments and made our way to the lobby. When we got there we headed for the clerk's desk, bumping together and shushing each other, trying to calm down some while Hook spoke to the clerk.

''We are the Hot Six,'' Hook shouted at the clerk, who stepped back quickly. ''And we playing at the Outer Planets Center for the Performing Arts' W. H. Blakely Memorial Traveling Grant Competition'' (we all threw in some ''oh yeahs!'' for such virtuosity) ''and we need your fastest car right now.''

''Well sir,'' the clerk said, ''all the cars have the same speed capability.''

''Oh come now, *come* now,'' Hook said, ''are you telling me that you don't know of a single car that's set to go a mite faster than normal?''

''No sir, none except the cars reserved for emergencies—''

"Emergencies! Why, don't you know that's exactly what this is? An emergency!"

"An emergency," we all echoed, and Crazy began to climb over the desk, muttering in a low voice, "Emergency, emergency."

"If you don't give us one of them emergency cars," Hook continued in a lowered voice, "then we've come over fifteen hundred million miles for no reason at all."

The clerk looked past Hook and saw us staring at him with the intensity that the White Brother can give you; looked at Crazy, who was clawing at the buttons on top of the counter. He shrugged. "One of the special cars will be waiting for you at the departure gate."

"Make it a big one," Hook said, "we got a lot of stuff to carry."

We went to the departure gate and found a sixteen-person car, painted bright red, waiting for us. We threw all the instruments in the back and clambered in; Hook set the controls and fired us out into the Titania Gap.

The Gap is a long, straight canyon whose origins are unknown. It looks like it was carved into Titania some eons back by a good-sized rock (say about the size of Demeter) that nearly missed it. It's about two hundred miles long, four to ten miles wide, and nearly that deep, and almost the entire colony on Titania is set down in the skinny end of it. So when we popped out the wall of our hotel and shot down our track, we were greeted with the sight of the whole colony, covering the floor and climbing the walls of a canyon that would have swallowed most of the rocks we had lived on. There was only the fine lacing of car tracks looping through space to keep us from dropping two or three miles. Above us the swirling greens of Uranus blocked off most of the sky we could see.

"Shit, this thing *is* fast," Hook said, after the car had taken a long drop and thrown us back in our seats. Crazy whooped and climbed over the seats back to his tuba case, from which he pulled another milky-white bottle. Fingers cheered and started singing, half-tempo like he always starts, "I Don't Know Where I'm Going But I'm On My Way," and Hook joined him.

"I feel pretty good," Sidney said from his window seat.

I sat back and watched the other cars slide along their strands, listening to the band keep loose. The front line, I thought, would be okay. I had been playing with Hook and Sidney since I was twelve years old—twelve years now—and Hook and Sidney had been playing together longer than that; we were the best front line there was, without a doubt, maybe the best there had ever been. And our back line was almost as good. Washboard never stopped hitting; even now he was clicking out rhythms on the side of the car, metal studs already taped to his fingers. Crazy was unreliable, we'd had to play many times without him because of his wild drinking; he didn't have the virtuoso command of the tuba that old Clarence Miles, our first tuba man, had had before he was paralyzed; but nobody could pump as much air through a tuba as Crazy could, and his mad stomping and blowing was one of the trademarks of the Hot Six. Fingers—he was probably our weakest spot. He's a bit slow to understand things, and he only has eight fingers now; maybe the best thing about his playing is that all eight of those fingers hit the keys a good part of the time. That's the only way a piano man gets heard in a jazz band, especially a fine loud one like ours.

Hook slammed us into one of the track intersections without slowing down, and we dropped through it with a sickening jolt. I had visions of the whole band plummeting down the Gap like a puny imitation of the rock that had carved it.

"Goddammit Hook, what's the rush?" I asked. "We're not that late."

"Don't worry," he said. "This is just a fancy ore car here, I got it in hand."

"Yeah, don't worry, Shaky," Crazy chipped in. "Why you worrying? You ain't going to get shaky again, are you Shaky?" They all laughed, Hook hardest of all; he had named me that because I was so scared when I first played with the band that my tone had a vibrato in it.

"I feel *real* good," said Sidney.

Then we turned a curve and were pointed right at the Performing Arts Center. It stuck up from the canyon floor like one of the natural spires, a huge stack right at the end of the colony, the last structure before the black U of the Gap stretched out, lightless and empty. The car hit the final swoop of track up to it, and scarcely slowed down. Nobody said anything; Fingers stopped singing. As we drew closer, and the side of the building blocked out our view of the Gap, Hook finished the verse:

"And I got no place to go to
And I got no place to stay
And I don't know where I'm going
But I'm on my way."

The waiting room backstage was crowded with a menagerie of about forty brightly dressed performers, all wandering in and out of practice rooms and talking loud, trying to work off tension. As soon as we walked in the door I could feel a heat on my cheeks, on account of all the eyes focusing on us. Everyone was happy to have something to think about besides the upcoming few hours, and as I looked at us all, standing in the doorway gawking, I could see we were good for that. Even in our best clothes (supplied by JM) we looked like exactly what we were: bulky, roughshod, unkempt, maimed, oh, we were miners, clear enough; and under the stares of that rainbow of costumes I suppose we should have quailed. But the energy we got from adrenaline and the White Brother and our wild flight down the Gap gave us a sort of momentum; and when Hook and Crazy looked at each other and burst out laughing, it was them that quailed. Glances turned away from us, and we strode into the room feeling on top of things.

I walked over to a circle of chairs that was empty and sat down. I got my trumpet out of its case and stuck my very shallowest mouthpiece into it; hit 'em high and hard, I thought. The rest of the band was doing the same around me, talking in mutters and laughing every time their eyes met. I looked around and saw that now our fellow performers were trying to watch us without looking. As my gaze swept the room it pushed eyes down and away like magic. When Washboard pulled his washboard out of his box and compulsively rippled his studded fingers down the slats to pop the cowbell, there was an attentive, amazed silence—very undeserved, I thought, considering how strange some of the other instruments in the room appeared—if that was really what they were. I walked over to the piano in a corner of the room, and nearly fell at an unexpected step down. I hit B-flat. My C was in tune with it. Hook, Sidney, and Crazy hit a variety of thirds and fifths, intending to sound as haphazard and out of tune as possible. Sidney made a series of small adjustments to his clarinet, but Hook and Crazy laid their brass down, the better to observe the show going on around them. Washboard was already moving around the room, stepping from level to level and politely asking questions about the weird machinery.

"Hey, look at this!" Hook called across to me. He was waving a square of paper. I crossed back to him.

"It's a program," he explained, and began to read out loud, " 'Number Eighteen, the Hot Six Jazz Band, from Jupiter Metals, Pallas—an instrumental group specializing in traditional jazz, a twentieth-century style of composition and performance characterized by vigorous improvisation.' Ha!

Vigorous improvisation!'' He laughed again. ''I'll vigorously improvise those—''

''Who's that up there?'' Fingers asked, pointing with his good hand at the video screen they had up on one wall. The performer on stage at the moment was a red-robed singer, warbling out some polytonal stuff that many of the people in the room looked like they wanted to hear, judging by the way they stared at Hook. The harmonies and counterpoints the performer was singing with himself were pretty complex, but he had a box surgically implanted in one side of his neck that was clearly helping his vocal cords, so even though he was sliding from Crazy's tuning note up to the A above high C while holding a C-major chord, I wasn't much impressed.

'' 'Number Sixteen,' '' Hook read (and my heart sledged in my chest all of a sudden; only two to go), '' 'Singer Roderick Flen-Jones, from Rhea, a vocalist utilizing the Sturmond Larynx-Synthesizer in four fugues of his own composition.''

''Shit,'' Crazy remarked at a particularly high turn, ''he sounds like a dog whistle.''

''Pretty lightweight,'' Washboard agreed.

''Lightweight? Man, he's *featherweight!*'' Crazy shouted, and laughed loudly at his own joke; he was feeling pretty good. I noticed we were causing a general exodus from the main waiting room. People were drifting into the practice chambers to get away from us, and there was a growing empty space surrounding our group of chairs. I caught Hook's eye and he seemed to get my meaning. He shrugged a ''Fuck them,'' but he got Crazy to pick up his tuba and go over some turns with him, which calmed things down somewhat.

I sat down beside a guy near our chairs who was dressed up in one of the simpler costumes in the room, a brown-and-gold robe. He had been watching us with what seemed like friendly interest the whole time we'd been there.

"You look like you're having fun," he said.

"Sure," I agreed. "How about you?"

"I'm a little scared to be enjoying myself fully."

"I know the feeling. What's that?" I asked, pointing to the instrument in his lap.

"Tone-bar," he said, running his fingers over it; without amplification it made only the ghost of a rippling glissando.

"Is that a new thing?" I asked.

"Not this time. Last time it was."

"You've tried this before?"

"Yes," he said, "I won, too."

"You won!" I exclaimed. "You got one of the grants?" He nodded. "So what are you doing back here?"

"That grant only gets you from place to place. It doesn't guarantee you're going to make enough to keep traveling once you're done with it."

"Well, will these folks give a grant twice?"

"They've never done it before," he said, and looked up from his tone-bar to smile lopsidedly at me. "So I've got quite a job today, don't I."

"I guess," I said.

We watched the video for a while. As the singer juggled the three parts of his fugue Tone-bar shook his head. "Amazing, isn't he," he said.

"Oh yeah," I said. "The question is, do you listen to music to be amazed."

He laughed. "I don't know, but the audience thinks so."

"I bet they don't," I said.

This time he didn't laugh. "So did I."

Number Sixteen was leaving the stage and being replaced by Number Seventeen. That meant we wouldn't be on for an hour or so. I wished we were going on sooner; all the excitement I had felt was slowly collecting into a tense knot below my diaphragm. And I could see signs of the same thing happening to the others. Not Crazy; he was still rowdy as ever; he was marching about the room with his tuba, blasting it in the technicians' ears and annoying as many people as possible. But I had seen Fingers wandering toward the piano, undoubtedly planning to join Hook and Crazy in the phrases they were working on; some character wrapped in purple-and-blue sheets sat down just ahead of him and began to play some fast complicated stuff, classical probably, with big dramatic hand-over-hands all up and down the keys. Fingers turned around and sat back down, hands hidden in his lap, and watched the guy play; and when the guy got up Fingers just sat there, looking down at his lap like he hadn't noticed.

And Sidney got quieter and quieter. He stared up at the video and watched a quartet of people fidget around a big box that they all played together, and as he stared he sank into his chair and closed around his clarinet. He was getting scared again. All the excitement and energy the band had generated on the trip over had disappeared, leaving only Washboard's insistent tapping and Crazy's crazy antics, which were gaining us more and more enemies among the other performers.

While I was still wondering what to do about this (because I felt like I was at least as scared as Sidney) Crazy made his way back to our corner of the room, did a quick side shuffle, and slammed into another musician.

"Hey!" Crazy yelled. "Watch it!"

I groaned. The guy he had knocked over was dressed in some material that shifted color when he moved; he had been making loud comments about us from the practice rooms ever since we had arrived. Now he got his footing and carefully lifted his instrument (a long many-keyed brass box that turned one arm back into itself) from the floor.

"You stupid, clumsy, drunken oaf," he said evenly.

"Hey," Crazy said, ignoring the description, "what's that you got there?"

"Ignorant fool," the musician said. "It's a Klein synthesizer, an instrument beyond your feeble understanding."

"Oh yeah?" Crazy said. "Sounds a little one-sided to me." He burst out laughing.

"It is unfortunate," the other replied, "that the Blakely Foundation finds it necessary to exhibit even the most *atavistic* forms of music at this circus." He turned and stalked over to the piano.

"Atavistic!" Crazy repeated, looking at us. "What's that mean?"

I shrugged. "It means primitive," said Tone-bar. Hook started to laugh.

"Primitive!" Crazy bellowed. "I'm going to go hit that guy and let him think it over." He turned to follow the musician, tuba still in his arms; and before anyone could move, he missed the step down and crashed to the floor, as loud as fifty cymbals all hit at once.

We leaped over and pulled the tuba off him. It was hardly dented; somehow he had twisted so it fell mostly on him.

"You okay?" Hook said anxiously, pushing back the rest of us. From somewhere in the room there was a laugh.

Crazy didn't move. We stood around him. "God damn it," Hook said, "the bastard is out cold." He looked like he wanted to kick him.

"And look!" Sidney said, lifting Crazy's left arm carefully. Right behind his hand (his fingering hand) was a bluish lump that stretched his skin tight. "He's hurt that wrist bad," Sidney said. "He's out of it."

"Fuck," Hook said quietly. I sat down beside him, stunned by our bad luck. There was a crowd gathered around us but I didn't pay them any attention. I watched Crazy's wrist swell out to the same width as his hand; that was our whole story, right there. We'd put him on stage in a lot of strange conditions before, but a man can't play without his fingering hand. . . .

"Hey, Wright is here today," Tone-bar said. He was frowning with what looked like real concern. "Doesn't he know some old jazz?" None of us answered him. "No, seriously," he said. "This kid Wright is an absolute genius, he'll probably be able to fill in for you." Still none of us spoke. "Well, I know where his box is," he finally continued. "I'll try to find him." He worked his way through the crowd and hurried out the door.

I sat there, feeling the knot in my stomach become a solid bar, and watched a few of the stagehands lift Crazy up and carry him out. We were beat before we began. You can play jazz without a tuba player—we had often had to—but the trombone has to take a lot of the bass line, nobody can be as free with the rhythm, the sound is tinny, there's no power to it, there's no *bottom!* Sidney looked over at Hook and said, with a sort of furtive relief, "Well, you said we didn't have a chance," but Hook just shook his head, eyes glistening, and said quietly, "I wanted to show 'em."

I sat and wondered if I was going to be sick. Crazy had crazied us right back to the rocks, and on top of my knotted stomach my heart pounded loud and slow as if saying "ka-Doom, ka-Doom, ka-DOOM." I thought of all the stories I'd heard of Vesta, the barren graveyard of the asteroids, and hoped I didn't live long enough to be sent there.

There was a long silence. None of us moved. The other performers circled about as quietly, making sure not to look at us. Slowly, very slowly, Sidney began to pull apart his clarinet.

"I got him!" came a wild voice. "He can do it!" Tone-bar came flying in the door, pulling a skinny kid by the arm. He halted and the kid slammed into his back. With a grin Tone-bar stepped aside and waved an arm.

"Perhaps the finest musician of our—" he began, but the kid interrupted him:

"I hear you need a tuba man," he said and stepped

forward. He was a few years younger than me even, and the grin on his adolescent face looked like it was clamped over a burst of laughter. When he pushed all his long black tangles of hair back I saw that the pupils of his eyes were flinching wildly just inside the line of the irises; he was clearly spaced, probably had never seen a tuba before.

"Come on, man," I said. "Where did you learn to play jazz tuba?"

"Pluto," he said, and laughed.

I stared at him. I couldn't believe it. As far as I knew, Dixieland jazz was only played in the bars on Jupiter Metals' rocks; I would have bet I knew, or knew of, every Dixieland musician alive. And this kid didn't come from the mines. He was too skinny, too sharp-edged, he didn't have the look.

"I didn't even know anyone played traditional jazz anymore," he said. "I thought I was the only one."

"I don't believe it," I said.

"We don't got a whole lot of choice, Shaky, we're running out of time," said Hook. "Hey kid—you know 'Panama'?"

"Sure," he said, and sang the opening bars. "Bum-bum, da da da-da, da da-da-da da."

"Son of a bitch," I said.

"I can do it," the kid said. "I *want* to do it."

"All right," Hook said. "Might as well take him." I looked at Hook in surprise and saw that he was grinning again; clearly there was something about the kid, the intensity of those black-hole eyes perhaps, that had him convinced. He slapped the kid on the shoulder and nearly knocked him down. "Come on!" he shouted. "Time to go!"

"Time to go!" I cried. "What the hell happened to Number seventeen?"

"They getting off! Let's go play!"

And the stagehands were already carrying stuff for us, watching the kid and gabbling excitedly.

"Shit," I exclaimed, and stuck my hand out to the kid. We shook. "Welcome to the Hot Six. Solos all sixteen bars, including yours if you want, choruses and refrains all repeated, don't worry about the tags; we'll have to stick to the old songs, do you know 'St. Louis Blues'? 'That's a Plenty'? 'Didn't He Ramble'? 'Milenburg Joys'? 'Mahogany Hall Stomp'? 'Want a Big Butter-and-Egg Man'? 'Ain't You Coming Back to Dixieland'?" and, miraculously, he kept yelling "Yes! Yes! Yes!" as he struggled with the tuba, still almost laughing, and then we were in the hall and didn't have time for any more—

We got out on stage and it was hot as a smelting chamber. The audience was just a blue-black blur outside the lights, which were glaring down exactly like the arc lamps set around a tunnel end. I could tell seats went way up above us (*they going to be looking down on you*) and then we were all standing there set to go and a big amplified voice said, "*From Jupiter Metals, Pallas, the Hot Six,*" and suddenly we all had our horns to our mouths. I put mine down and said, " 'In the Alley Blues,' " which, amplified, sounded like a single word, then put the horn up and commenced playing.

We sounded horrible. They had indirect mikes on all of us, and just playing normal mezzo forte we were *booming* out into the huge cavern of the auditorium, so we could hear very clearly how bad we sounded. Hook was solid, and so was the kid, which was a relief; but my tone was quivering with just the slightest vibrato, and sometimes I couldn't hear Sidney at all. And his fear was spreading to the rest of us. We knew he had to be petrified to even miss a note.

We brought "In the Alley" to a quick finish, and the applause was *loud*. That made me realize how big the audience was (twenty thousand, Tone-bar said) and I was more scared than ever. I could feel their eyes pressing on me, just like I can sometimes feel the vacuum when I look out a view window. I figured we'd better play one of the best songs next, so we'd get as much help from the material as possible. " 'Weary Blues,' " I said, meaning to say it to the band, since we had planned to play "Ganymede." But the mikes picked me up anyway and I heard "Weary Blues" bounce back out of the cavern, so I just raised my horn to my lips and started; and it was probably two bars before everyone caught on and joined in. That didn't help any.

And I myself was having trouble. The more I could hear the vibrato wavering down the middle of my tone, the worse it got, and the more I could hear it . . . it began to sound like an oscilloscopic saw, and I hoped it wouldn't get out of control and break the tone completely. We got to the refrain, where "Weary" usually starts rolling. I could tell that everyone was so scared they couldn't think about what they were playing, so the notes were coming out right by instinct, but there was no feel in them, it was like they were being played by a music box, every note made by a piece of metal springing loose.

"Weary Blues" ended and again the applause was triple forte. I stepped over to Hook and shouted, under my breath, "Let's do 'I Guess I'll Have to Change My Plans.' " He couldn't hear me, so I said it louder and the mikes caught me, " 'I Guess I'll Have to Change My Plans,' " I announced. There was a long flurry of laughter from the audience. Hook started the intro to "Plans," as calm as though he were playing to a crowded bar. We slid into the song and I realized how much easier it is to play fast when you're nervous. Hook was doing fine, but his backup was trembling, barely hitting the chords. With the leisure of playing accompaniment I could look up and see the silver line of boxes that held our judges, hanging high above us; and that didn't help either.

We moved quickly into "That's a Plenty," and I could tell

we'd calmed down enough to think about the music; after your body pumps full of adrenaline, soaks you in sweat, and shakes you like the ague, there's not much more it can do, you've *got* to calm down some; but that maybe wasn't helping us, since now we had to make the music ourselves, rather than leave it to instinct. I was still shaky enough that when I got to the triple-tonguing in the trumpet break, it actually seemed slow to me, and next time around I fitted in another note, hammering them with two double-tongues. This seemed to perk up the band ("Put chills down my spine," the kid said later), but we still sounded ragged; I knew if we continued like this we were in trouble. And Sidney was still *missing phrases*. I don't think I'd ever heard him miss more than a note or two in my whole life, and here he was squeaking through bars at a time, playing like he had a crimp on his throat.

When we finished the kid waved me over to him. He raised a hand in the air and lowered it, which was apparently the signal needed to get the mike men off us. The kid was completely relaxed. He looked like he was having a good time.

"Your clarinet player is dying," he said. "Does he know 'Burgundy Street Blues'?"

"Sure," I said.

"Maybe you should have him play that. If he had to play a song by himself he'd be sure to calm down some."

I turned around. "Sidney, you ready to play 'Burgundy Street'?"

He shook his head vehemently.

"Come on, Sidney," Hook said from beside him. "That's your song." He turned to the audience, and the kid quickly lifted a hand. " 'The Burgundy Street Blues,' " Hook announced.

Now "Burgundy Street," like "Just a Closer Walk With Thee" or "Bucket's Got a Hole in It," is a single-strain tune, just an eight-bar melody; and it's the variations that a clarinet player works in as he repeats it, again and again, that make the song something special. The first couple of times Sidney went through it, I could barely hear him. He was playing the melody, as simple as possible, and the sound he was making was more breath than tone. I didn't think he'd finish. He shifted toward us as if he wanted to turn his back on the audience, but Hook threw in a couple bars of harmony to bolster him, and when he started the strain a third time he took hold of himself and bore down; and that time, though the notes quivered and never got over pianissimo, he could be heard.

The kid was hopping up and down beside me as if he couldn't wait to start playing again. "Damn that man plays fine clarinet," he whispered to me. Suddenly I realized that if you didn't know Sidney you might think he was playing warbly on purpose, in which case it sounded all right. Apparently this occurred to Sidney too. Each time around he played a little louder, tried a few more variations, gathered a little more confidence. The fifth time around he usually played a variation filled with chromatic runs; he went ahead and tried them, and they came out sharp and well articulated. Amplified like he was, he could hear as clearly as anyone how good he sounded—he was learning what I'd already discovered, that even though you're scared, the notes come out. He began to take advantage of the new acoustics, building up till he filled the auditorium with sound, then dropping back so fast the mike men were lost, and he was as silent as piano keys pushed down.

And as he went on, I could see him begin to forget his surroundings and become what he was, a musician working on the song, putting together phrases, playing with the sounds he could make. His forehead wrinkled and smoothed as he carved an especially difficult passage; he closed his eyes, and the notes took on a life that hadn't been there before. He was lost in it now, completely lost in it, and the last time around he bent the notes like only a fine clarinet player can bend them, soaring them out into the cavern; a sound human and inhuman, music.

When he was done everyone was clapping, even me, and I realized that I had only thought the earlier applause was loud because I'd never heard that many people clap at once before. Now it was louder than when a ship takes off over a tunnel you're in. . . .

We played "Panama" next, and the difference was hard to believe. Sidney was back in form, winding about the upper registers with quick-fingered ingenuity, and as he pulled together so did the band. And the kid, as if he'd only been waiting for Sidney, began to let loose. He'd abandoned his steady *oomph-oomph-oomph-oomph* and was sliding up and down the bass clef, playing like a fourth member of the front line, and *leading* the tempo. Normally I set the tempo, and Crazy and Washboard listen to me and pick it up. But the kid wasn't paying any attention to me; his notes were hitting just a touch ahead of mine, and if there's anyone who can take the tempo away from the trumpet it's the tuba. I tried to play as fast as him but he kept ahead; by the time he let Washboard and me catch up with him we were playing "Panama" faster than we'd *ever* played it, and excited as we were, we were equal to it. When we finished, the applause seemed to push us to the back of the stage.

We played the "St. Louis Blues," and then the "Milenburg Joys," and then "Sweet Georgia Brown," and each time the kid took over, pumping wildly away at the tuba, and pushed us to our limit. Sidney responded like that was the way he'd always wanted to play, arching high wails between phrases and helping the kid to drive us on. And the audience was with us! Maybe the earlier groups had been too modern, maybe too many of them had been playing to the judges; whatever the reason, the audience was with us now. An hour ago none of them had even heard of Dixieland jazz, and now they were cheering after the solos and clapping in the choruses; and we had to start "Sweet Georgia Brown" by playing through the applause.

Then we were set for the finale. *"For all of you music lovers in the house,"* I said, knowing they wouldn't get the reference to Satchmo but saying it anyway, *"we going to beat out* 'The Muskrat Ramble.' "

"The Muskrat Ramble." Our best song, maybe *the* best song. We started up the "Ramble" and the band fell together and meshed like parts of a beautiful machine. All those years of playing in those bars: all the years of getting off work and going down and playing tired, playing with nobody listening but us, playing with nothing to keep us going but the music; all that came from inside us now, in a magic combination of fear, and anger, and the wild exhilaration of knowing we were the best there was at what we were doing. Hook was looping his part below me, Sidney leaping about above, the kid pushing us every note; and to keep up with the weave we were making I had to play hard and fast right down the middle of the song, lifting and growling and breaking my notes off, showing them all that there was a man *working* behind that horn, blowing as clear and sharp and excited as old Dipper-mouth Satchel-mouth Satchmo Louie Louis Daniel Armstrong himself. When we played the final round of the refrain everyone played their solo at once, only Fingers and Washboard held us down at all, and the old "Muskrat Ramble" lifted up and played itself, carrying us along as if it made us and not the other way around. Hook played the trombone coda and we tagged it; then the kid surprised us and repeated the coda, and we barely got our horns back up to tag it again; then we all played the coda and popped it solid, the end.

I motioned the band off. We were done; there was no way we could top that. We started for the wings and the roar of the audience soared up to a gooseflesh howl. We hurried off, waving our arms and shouting as loud as anyone there, jumping up and down and slapping each other on the back, chased by a wall of sound that shook the building.

We waited; tired, happy, tense, we waited:

And God damn me if we didn't win one of those grants, a four-year tour of the Solar System; oh, we leaped about that waiting room and shouted and hit each other; Fingers and Washboard marched about singing and smashing out rhythms on the walls and furniture; Hook stood on a table and sprayed champagne on us; the kid rolled on the floor and laughed and laughed, "Now you're in for it," he choked out, "you're in for it now!" but we didn't know what he meant then, we just poured champagne on his head and laughed at him, even old Sidney was jumping up and down, wisps of hair flying over his ears, singing (I'd never heard him sing) a scat solo he was making up as he went along, shouting it out while tears and champagne ran down his face:

"bo bo de zed,
we leaving the tunnels!
woppity bip,
we going to see Earth!
yes we (la da de dip)
going (ze be de be dop)
home!"

—1975

Stone Eggs

Tom Finn got on the Greyhound bus intending never to get off. He had purchased a month pass in Chicago and gotten on bus 782. He planned to take the southern route to California, go up the Pacific coast, back to the Great Lakes, and on to New England. Or wherever. When he bought the next pass he would think about it.

In the bus it was cool. The air from the vent played on his arm. All the windows except the windshield were tinted dark green, polarizing the light and reducing the outside world to a wash of grays. Tom liked it that way.

They stopped in the run-down parts of towns where the bus depots were, to change passengers and eat meals. Joplin, Missouri; Tulsa, Oklahoma; Amarillo, Texas. Half an hour for lunch, an hour for dinner. He fell into the routine with relief.

He got on a New York-to-Los Angeles bus, and a group of passengers stayed on it for two or three days. He watched them as they lived their lives on the bus, talking and getting to know each other. Finn never introduced himself to anyone, or talked. At night people slumped in their seats, unselfconsciously sleeping. Some kept on their little overhead lights and talked all night long. Tom Finn could not sleep in a sitting position, so at night he unobtrusively crawled under his seat and slept curled on the floor, using his tennis shoes for a pillow. It was comfortable enough. In the mornings he scrambled up onto his seat and stared back at the few bleary-eyed strangers who were awake at dawn. A thin-faced young black man. A girl with stringy hair and dirty clothes. An old couple. The poor, in all their variety. . . . Then back to the little toilet room, which grew more fetid by the hour.

As they crossed New Mexico he looked out at the parched gray land, dozed, observed the occupants of the seat ahead of him. A fat young woman struggled vainly to control her four sons, slapping them and threatening them with worse. The boys—aged eight, seven, four, and one, Finn guessed—ignored her, except for the infant, who cried or slept or sucked a bottle. The mother had scarcely slept in the three days Finn had sat behind her. He watched the oldest son, who tormented the four-year-old incessantly, and wondered if the boy was naturally evil or if his meanness was the result of his upbringing. Naturally evil? . . . The boy would grow up to be a runaway, he thought. Finn was a runaway.

That evening the bus pulled off Highway 8, in the south Arizona desert, for a dinner stop. The offramp circled down to a road that stretched off into the desert to the north and extended to the south no farther than a small group of buildings just off the freeway. Approaching the group of buildings, Tom read a sign: DATELAND RESTAURANT, POST OFFICE, AND CURIO SHOP.

He joined the file of people getting off the bus. "One hour, now," the bus driver said. Although it was nearly dusk the air was still hot and dry. Finn walked across the gravel parking lot to the door of the café. There were two middle-aged men sitting at the counter. All the booths were empty. The waitresses were talking to each other. Tom saw that it was yet another restaurant that could not survive without its Greyhound concession. He sat in one of the booths, and a waitress took his order. He ordered a hamburger, fries, and a Coke. While he waited he flipped through the selections listed in his table jukebox console. Country-western, old rock and roll, songs in Spanish. Behind him sat the mother and her four boys. "Stop that. Stop that or I'll hit you in front of everybody." When his food came he ate quickly, paid his bill and left.

The main building was in the shape of an L; the long side was the café, the short side was the curio shop. Finn walked over to the curio shop, thinking to get out of the heat. Beside the door was a thermometer in an old tin Coca-Cola sign. It read 104 degrees. He went into the shop.

Quite a few people from the bus were already there, wandering about. Tom did the same. The curio shop offered for sale string ties with clasps made of clear plastic that held embalmed scorpions; cactus-growing kits; postcards with pictures of donkeys and cactus flowers and Jackalopes; turquoise rings, the turquoise white and cracked; candy in yellowed cellophane; and stone eggs. Everything in the shop had obviously been there for years and years; all those chill air-conditioned days and long hot nights had desiccated every item. No one from the bus was buying anything. The cashier stared out the window. It reminded Finn of things he could not afford to think of, and feeling that he might scream, or start to cry, he left the shop.

The heat outside relaxed him. The sun was about to set. Behind Dateland there was an old road leading off over a hill to the east. Finn began to walk on it. He was fascinated by the thin roads, asphalt or gravel or dirt, that crisscrossed the great American desert. He had seen a lot of them from the bus. Who had built them, and when? It was easy to imagine Interstate 8 being built: hundreds of men, huge yellow bulldozers and earthmovers, a whole community, moving along through the desert and excreting the highway behind it. But what about these little roads, stretching from nowhere to nowhere under the broiling sun? Finn couldn't imagine their construction. He stared down at the faded, cracked asphalt as he walked. Sand silted over the edges of the road. It could have been built a thousand years ago. These are the ruins of the twentieth century, he thought. Already here.

The road ended in a settlement of foundations. Rectangles of cement, half covered by sand, with fixture pipes rusting through at one corner of each foundation. The sun was below the hill now, and the settlement was in shadow. It was still very hot. Finn walked around the area, looking at the cement and the dry grass that had overgrown it and died. Wind gusted through the shadows, rustling the grass. In the east the sky was a deep blue.

Eventually he sat down on a concrete block and let the desert fill him. Occasionally the faint diesel roar of a truck wafted over from the interstate to the north. In the western sky the evening star appeared. This was his life, Tom Finn thought, this desert, this community in ruins before it had ever been occupied. . . . Through his tears it seemed the homes that somebody had planned to put there did indeed stand, as clear glass houses that revealed everything about their owners, brittle things that could be shattered with a blink of the eye. And each blink brought the houses crashing to the ground, and the faint stars with them so that they should have been great pyres burning around him on the desert floor.

Then the evening star dropped like a stone over the western horizon, and it didn't come back no matter how hard Finn blinked. As if it had been a meteor. Just a shooting star, Finn thought. But fear rustled through him like the wind, and he got up and walked quickly back over the old abandoned road. Something had happened. . . .

From the hill he could see the back of Dateland. The

parking lot was empty. Finn cursed out loud. He had missed the bus! Sitting out there thinking about his mess of a life he had missed his bus. He hurried down the hill, cursing still. He would have to wait in that café for the next bus, and call ahead to get the Greyhound people to recover his suitcase. Damn it! Hadn't the bus driver counted his passengers? Had no one noticed his absence?

But when he got to the building, he forgot his anger.

Dateland was empty. Boarded up, faded, sand-drifted, empty.

The sun had been down for a while now, and Finn found himself shivering. Absently he walked over to look at the thermometer by the curio-shop door; it was broken. He turned the doorknob and pushed the door in; a gust of wind pulled it out of his hand, and it hit the counter inside with a wooden *thwack*. Finn stuck his head in the door and looked around, afraid to enter. Everything in the curio shop was the same, except dustier. A handful of Jackalope postcards tumbled to the floor, caught by the wind, and Finn jumped back with his heart racing.

It took all his courage to open the door to the café. It too was deserted. Parts of it had been removed: the jukeboxes, the kitchen fixtures, the drink machines. The vinyl booth seats were cracked like dried mud. Overcome by sudden terror, Finn rushed out of the café to the safety of the gravel parking lot. But it was getting dark; the vast network of stars revealed itself; Dateland stood behind him dark and empty, like a house in a child's nightmare. He shivered uncontrollably. The dry wind made little noises against the building. A loose plank somewhere slapped woodenly a few times. He was afraid. "What's going on here?" he cried out miserably. No answer but wind.

He ran up the road to the freeway onramp. The spare concrete of Interstate 8 was tremendously reassuring. Nothing there had changed. The highway was empty in both directions, but that was not unusual. He walked up the onramp until he was out on the westbound lanes, ready to stop the next car that came by. He could just see Dateland over the shoulder of the eastbound lanes, a dark mass in the starlit desert sand.

Hours passed, and no cars drove by. He was frightened again. It got colder, and he sat on the blacktop edging the white concrete of the lanes, where it was still warm with the day's heat.

Then to the east he saw headlights approaching, and he jumped up stiffly, adrenaline pumping up his heartbeat. "Now stop," he muttered, "please stop, please stop, please stop. . . ."

Just before they would have reached him the lights slowed, turned on the big circular offramp leading down to Dateland. It was a Greyhound bus.

He ran down the onramp and along the road back to Dateland. Another bus! His pass was still in his pocket. . . .

The bus was pulling back out of the parking lot when he ran up. "*Wait,*" he screamed, the word torn out of him like no other had ever been in his life. The headlights caught him for a moment, the bus stopped, the door at the front *whooshed* open.

He jumped onto the first step, grabbed the chrome handrail and pulled himself up the steps to the main aisle. There was only one passenger on the bus, an old woman sitting in the seat behind the driver. The driver looked up at him. "Sit down," he said. "Can't go until you sit down."

Finn sat in the front seat, across from the old woman and the driver. He felt his bus pass in his pocket; but the driver was turning onto the onramp, oblivious to him. He sat back, happy to be leaving Dateland. Yet he was afraid to ask the two people across from him what they knew of it.

"So you found a new doctor, eh?" the driver said when they were on the freeway and up to speed. He was looking in his mirror at the old woman.

"Yes, I did," she replied. "The best you can find, these days anyway. A Jack Mathewson, from Gila Bend. Trained by Westinghouse. He says he'll replace the pivot in my lower back with a new part made by G.E."

"That might work," the driver said. "Got a G.E. pivot myself."

Tom Finn, pressed back against his window, stared at the two people across from him. The old woman . . . her eyes were glass. The bus passed under a light over the freeway, and he saw that her skin was some kind of plastic. He tried to control his breathing. . . .

"The plain fact is," the old woman-thing said, "it's hell to grow old. Nothing to be done about it."

"Nope," the driver agreed.

"Forty-seven years as a librarian, and me with a bad back. Sometimes you wonder why we were designed to feel pain at all."

"Keeps us alive."

"*I* think it was because people didn't want us to have any advantages," she said, looking for an instant at Finn. "Ah, well. All of my typemates dead and gone for years now. And Westinghouse has no more parts for my type, they say."

"G.E. parts are just as good. But I know what you mean. All my typemates are gone too. Last century was the good one for simulacra."

"Don't you know it!"

Tom Finn got up unsteadily and walked down the aisle to the back of the bus, thinking that he might throw up in the toilet. But when he got to the door, he couldn't bring himself to open it; he imagined looking into the coppery mirror and seeing his reflection grin at him with steel teeth—imagined unzipping, and finding only smooth metal. Had he always been a machine, and only dreamed, out there in the desert, of being something else? For a long time he stood there swaying with the bus. A part of his mind noticed that the bus's engine didn't sound like the old piston-driven ones used to. The *old* piston-driven ones? Furtively he looked up the bus at the two figures, still talking in low tones. Something had happened, back there at Dateland . . . he couldn't bear to look down at himself. After a while he forced himself (for the sake of appearances! he thought) to return to the front of the bus. He watched the simulacra talking to each other, and listened to their words for a long time, wondering how to ask what year it was. Finally exhaustion overcame him and he was lulled to sleep by their voices and the hum of the bus.

He was awakened by the sound of the bus downshifting. They were on the curve of another offramp. He jerked up and looked around. They were still in the desert; it was light, just before sunrise. Just off the freeway was their destination, another little isolated café. Finn saw the sign on the building and felt faint; DATELAND RESTAURANT, POST OFFICE, AND CURIO SHOP.

"Isn't this where I got on?" he croaked, his mouth dry with sleep and fear. They were the first words he had spoken since getting on the bus.

The driver turned his plastic head (it was obvious in the dawn) to glance at him, and laugh. "You think I drive this bus in circles? We're west of Yuma now. There's lots of places that look like that in this desert."

The old woman was asleep, or turned off, still upright in her seat across from Finn. Finn felt his own pump hammering the fluids through him, and all of a sudden it was too much. He gave in to it.

Without thinking he got off the bus when it stopped. Walked over to the door of the curio shop. Without surprise he registered the fact that the bus was driving off, back to the freeway. The thermometer by the door was still broken, the paint on the tin almost gone. It still read 104. He opened the door and walked inside the curio shop. All the goods were still there, safe and untouched, covered with dust. Finn swallowed hard. There was something about the place, something he had sensed when he first entered it so many years ago. . . .

The sun broke over the horizon, flooding the shop with dusty white light. Behind the cashier's booth there was a closet. In it he found a broom and a feather duster, and he went to work cleaning up. All of the arrowheads, the turquoise and onyx and malachite rings, the cactus-growing kits, the postcards, the stone eggs. All as clean as new.

A couple of hours later he stood, sweaty and grimy, in a clean and orderly curio shop. White dust motes like talcum swirled in the air, made bright and palpable by the low morning sun. He walked outside into the fresh air, which was still cool. Glancing in the café door, he shook his head; he'd have to attend to that later.

Another Greyhound swooped down the circular offramp. He hurried back to the curio-shop door. Maybe somebody would buy something. Nervously he watched as people stepped down from the bus. Some of them walked toward cars that Finn had assumed were wrecks, on the other side of the gravel lot; they drove away to the north, under the freeway and out of sight. But several more, observing him standing in the shop doorway, approached the shop. Finn stepped back inside, to clear the entrance.

One by one they filed past. "Opening the old place up again, eh?" a man said.

"Yes," Finn replied, and cleared his throat. "I'm going to give it a try." He stared at the man. In the klieg-light glare of the horizontal sun the man's blue eyes were quite clearly glass. But that look on his face, that curiosity . . . Finn blinked and the man blinked too, and Finn saw the film of tears and the tiny red veins. An iris could look like crystal from some angles, he knew that. . . . Eventually Finn shook himself and followed the man in. He couldn't tell. He didn't care.

"Oh, look," a young woman said to her companion, an older woman.

"That would look nice in your room," the older woman said. Finn could hear the years in her voice, and he was reminded of the old woman on his bus.

"I want this," the young woman said to Finn. "How much is it?"

She held out one of the stone eggs. He took it from her cool hand. It was smooth and brown, mottled by black cracking deep in the stone. Finn looked around: no cash register.

"Um," he said, feeling in his pockets for change. "A dollar."

"Sold," she said, and laughed. The old woman smiled. While the young woman fumbled in her pocketbook, Finn cleaned the egg one last time with a rag he had found under a counter.

"You have to be careful with these," he warned her. "They're lighter than they look. And fragile? They'd break like glass if you dropped one."

"I'll remember." She handed him a dollar. George Washington still on the front, he saw. "Where are you living?"

"Well . . ." The men examining the postcards swiveled their heads to hear his answer. "There's some old foundations over the hill to the east. I'm going to set up out there."

"We live on the other side of the freeway; you should come visit."

"I will."

Then they trailed out of the shop, talking and leaving great swirls in the mote-coned morning air. Finn watched them from the doorway; they all balanced with unnatural carefulness across the gravel. He shrugged. When they were all gone, out of sight under the freeway, he went back inside. He would have to find a cash register, and start the air conditioner up again. He straightened up the postcards. Rearranged the stone eggs. After breakfast he would walk up the narrow road to the north.

—1979

Black Air 

They sailed out of Lisbon harbor with the flags snapping and the brass culverins gleaming under a high white sun, priests proclaiming in sonorous Latin the blessing of the Pope, soldiers in armor jammed on the castles fore and aft, and sailors spiderlike in the rigging, waving at the citizens of the town who had left their work to come out on the hills and watch the ships crowd out the sunbeaten roads, for this was the Armada, the Most Fortunate Invincible Armada, off to subjugate the heretic English to the will of God. There would never be another departure like it.

Unfortunately, the wind blew out of the northeast for a month after they left without shifting even a point on the compass, and at the end of that month the Armada was no closer to England than Iberia itself. Not only that, but the hard-pressed coopers of Portugal had made many of the Armada's casks of green wood, and when the ship's cooks opened them the meat was rotten and the water stank. So they trailed into the port of Corunna, where several hundred soldiers and sailors swam to the shores of Spain and were never seen again. A few hundred more had already died of disease, so from his sickbed on the flagship Don Alonso Perez de Guzman el Bueno, seventh Duke of Medina Sidonia and Admiral of the Armada, interrupted the composition of his daily complaint to Philip the Second, and instructed his soldiers to go out into the countryside and collect peasants to help man the ships.

One squad of these soldiers stopped at a Franciscan monastery on the outskirts of Corunna, to impress all the boys who lived there and helped the monks, waiting to join the order themselves. Although they did not like it the monks could not object to the proposal, and off the boys went to join the fleet.

Among these boys, who were each taken to a different ship, was Manuel Carlos Agadir Tetuan. He was seventeen years old; he had been born in Morocco, the son of West Africans who had been captured and enslaved by Arabs. In his short life he had already lived in the Moroccan coastal town of Tetuan, in Gibraltar, the Balearics, Sicily, and Lisbon. He had worked in fields and cleaned stables, he had helped make rope and later cloth, and he had served food in inns. After his mother died of the pox and his father drowned, he had begged in the streets and alleys of Corunna, the last port his father had sailed out of, until in his fifteenth year a Franciscan had tripped over him sleeping in an alley, inquired after him, and taken him to the refuge of the monastery.

Manuel was still weeping when the soldiers took him aboard *La Lavia*, a Levantine galleon of nearly a thousand tons. The sailing master of the ship, one Laeghr, took him in charge and led him below decks. Laeghr was an Irishman, who had left his country principally to practice his trade, but also out of hatred of the English who ruled Ireland. He was a huge man with a torso like a boar's, and arms as thick as the yardarms of the ship. When he saw Manuel's distress he showed that he was not without kindness; clapping a callused hand to the back of Manuel's neck he said, in accented but fluent Spanish, "Stop your snivelling, boy, we're off to conquer the damned English, and when we do your fathers at the monastery will make you their abbot. And before that happens a dozen English girls will fall at your feet and ask for the touch of those black hands, no doubt. Come on, stop it. I'll show you your berth first, and wait till we're at sea to show you your station. I'm going to put you in the main top, all our blacks are good topmen."

Laeghr slipped through a door half his height with the ease of a weasel ducking into one of its tiny holes in the earth. A hand half as wide as the doorway reemerged and pulled Manuel into the gloom. The terrified boy nearly fell down a broad-stepped ladder, but caught himself before falling onto Laeghr. Far below several soldiers laughed at him. Manuel had never been on anything larger than a Sicilian pataches, and most of his fairly extensive seagoing experience was of coastal carracks, so the broad deck under him, cut by bands of yellow sunlight that flowed in at open ports big as church windows, crowded with barrels and bales of hay and tubs of rope, and a hundred busy men, was a marvel. "Saint Anna save me," he said, scarcely able to believe he was on a ship. Why, the monastery itself had no room as large as the one he descended into now. "Get down here," Laeghr said in an encouraging way.

Once on the deck of that giant room they descended again, to a stuffy chamber a quarter the size, illuminated by narrow fans of sunlight that were let in by ports that were mere slits in the hull. "Here's where you sleep," Laeghr said, pointing at a dark corner of the deck, against one massive oak wall of the ship. Forms there shifted, eyes appeared as lids lifted, a dull voice said, "Another one you'll never find again in this dark, eh master?"

"Shut up, Juan. See boy, there are beams dividing your berth from the rest, that will keep you from rolling around when we get to sea."

"Just like a coffin, with the lid up there."

"Shut up, Juan."

After the sailing master had made clear which slot in particular was Manuel's, Manuel collapsed in it and began to cry again. The slot was shorter than he was, and the dividing boards set in the deck were cracked and splintered. The men around him slept, or talked among themselves, ignoring Manuel's presence. His medallion cord choked him, and he shifted it on his neck and remembered to pray.

His guardian saint, the monks had decided, was Anne, mother of the Virgin Mary and grandmother of Jesus. He owned a small wooden medallion with her face painted on it, which Abbot Alonso had given to him. Now he took the medallion between his fingers, and looked in the tiny brown dots that were the face's eyes. "Please, Mother Anna," he prayed silently, "take me from this ship to my home. Take me home." He clenched the tag in his fist so tightly that the back of it, carved so that a cross of wood stood out from its surface, left an imprinted red cross in his palm. Many hours passed before he fell asleep.

Two days later the Most Fortunate Invincible Armada left Corunna, this time without the flags, or the crowds of spectators, or the clouds of priestly incense trailing downwind. This time God favored them with a westerly wind, and they sailed north at good speed. The ships were arranged in a formation devised by the soldiers, orderly phalanxes rising and falling on the swells: the galleasses in front, the supply hulks in the center, and the big galleons on either flank. The thousands of sails stacked on hundreds of masts made a grand and startling sight, like a copse of white trees on a broad blue plain.

Manuel was as impressed by the sight as the rest of the men. There were four hundred men on *La Lavia*, and only thirty were needed at any one time to sail the ship, so all of the three hundred soldiers stood on the sterncastle observing the fleet, and the sailors who were not on duty or sleeping did the same on the slightly lower forecastle.

Manuel's duties as a sailor were simple. He was stationed at the port midships taffrail, to which were tied the sheets for the port side of the mainmast's sails, and the sheets for the big lateen-rigged sail of the foremast. Manuel helped five other men pull these ropes in or let them out, following Laeghr's instructions; the other men took care of the belaying knots, so Manuel's job came down to pulling on a rope when told to. It could have been more difficult, but Laeghr's plan to make him a topman like the other Africans aboard had come to grief. Not that Leaghr hadn't tried. "God made you Africans with a better head for heights, so you can climb trees to keep from being eaten by lions, isn't that right?" But when Manuel had followed a Moroccan named Habedeen up the halyard ladder to the main top, he found himself plunging about space, nearly scraping low foggy clouds, and the sea, embroidered with the wakes of the ships ahead, was more often than not *directly below him*. He had clamped, arms and legs, around a stanchion of the main top, and it had taken five men, laughing and cursing, to pry him loose and pull him down. With rich disgust, but no real physical force, Laeghr had pounded him with his cane and shoved him to the port taffrail. "You must be a Sicilian with a sunburn." And so he had been assigned his station.

Despite this incident he got on well with the rest of the crew. Not with the soldiers; they were rude and arrogant to the sailors, who stayed out of their way to avoid a curse or a blow. So three-quarters of the men aboard were of a different class, and remained strangers. The sailors therefore hung together. They were a mongrel lot, drawn from all over the Mediterranean, and Manuel was not unusual because of his recent arrival. They were united only in their dislike and resentment of the soldiers. "Those heroes wouldn't be able to conquer the Isle of Wight if we didn't sail them there,'' Juan said.

Manuel became acquainted first with the men at his post, and then with the men in his berth. As he spoke Spanish and Portuguese, and fair amounts of Arabic, Sicilian, Latin, and a Moroccan dialect, he could converse with everyone in his corner of the lower foredeck. Occasionally he was asked to translate for the Moroccans; more than once this meant he was the arbiter of a dispute, and he thought fast and mistranslated whenever it would help make peace. Juan, the one who had made the bitter comments to Laeghr on Manuel's arrival, was the only pure Spaniard in the berth. He loved to talk, and complained to Manuel and the others continuously. ''I've fought *El Draco* before, in the Indies,'' he boasted. ''We'll be lucky to get past that devil. You mark my words, we'll never do it.''

Manuel's mates at the main taffrail were more cheerful, and he enjoyed his watches with them and the drills under Laeghr's demanding instruction. These men called him Topman or Climber, and made jokes about his knots around the belaying pins, which defied quick untying. This inability earned Manuel quite a few swats from Laeghr's cane, but there were worse sailors aboard, and the sailing master seemed to bear him no ill will.

A life of perpetual change had made Manuel adaptable, and shipboard routine became for him the natural course of existence. Laeghr or Pietro, the leader at Manuel's station, would wake him with a shout. Up to the gundeck, which was the domain of the soldiers, and from there up the big ladder that led to fresh air. Only then could Manuel be sure of the time of day. For the first week it was an inexpressible delight to get out of the gloom of the lower decks and under the sky, in the wind and clean salt air; but as they proceeded north, it began to get too cold for comfort. After their watches were over, Manuel and his mates would retire to the galley and be given their biscuits, water and wine. Sometimes the cooks killed some of the goats and chickens and made soup. Usually, though, it was just biscuits, biscuits that had not yet hardened in their barrels. The men complained grievously about this.

"The biscuits are best when they're hard as wood, and bored through by worms," Habedeen told Manuel.

"How do you eat it then?" Manuel asked.

"You bang pieces of biscuit against the table until the worms fall out. You eat the worms if you want." The men laughed, and Manuel assumed Habedeen was joking, but he wasn't certain.

"I despise this doughy shit," Pietro said in Portuguese. Manuel translated into Moroccan Arabic for the two silent Africans, and agreed in Spanish that it was hard to stomach. "The worst part," he offered, "is that some parts are stale while others are still fresh."

"The fresh part was never cooked."

"No, that's the worms."

As the voyage progressed, Manuel's berthmates became more intimate. Farther north the Moroccans suffered terribly from the cold. They came belowdecks after a watch with their dark skins completely goose-pimpled, like little fields of stubble after a harvest. Their lips and fingernails were blue, and they shivered an hour before falling asleep, teeth chattering like the castanets in a fiesta band. Not only that, but the swells of the Atlantic were getting bigger, and the men, since they were forced to wear every scrap of clothing they owned, rolled in their wooden berths unpadded and unprotected. So the Moroccans, and then everyone in the lower foredeck, slept three to a berth, taking turns in the middle, huddling together like spoons. Crowded together like that the pitching of the ship could press them against the beams, but it couldn't roll them around. Manuel's willingness to join these bundlings, and to lie against the beams, made him well-liked. Everyone agreed he made a good cushion.

Perhaps it was because of his hands that he fell ill. Though his spirit had been reconciled to the crusade north, his flesh was slower. Hauling on the coarse hemp ropes every day had ripped the skin from his palms, and salt, splinters, belaying pins and the odd boot had all left their marks as well, so that after the first week he had wrapped his hands in strips of cloth torn from the bottom of his shirt. When he became feverish, his hands pulsed painfully at every nudge from his heart, and he assumed that the fever had entered him through the wounds in his palms.

Then his stomach rebelled, and he could keep nothing down. The sight of biscuits or soup revolted him; his fever worsened, and he became parched and weak; he spent a lot of time in the head, wracked by dysentery. "You've been poisoned by the biscuits," Juan told him. "Just like I was in the Indies. That's what comes of boxing fresh biscuits. They might as well have put fresh dough in those barrels."

Manuel's berthmates told Laeghr of his condition, and Laeghr had him moved to the hospital, which was at the stern of the ship on a lower deck, in a wide room that the sick shared with the rudder post, a large smoothed tree trunk thrusting through floor and ceiling. All of the other men were gravely ill. Manuel was miserable as they laid him down on his pallet, wretched with nausea and in great fear of the hospital, which smelled of putrefaction. The man on the pallet next to him was insensible, and rolled with the sway of the ship. Three candle lanterns lit the low chamber and filled it with shadows. One of the Dominican friars, a Friar Lucien, gave him hot water and wiped his face. They talked for a while, and the friar heard Manuel's confession, which only a proper priest should have done. Neither of them cared. The priests on board avoided the hospital, and tended to serve only the officers and the soldiers. Friar Lucien was known to be willing to minister to the sailors, and he was popular among them.

Manuel's fever got worse, and he could not eat. Days passed, and when he woke up the men around him were not the same men who had been there when he fell asleep. He became convinced he was going to die, and once again he felt despair that he had been made a member of the Most Fortunate Invincible Armada. "Why are we here?" he demanded of the friar in a cracked voice. "Why shouldn't we let the English go to hell if they please?"

"The purpose of the Armada is not only to smite the heretic English," said Lucien. He held a candle closer to his book, which was not a Bible, but a slender little thing which he kept hidden in his robes. Shadows leaped on the blackened beams and planks over them, and the rudder post squeaked as it turned against the leather collar in the floor. "God also sent us as a test. Listen:

" 'I assume the appearance of a refiner's fire, purging the dross of forms outworn. This is mine aspect of severity; I am as one who testeth gold in a furnace. Yet when thou hast been tried as by fire, the gold of thy soul shall be cleansed, and visible as fire: then the vision of thy Lord shall be granted unto thee, and seeing Him shall thou behold the shining one, who is thine own true self.'

"Remember that, and be strong. Drink this water here—come on, do you want to fail your God? This is part of the test."

Manuel drank, threw up. His body was no more than a tongue of flame contained by his skin, except where it burst out of his palms. He lost track of the days, and forgot the existence of anyone beyond himself and Friar Lucien. "I never wanted to leave the monastery," he told the friar, "yet I never thought I would stay there long. I've never stayed long any place yet. It was my home but I knew it wasn't. I haven't found my home yet. They say there is ice in England—I saw the snow in the Catalonian mountains, once, Father, will we go home? I only want to return to the monastery and be a father like you."

"We will go home. What you will become, only God knows. He has a place for you. Sleep now. Sleep, now."

By the time his fever broke his ribs stood out from his chest as clearly as the fingers of a fist. He could barely walk. Lucien's narrow face appeared out of the gloom clear as a memory. "Try this soup. Apparently God has seen fit to keep you here."

"Thank you Saint Anna for your intercession," Manuel croaked. He drank the soup eagerly. "I want to return to my berth."

"Soon."

They took him up to the deck. Walking was like floating, as long as he held on to railings and stanchions. Laeghr greeted him with pleasure, as did his stationmates. The world was a riot of blues; waves hissed past, low clouds jostled together in their rush east, tumbling between them shafts of sunlight that spilled onto the water. He was excused from active duty, but he spent as many hours as he could at his station. He found it hard to believe that he had survived his illness. Of course, he was not entirely recovered; he could not yet eat any solids, particularly biscuit, so that his diet consisted of soup and wine. He felt weak, and perpetually light-headed. But when he was on deck in the wind he was sure that he was getting better, so he stayed there as much as possible. He was on deck, in fact, when they first caught sight of England. The soldiers pointed and shouted in great excitement, as the point Laeghr called The Lizard bounced over the horizon. Manuel had grown so used to the sea that the low headland rising off their port bow seemed unnatural, an intrusion into a marine world, as if the deluge was just now receding and these drowned hillsides were just now shouldering up out of the waves, soaking wet and covered by green seaweed that had not yet died. And that was England.

A few days after that they met the first English ships—faster than the Spanish galleons, but much smaller. They could no more impede the progress of the Armada than flies could slow a herd of cows. The swells became steeper and followed each other more closely, and the changed pitching of *La Lavia* made it difficult for Manuel to stand. He banged his head once, and another time ripped away a palmful of scabs, trying to keep his balance in the violent yawing caused by the chop. Unable to stand one morning, he lay in the dark of his berth, and his mates brought him cups of soup. That went on for a long time. Again he worried that he was going to die. Finally Laeghr and Lucien came below together.

"You must get up now," Laeghr declared. "We fight within the hour, and you're needed. We've arranged easy work for you."

"You have only to provide the gunners with slow match," said Friar Lucien as he helped Manuel to his feet. "God will help you."

"God will have to help me," Manuel said. He could see the two men's souls flickering above their heads: little triple knots of transparent flame that flew up out of their hair and lit the features of their faces. "The gold of thy soul shall be cleansed, and visible as fire," Manuel recalled. "Hush," said Lucien with a frown, and Manuel realized that what Lucien had read to him was a secret.

Amidships Manuel noticed that now he was also able to see the air, which was tinged red. They were on the bottom of an ocean of red air, just as they were on top of an ocean of blue water. When they breathed they turned the air a darker red; men expelled plumes of air like horses breathing out clouds of steam on a frosty morning, only the steam was red.

Manuel stared and stared, marveling at the new abilities God had given his sight.

"Here," Laeghr said, roughly directing him across the deck. "This tub of punk is yours. This is slow match, understand?" Against the bulkhead was a tub full of coils of closely braided cord. One end of the cord was hanging over the edge of the tub burning, fizzing the air around it to deep crimson. Manuel nodded: "Slow match."

"Here's your knife. Cut sections about this long, and light them with a piece of it that you keep beside you. Then give sections of it to the gunners who come by, or take it to them if they call for it. But don't give away all your lit pieces. Understand?"

Manuel nodded that he understood and sat down dizzily beside the tub. One of the largest cannon poked through a port in the bulkhead just a few feet from him. Its crew greeted him. Across the deck his stationmates stood at their taffrail. The soldiers were ranked on the fore- and sterncastles, shouting with excitement, gleaming like shellfish in the sun. Through the port Manuel could see some of the English coast.

Laeghr came over to see how he was doing. "Hey, don't you lop your fingers off there, boy. See out there? That's the Isle of Wight. We're going to circle and conquer it, I've no doubt, and use it as our base for our attack on the mainland. With these soldiers and ships they'll *never* get us off that island. It's a good plan."

But things did not progress according to Laeghr's plan. The Armada swung around the east shore of the Isle of Wight, in a large crescent made of five distinct phalanxes of ships. Rounding the island, however, the forward galleasses encountered the stiffest English resistance they had met so far. White puffs of smoke appeared out of the ships and were quickly stained red, and the noise was tremendous.

Then the ships of *El Draco* swept around the southern

point of the island onto their flank, and suddenly *La Lavia* was in the action. The soldiers roared and shot off their arquebuses, and the big cannon beside Manuel leaped back in its truck with a bang that knocked him into the bulkhead. After that he could barely hear. His slow match was suddenly in demand; he cut the cord and held the lit tip to unlit tips, igniting them with his red breath. Cannonballs passing overhead left rippling wakes in the blood air. Grimy men snatched the slow match and dashed to their guns, dodging tackle blocks that thumped to the deck. Manuel could see the cannonballs, big as grapefruit, flying at them from the English ships and passing with a whistle. And he could see the transparent knots of flame, swirling higher than ever about the men's heads.

Then a cannonball burst through the porthole and knocked the cannon off its truck, the men to the deck. Manuel rose to his feet and noticed with horror that the knots of flame on the scattered gunners were gone; he could see their heads clearly now, and they were just men, just broken flesh draped over the plowed surface of the deck. He tried, sobbing, to lift a gunner who was bleeding only from the ears. Laeghr's cane lashed across his shoulders: "Keep cutting match! There's others to attend to these men!" So Manuel cut lengths of cord and lit them with desperate puffs and shaking hands, while the guns roared, and the exposed soldiers on the castles shrieked under a hail of iron, and the red air was ripped by passing shot.

The next few days saw several battles like that as the Armada was forced past the Isle of Wight and up the Channel. His fever kept him from sleeping, and at night Manuel helped the wounded on his deck, holding them down and wiping the sweat from their faces, nearly as delirious as they were. At dawn he ate biscuits and drank his cup of wine and went to his tub of slow match to await the next engagement.

La Lavia, being the largest ship on the left flank, always took the brunt of the English attack. It was on the third day that *La Lavia*'s mainmast topgallant yard fell on his old taffrail crew, crushing Hanan and Pietro. Manuel rushed across the deck to help them, shouting his anguish. He got a dazed Juan down to their berth and returned amidships. Around him men were being dashed to the deck, but he didn't care. He hopped through the red mist that nearly obscured his sight, carrying lengths of match to the gun crews, who were now so depleted that they couldn't afford to send men to him. He helped the wounded below to the hospital, which had truly become an antechamber of hell; he helped toss the dead over the side, croaking a short prayer in every case; he ministered to the soldiers hiding behind the bulwarks of the bulkheads, waiting vainly for the English to get within range of their arquebuses. Now the cry amidships was "Manuel, match here! Manuel, some water! Help, Manuel!" In a dry fever of energy Manuel hurried to their aid.

He was in such perpetual haste that in the middle of a furious engagement he nearly ran into his patroness, Saint Anna, who was suddenly standing there in the corner of his tub. He was startled to see her.

"Grandmother!" he cried. "You shouldn't be here, it's dangerous."

"As you have helped others, I am here to help you," she replied. She pointed across the purplish chop to one of the English ships. Manuel saw a puff of smoke appear from its side, and out of the puff came a cannonball, floating in an arc over the water. He could see it as clearly as he could have seen an olive tossed at him from across a room: a round black ball, spinning lazily, growing bigger as it got closer. Now Manuel could tell that it was coming at him, *directly* at him, so that its trajectory would intersect his heart. "Um, blessed Anna," he said, hoping to bring this to his saint's attention. But she had already seen it, and with a brief touch to his forehead she floated up into the maintop, among the unseeing soldiers. Manuel watched her, eyeing the approaching cannonball at the same time. At the touch of her hand a rigging block fell away from the end of the main yard; it intercepted the cannonball's flight, knocking the ball downward into the hull where it stuck, half embedded in the thick wood. Manuel stared at the black half sphere, mouth open. He waved up at Saint Anna, who waved back and flew up into the red clouds toward heaven. Manuel kneeled and said a prayer of thanks to her and to Jesus for sending her and went back to cutting match.

A night or two later—Manuel himself was not sure, as the passage of time had become for him something plastic and elusive and, more than anything else, meaningless—the Armada anchored at Calais Roads, just off the Flemish coast. For the first time since they had left Corunna *La Lavia* lay still, and listening at night Manuel realized how much the constant chorus of wooden squeaks and groans was the voice of the crew, and not of the ship. He drank his ration of wine and water quickly, and walked the length of the lower deck, talking with the wounded and helping when he could to remove splinters. Many of the men wanted him to touch them, for his safe passage through some of the worst scenes of carnage had not gone unnoticed. He touched them, and when they wanted, said a prayer. Afterwards he went up on deck. There was a fair breeze from the southwest, and the ship rocked ever so gently on the tide. For the first time in a week the air was not suffused red: Manuel could see stars, and distant bonfires on the Flemish shore, like stars that had fallen and now burnt out their life on the land.

Laeghr was limping up and down amidships, detouring from his usual path to avoid a bit of shattered decking.

"Are you hurt, Laeghr?" Manuel inquired.

For answer Laeghr growled. Manuel walked beside him.

After a bit Laeghr stopped and said, "They're saying you're a holy man now because you were running all over the deck these last few days, acting like the shot we were taking was hail and never getting hit for it. But I say you're just too foolish to know any better. Fools dance where angels would hide. It's part of the curse laid on us. Those who learn the rules and play things right end up getting hurt—sometimes from doing just the things that will protect them the most. While the blind fools who wander right into the thick of things are never touched."

Manuel watched Laeghr's stride. "Your foot?"

Laeghr shrugged. "I don't know what will happen to it."

Under a lantern Manuel stopped and looked Laeghr in the eye. "Saint Anna appeared and plucked a cannonball that was heading for me right out of the sky. She saved my life for a purpose."

"No." Laeghr thumped his cane on the deck. "Your fever has made you mad, boy."

"I can show you the shot!" Manuel said. "It stuck in the hull!" Laeghr stumped away.

Manuel looked across the water at Flanders, distressed by Laeghr's words, and by his hobbled walk. He saw something he didn't comprehend.

"Laeghr?"

"What?" came Laeghr's voice from across midships.

"Something bright . . . the souls of all the English at once, maybe. . . ." His voice shook.

"What?"

"Something coming at us. Come here, master."

Thump, thump, thump. Manuel heard the hiss of Laeghr's indrawn breath, the muttered curse.

"Fireships," Laeghr bellowed at the top of his lungs. "Fireships! Awake!"

In a minute the ship was bedlam, soldiers running everywhere. "Come with me," Laeghr told Manuel, who followed the sailing master to the forecastle, where the anchor hawser descended into the water. Somewhere along the way Laeghr had gotten a halberd, and he gave it to Manuel. "Cut the line."

"But master, we'll lose the anchor."

"Those fireships are too big to stop, and if they're hellburners they'll explode and kill us all. Cut it."

Manuel began chopping at the thick hawser, which was very like the trunk of a small tree. He chopped and chopped, but only one strand of the huge rope was cut when Laeghr seized the halberd and began chopping himself, awkwardly to avoid putting his weight on his bad foot. They heard the voice of the ship's captain— "Cut the anchor cable!" And Laeghr laughed.

The rope snapped, and they were floating free. But the fireships were right behind them. In the hellish light Manuel could see English sailors walking about on their burning decks, passing through the flames like salamanders or demons. No doubt they were devils. The fires towering above the eight fireships shared the demonic life of the English; each tongue of yellow flame contained an English demon eye looking for the Armada, and some of these leaped free of the blaze that twisted above the fireships, in vain attempts to float onto *La Lavia* and incinerate it. Manuel held off these embers with his wooden medallion, and the gesture that in his boyhood in Sicily had warded off the evil eye. Meanwhile, the ships of the fleet were cut loose and drifting on the tide, colliding in the rush to avoid the fireships. Captains and officers screamed furiously at their colleagues on other ships, but to no avail. In the dark and without anchors the ships could not be regathered, and as the night progressed most were blown out into the North Sea. For the first time the neat phalanxes of the Armada were broken, and they were never to be reformed again.

*   *   *

When it was all over *La Lavia* held its position in the North Sea by sail, while the officers attempted to identify the ships around them, and find out what Medina Sidonia's orders were. Manuel and Juan stood amidships with the rest of their berthmates. Juan shook his head. "I used to make corks in Portugal. We were like a cork back there in the Channel, being pushed into the neck of a bottle. As long as we were stuck in the neck we were all right—the neck got narrower and narrower, and they might never have gotten us out. Now the English have pushed us right down into the bottle itself. We're floating about in our own dregs. And we'll never get out of the bottle again."

"Not through the neck, anyway," one of the others agreed.

"Not any way."

"God will see us home," Manuel said.

Juan shook his head.

Rather than try to force the Channel, Admiral Medina Sidonia decided that the Armada should sail around Scotland, and then home. Laeghr was taken to the flagship for a day to help chart a course, for he was familiar with the north as none of the Spanish pilots were.

The battered fleet headed away from the sun, ever higher into the cold North Sea. After the night of the fireships Medina Sidonia had restored discipline with a vengeance. One day the survivors of the many Channel battles were witness to the hanging from the yardarm of a captain who had let his ship get ahead of the Admiral's flagship, a position which was now forbidden. A carrack sailed through the fleet again and again so every crew could see the corpse of the disobedient captain, swinging freely from its spar.

Manuel observed the sight with distaste. Once dead, a man was only a bag of bones; nowhere in the clouds overhead could he spot the captain's soul. Perhaps it had plummeted into the sea, on its way to hell. It was an odd transition, death. Curious that God did not make more explicit the aftermath.

So *La Lavia* faithfully trailed the Admiral's flagship, as did the rest of the fleet. They were led farther and farther north, into the domain of cold. Some mornings when they came on deck in the raw yellow of the dawn the riggings would be rimed with icicles, so that they seemed strings of diamonds. Some days it seemed they sailed across a sea of milk, under a silver sky. Other days the ocean was the color of a bruise, and the sky a fresh pale blue so clear that Manuel gasped with the desire to survive this voyage and live. Yet he was as cold as death. He remembered the burning nights of his fever as fondly as if he were remembering his first home on the coast of North Africa.

All the men were suffering from the cold. The livestock was dead, so the galley closed down: no hot soup. The Admiral imposed rationing on everyone, including himself; the deprivation kept him in his bed for the rest of the voyage. For the sailors, who had to haul wet or frozen rope, it was worse. Manuel watched the grim faces, in line for their two biscuits and one large cup of wine and water—their daily ration—and concluded that they would continue sailing north until the sun was under the horizon and they were in the icy realm of death, the north pole where God's dominion was weak, and there they would give up and die all at once. Indeed, the winds drove them nearly to Norway, and it was with great difficulty that they brought the shot-peppered hulks around to a westerly heading.

When they did, they discovered a score of new leaks in *La Lavia*'s hull, and the men, already exhausted by the effort of bringing the ship about, were forced to man the pumps around the clock. A pint of wine and a pint of water a day were not enough. Men died. Dysentery, colds, the slightest injury; all were quickly fatal.

Once again Manuel could see the air. Now it was a thick

blue, distinctly darker where men breathed it out, so that they all were shrouded in dark blue air that obscured the burning crowns of their souls. All of the wounded men in the hospital had died. Many of them had called for Manuel in their last moments; he had held their hands or touched their foreheads, and as their souls had flickered away from their heads like the last pops of flame out of the coals of a dying fire, he had prayed for them. Now other men too weak to leave their berths called for him, and he went and stood by them in their distress. Two of these men recovered from dysentery, so his presence was requested even more frequently. The captain himself asked for Manuel's touch when he fell sick; but he died anyway, like most of the rest.

One morning Manuel was standing with Laeghr at the midships bulkhead. It was chill and cloudy, the sea was the color of flint. The soldiers were bringing their horses up and forcing them over the side, to save water.

"That should have been done as soon as we were forced out of the Sleeve," Laeghr said. "Waste of water."

"I didn't even know we had horses aboard," Manuel said.

Laeghr laughed briefly. "Boy, you are a prize of a fool. One surprise after another."

They watched the horses' awkward falls, their rolling eyes, their flared nostrils expelling clouds of blue air. Their brief attempts to swim.

"On the other hand, we should probably be eating some of those," Laeghr said.

"Horse meat?"

"It can't be that bad."

The horses all disappeared, exchanging blue air for flint water. "It's cruel," Manuel said.

"In the horse latitudes they swim for an hour," Laeghr said. "This is better." He pointed to the west. "See those tall clouds?"

"Yes."

"They stand over the Orkneys. The Orkneys or the Shetlands, I can't be sure anymore. It will be interesting to see if these fools can get this wreck through the islands safely." Looking around, Manuel could only spot a dozen or so ships; presumably the rest of the Armada lay over the horizon ahead of them. He stopped to wonder about what Laeghr had just said, for it would naturally be Laeghr's task to navigate them through the northernmost of the British Isles; at that very moment Laeghr's eyes rolled like the horses' had, and he collapsed on the deck. Manuel and some other sailors carried him down to the hospital.

"It's his foot," said Friar Lucien. "His foot is crushed and his leg has putrefied. He should have let me amputate."

Around noon Laeghr regained consciousness. Manuel, who had not left his side, held his hand, but Laeghr frowned and pulled it away.

"Listen," Laeghr said with difficulty. His soul was no more than a blue cap covering his tangled salt-and-pepper hair. "I'm going to teach you some words that may be useful to you later." Slowly he said, *"Tor conaloc an dhia,"* and Manuel repeated it. "Say it again." Manuel repeated the syllables over and over, like a Latin prayer. Laeghr nodded. *"Tor conaloc an naom dhia*. Good. Remember the words always." After that he stared at the deckbeams above, and would answer none of Manuel's questions. Emotions played over his face like shadows, one after another. Finally he took his gaze from the infinite and looked at Manuel. "Touch me, boy."

Manuel touched his forehead, and with a sardonic smile Laeghr closed his eyes: his blue crown of flame flickered up through the deck above and disappeared.

They buried him that evening, in a smoky, hellish brown sunset. Friar Lucien said the shortened Mass, mumbling in a voice that no one could hear, and Manuel pressed the back of his medallion against the cold flesh of Laeghr's arm, until the impression of the cross remained. Then they tossed him overboard. Manuel watched with a serenity that surprised him. Just weeks ago he had shouted with rage and pain as his companions had been torn apart; now he watched with a peace he did not understand as the man who had taught him and protected him sank into the iron water and disappeared.

A couple of nights after that Manuel sat apart from his remaining berthmates, who slept in one pile like a litter of kittens. He watched the blue flames wandering over the exhausted flesh, watched without reason or feeling. He was tired.

Friar Lucien looked in the narrow doorway and hissed. "Manuel! Are you there?"

"I'm here."

"Come with me."

Manuel got up and followed him. "Where are we going?"

Friar Lucien shook his head. "It's time." Everything else he said was in Greek. He had a little candle lantern with three sides shuttered, and by its illumination they made their way to the hatch that led to the lower decks.

Manuel's berth, though it was below the gun deck, was not on the lowest deck of the ship. *La Lavia* was very much bigger than that. Below the berth deck were three more decks that had no ports, as they were beneath the waterline. Here in perpetual gloom were stored the barrels of water and biscuit, the cannonballs and rope and other supplies. They passed by the powder room, where the armorer wore felt slippers so that a spark from his boots might not blow up the ship. They found a hatchway that held a ladder leading to an even lower deck. At each level the passages became narrower, and they were forced to stoop. Manuel was astounded when they descended yet again, for he would have imagined them already on the keel, or in some strange chamber suspended beneath it; but Lucien knew better. Down they went, through a labyrinth of dank black wooden passageways. Manuel was long lost, and held Lucien's arm for fear of being separated from him, and becoming hopelessly trapped in the bowels of the ship. Finally they came to a door that made their narrow hallway a dead end. Lucien rapped on the door and hissed something, and the door opened, letting out enough light to dazzle Manuel.

After the passageways, the chamber they entered seemed very large. It was the cable tier, located in the bow of the ship just over the keel. Since the encounter with the fireships, *La Lavia* had little cable, and what was left lay in the corners of the room. Now it was lit by candles set in small iron candelabra that had been nailed to the side beams. The floor was covered by an inch of water, which reflected each of the candle flames as a small spot of white light. The curving walls dripped and gleamed. In the center of the room a box had been set on end, and covered with a bit of cloth. Around the box stood several men: a soldier, one of the petty officers, and some sailors Manuel knew only by sight. The transparent knots of cobalt flame on their heads added a bluish cast to the light in the room.

"We're ready, Father," one of the men said to Lucien. The friar led Manuel to a spot near the upturned box, and the others arranged themselves in a circle around him. Against the aft wall, near gaps where floor met wall imperfectly, Manuel spotted two big rats with shiny brown fur, all ablink and twitch-whiskered at the unusual activity. Manuel frowned and one of the rats plopped into the water covering the floor and swam under the wall, its tail swishing back and forth like a small snake, revealing to Manuel its true nature. The other rat stood its ground and blinked its bright little round eyes as it brazenly returned Manuel's unwelcoming gaze.

From behind the box Lucien looked at each man in turn, and read in Latin. Manuel understood the first part: "I believe in God the Father Almighty, maker of heaven and earth, and of all things visible and invisible . . .'' From there Lucien read on, in a voice powerful yet soothing, entreatful yet proud. After finishing the creed he took up another book, the little one he always carried with him, and read in Spanish:

" 'Know ye, O Israel, that what men call life and death are as beads of white and black strung upon a thread; and this thread of perpetual change is mine own changeless life, which bindeth together the unending string of little lives and little deaths.

" 'The wind turns a ship from its course upon the deep: the wandering winds of the senses cast man's mind adrift on the deep.

" 'But lo! That day shall come when the light that *is* shall still all winds, and bind every hideous liquid darkness; and all thy habitations shall be blest by the white brilliance which descendeth from the crown.' ''

While Lucien read this, the soldier moved slowly about the chamber. First he set on the top of the box a plate of sliced biscuit; the bread was hard, as it became after months at sea, and someone had taken the trouble to cut slices, and then polish them into wafers so thin that they were translucent, and the color of honey. Occasional wormholes gave them the look of old coins, that had been beaten flat and holed for use as jewelry.

Next the soldier brought forth from behind the box an empty glass bottle with its top cut off so that it was a sort of bowl. Taking a flask in his other hand, he filled the bowl to the midway point with *La Lavia*'s awful wine. Putting the flask down, he circled the group while the friar finished reading. Every man there had cuts on his hands that more or less continuously leaked blood, and each man pulled a cut open over the bottle held to him, allowing a drop to splash in, until the wine was so dark that to Manuel, aware of the blue light, it was a deep violet.

The soldier replaced the bottle beside the plate of wafers on the box. Friar Lucien finished his reading, looked at the box, and recited one final sentence: "O lamps of fire! Make bright the deep caverns of sense; with strange brightness give heat and light together to your beloved, that we may be one with you." Taking the plate in hand, he circled the chamber, putting a wafer in the mouths of the men. "The body of Christ, given for you. The body of Christ, given for you."

Manuel snapped the wafer of biscuit between his teeth and chewed it. At last he understood what they were doing. This was a communion for the dead: a service for Laeghr, a service for all of them, for they were all doomed. Beyond the damp curved wall of their chamber was the deep sea, pressing against the timbers, pressing in on them. Eventually they would all be swallowed, and would sink down to become food for the fishes, after which their bones would decorate the floor of the ocean, where God seldom visited. Manuel could scarcely get the chewed biscuit past the lump in his throat. When Friar Lucien lifted the half bottle and put it to his lips, saying first, "The blood of Christ, shed for you," Manuel stopped him. He took the bottle from the friar's hand. The soldier stepped forward, but Lucien waved him away. Then the friar kneeled before Manuel and crossed himself, but backwards as Greeks did, left to right rather than the proper way. Manuel said, "You are the blood of Christ," and held the half bottle to Lucien's lips, tilting it so he could drink.

He did the same for each of the men, the soldier included. "You are the Christ." This was the first time any of them had partaken of this part of the communion, and some of them could barely swallow. When they had all drunk, Manuel put the bottle to his lips and drained it to the dregs. "Friar Lucien's book says, all thy habitations shall be blest by the white brilliance that is the crown of fire, and we shall all be made the Christ. And so it is. We drank, and now we are the Christ. See''—he pointed at the remaining rat, which was now on its hind legs, washing its forepaws so that it appeared to pray, its bright round eyes fixed on Manuel—''even the beasts know it.'' He broke off a piece of biscuit wafer, and leaned down to offer it to the rat. The rat accepted the fragment in its paws, and ate it. It submitted to Manuel's touch. Standing back up, Manuel felt the blood rush to his head. The crowns of fire blazed on every head, reaching far above them to lick the beams of the ceiling, filling the room with light— ''He is here!'' Manuel cried, ''He has touched us with light, see it!'' He touched each of their foreheads in turn, and saw their eyes widen as they perceived the others' burning souls in wonder, pointing at each other's heads; then they were all embracing in the clear white light, hugging one another with the tears running down their cheeks and giant grins splitting their beards. Reflected candlelight danced in a thousand parts on the watery floor. The rat, startled, splashed under the gap in the wall, and they laughed and laughed and laughed.

Manuel put his arm around the friar, whose eyes shone with joy. ''It is good,'' Manuel said when they were all quiet again. ''God will see us home.''

They made their way back to the upper decks like boys playing in a cave they know very well.

The Armada made it through the Orkneys without Laeghr, though it was a close thing for some ships. Then they were out in the North Atlantic, where the swells were broader, their troughs deeper, and their tops as high as the castles of *La Lavia*, and then higher than that.

Winds came out of the southwest, bitter gales that never ceased, and three weeks later they were no closer to Spain than they had been when they slipped through the Orkneys. The situation on *La Lavia* was desperate, as it was all through the fleet. Men on *La Lavia* died every day, and were thrown overboard with no ceremony except the impression of Manuel's medallion into their arms. The deaths made the food and water shortage less acute, but it was still serious. *La Lavia* was now manned by a ghost crew, composed mostly of soldiers. There weren't enough of them to properly man the pumps, and the Atlantic was springing new leaks every day in the already broken hull. The ship began taking on water in such quantities that the acting captain of the ship—who had started the voyage as third mate—decided that they must make straight for Spain, making no spare leeway for the imperfectly known west coast of Ireland. This decision was shared by the captains of several other damaged ships, and they conveyed their decision to the main body of the fleet, which was reaching farther west before turning south to Spain. From his sickbed Medina Sidonia gave his consent, and *La Lavia* sailed due south.

Unfortunately, a storm struck from just north of west soon after they had turned homeward. They were helpless before it. *La Lavia* wallowed in the troughs and was slammed by crest after crest, until the poor hulk lay just off the lee shore, Ireland.

It was the end, and everyone knew it. Manuel knew it because the air had turned black. The clouds were like thousands of black English cannonballs, rolling ten deep over a clear floor set just above the masts, and spitting lightning into the sea whenever two of them banged together hard enough. The air beneath them was black as well, just less thick: the wind as tangible as the waves, and swirling around the masts with smoky fury. Other men caught glimpses of the lee shore, but Manuel couldn't see it for the blackness. These men called out in fear; apparently the western coast of Ireland was sheer cliff. It was the end.

Manuel had nothing but admiration for the third-mate-now-captain, who took the helm and shouted to the lookout in the top to find a bay in the cliffs they were drifting toward. But Manuel, like many of the men, ignored the mate's commands to stay at post, as they were clearly pointless. Men embraced each other on the castles, saying their farewells; others cowered in fear against the bulkheads. Many of them approached Manuel and asked for a touch, and Manuel brushed their foreheads as he angrily marched about the forecastle. As soon as Manuel touched them, some of the men flew directly up toward heaven while others dove over the side of the ship and became porpoises the moment they struck the water, but Manuel scarcely noticed these occurrences, as he was busy praying, praying at the top of his lungs.

''*Why* this storm, Lord, *why?* First there were winds from the north holding us back, which is the only reason I'm here in the first place. So you wanted me here, but why why why? Juan is dead and Laeghr is dead and Pietro is dead and Habedeen is dead and soon we will all be dead, and why? It isn't just. You promised you would take us home.'' In a fury he took his slow match knife, climbed down to the swamped midships, and went to the mainmast. He thrust the knife deep into the wood, stabbing with the grain. ''There! I say *that* to your storm!''

''Now, that's blasphemy,'' Laeghr said as he pulled the knife from the mast and threw it over the side. ''You know what stabbing the mast means. To do it in a storm like this—you'll offend gods a lot older than Jesus, and more powerful, too.''

''Talk about blasphemy,'' Manuel replied. ''And you wonder why you're still wandering the seas a ghost, when you say things like that. You should take more care.'' He looked up and saw Saint Anna, in the maintop giving directions to the third mate. ''Did you hear what Laeghr said?'' he shouted up to her. She didn't hear him.

''Do you remember the words I taught you?'' Laeghr inquired.

"Of course. Don't bother me now, Laeghr, I'll be a ghost with you soon enough." Laeghr stepped back, but Manuel changed his mind, and said, "Laeghr, why are we being punished like this? We were on a crusade for God, weren't we? I don't understand."

Laeghr smiled and turned around, and Manuel saw then that he had wings, wings with feathers intensely white in the black murk of the air. He clasped Manuel's arm. "You know all that I know." With some hard flaps he was off, tumbling east swiftly in the black air, like a gull.

With the help of Saint Anna the third mate had actually found a break in the cliffs, a quite considerable bay. Other ships of the Armada had found it as well, and they were already breaking up on a wide beach as *La Lavia* limped nearer shore. The keel grounded and immediately things began breaking. Soupy waves crashed over the canted midships, and Manuel leaped up the ladder to the forecastle, which was now under a tangle of rigging from the broken foremast. The mainmast went over the side, and the lee flank of the ship splintered like a match tub and flooded, right before their eyes. Among the floating timbers Manuel saw one that held a black cannonball embedded in it, undoubtedly the very one that Saint Anna had deflected from its course toward him. Reminded that she had saved his life before, Manuel grew calmer and waited for her to appear. The beach was only a few shiplengths away, scarcely visible in the thick air; like most of the men, Manuel could not swim, and he was searching with some urgency for a sight of Saint Anna when Friar Lucien appeared at his side, in his black robes. Over the shriek of the dark wind Lucien shouted, "If we hold on to a plank we'll float ashore."

"You go ahead," Manuel shouted back. "I'm waiting for Saint Anna." The friar shrugged. The wind caught his robes and Manuel saw that Lucien was attempting to save the ship's liturgical gold, which was in the form of chains that were now wrapped around the friar's middle. Lucien made his way to the rail and jumped over it, onto a spar that a wave was carrying away from the ship. He missed his hold on the rounded spar, however, and sank instantly.

The forecastle was now awash, and soon the foaming breakers would tear it loose from the keel. Most of the men had already left the wreck, trusting to one bit of flotsam or other. But Manuel still waited. Just as he was beginning to worry he saw the blessed grandmother of God, standing among figures on the beach that he perceived but dimly, gesturing to him. She walked out onto the white water, and he understood. "We are the Christ, of course! I will walk to shore as He once did." He tested the surface with one shoe; it seemed a little, well, infirm, but surely it would serve—it would be like the floor of their now-demolished chapel, a sheet of water covering one of God's good solids. So Manuel walked out onto the next wave that passed at the level of the forecastle, and plunged deep into the brine.

"Hey!" he spluttered as he struggled back to the surface. "Hey!" No answer from Saint Anna this time; just cold salt water. He began the laborious process of drowning, remembering as he struggled a time when he was a child, and his father had taken him down to the beach in Morocco, to see the galley of the pilgrims to Mecca rowing away. Nothing could have been less like the Irish coast than that serene, hot, tawny beach, and he and his father had gone out into the shallows to splash around in the warm water, chasing lemons. His father would toss the lemons out into the deeper water, where they bobbed just under the surface, and then Manuel would paddle out to retrieve them, laughing and choking on water.

Manuel could picture those lemons perfectly, as he snorted and coughed and thrashed to get his head back above the freezing soup one more time. Lemons bobbing in the green sea, lemons oblong and bumpy, the color of the sun when the sun is its own width above the horizon at dawn . . . bobbing gently just under the surface, with a knob showing here or there. Manuel pretended he was a lemon, at the same time that he tried to remember the primitive dog paddle that had gotten him around in the shallows. Arms, pushing downward. It wasn't working. Waves tumbled him, lemonlike, in toward the strand. He bumped on the bottom and stood up. The water was only waist deep. Another wave smashed him from behind and he couldn't find the bottom again. Not fair! he thought. His elbow ran into sand, and he twisted around and stood. Knee deep, this time. He kept an eye on the treacherous waves as they came out of the black, and trudged through them up to a beach made of coarse sand, covered by a mat of loose seaweed.

Down on the beach a distance were sailors, companions, survivors of the wrecks offshore. But there among them—soldiers on horses. English soldiers, on horses and on foot—Manuel groaned to see it—wielding swords and clubs on the exhausted men strewn across the seaweed. "No!" Manuel cried, "No!" But it was true. "Ah, God," he said, and sank till he was sitting. Down the strand soldiers clubbed his brothers, splitting their fragile eggshell skulls so that the yolk of their brains ran into the kelp. Manuel beat his insensible fists against the sand. Filled with horror at the sight, he watched horses rear in the murk, giant and shadowy. They were coming down the beach toward him. "I'll make myself invisible," he decided. "Saint Anna will make me invisible." But remembering his plan to walk on the water, he determined to help the miracle by staggering up the beach and burrowing under a particularly tall pile of seaweed. He was invisible without it, of course, but the cover of kelp would help keep him warm. Thinking such thoughts, he shivered and shivered and on the still land fell insensible as his hands.

* * *

When he woke up, the soldiers were gone. His fellows lay up and down the beach like white driftwood; ravens and wolves already converged on them. He couldn't move very well. It took him half an hour to move his head to survey the beach, and another half hour to free himself from his pile of seaweed. And then he had to lie down again.

When he regained consciousness, he found himself behind a large log, an old piece of driftwood that had been polished silver by its years of rolling in sand. The air was clear again. He could feel it filling him and leaving him, but he could no longer see it. The sun was out; it was morning, and the storm was over. Each movement of Manuel's body was a complete effort, a complete experience. He could see quite deeply into his skin, which appeared pickled. He had lost all of his clothes, except for a tattered shred of trousers around his middle. With all his will he made his arm move his hand, and with his stiff forefinger he touched the driftwood. He could feel it. He was still alive.

His hand fell away in the sand. The wood touched by his finger was changing, becoming a bright green spot in the surrounding silver. A thin green sprig bulged from the spot, and grew up toward the sun; leaves unfolded from this sprout as it thickened, and beneath Manuel's fascinated gaze a bud appeared and burst open: a white rose, gleaming wetly in the white morning light.

He had managed to stand, and cover himself with kelp, and walk a full quarter of a mile inland, when he came upon people. Three of them to be exact, two men and a woman. Wilder looking people Manuel couldn't imagine: the men had beards that had never been cut, and arms like Laeghr's. The woman looked exactly like his miniature portrait of Saint Anna, until she got closer and he saw that she was dirty and her teeth were broken and her skin was brindled like a dog's belly. He had never seen such freckling before, and he stared at it, and her, every bit as much as she and her companions stared at him. He was afraid of them.

"Hide me from the English, please," he said. At the word *English* the men frowned and cocked their heads. They jabbered at him in a tongue he did not know. "Help me," he said. "I don't know what you're saying. Help me." He tried Spanish and Portuguese and Sicilian and Arabic. The men were looking angry. He tried Latin, and they stepped back. "I believe in God the Father Almighty, Maker of Heaven and Earth, and in all things visible and invisible." He laughed, a bit hysterically. "Especially invisible." He grabbed his medallion and showed them the cross. They studied him, clearly at a loss.

"*Tor conaloc an dhia,*" he said without thinking. All four of them jumped. Then the two men moved to his sides to hold him steady. They chattered at him, waving their free arms. The woman smiled, and Manuel saw that she was young. He said the syllables again, and they chattered at him some more. "Thank you, Laeghr," he said. "Thank you, Anna. Anna," he said to the girl, and reached for her. She squealed and stepped back. He said the phrase again. The men lifted him, for he could no longer walk, and carried him across the heather. He smiled and kissed both men on the cheek, which made them laugh, and he said the magic phrase again and started to fall asleep and smiled and said the phrase. *Tor conaloc an dhia*. The girl brushed his wet hair out of his eyes; Manuel recognized the touch, and he could feel the flowering begin inside him.

—give mercy for God's sake—

—1982